T0129874

GOLD DUST

MARION BUICK

authorHOUSE®

AuthorHouse™
1663 Liberty Drive
Bloomington, IN 47403
www.authorhouse.com
Phone: 1 (800) 839-8640

Published by AuthorHouse 12/11/2018

ISBN: 978-1-5462-6511-5 (sc)
ISBN: 978-1-5462-6510-8 (e)

Print information available on the last page.

PART ONE

1803 - CHARLESTON, SOUTH CAROLINA

CHAPTER ONE

"AMANDA, AMANDA, COME here, come here quick!" was the cry from the bedroom where Juliet Springer had just given birth to a beautiful baby girl. "Come here and see".

"Oh, I do see, I do see" replied Amanda, the cook, scurrying from the parlor where she had just delivered coffee to the men anxiously awaiting the delivery. Hazel pointed to the bassinet lying next to the exhausted mother. Amanda looked inside and, just as she reached in to pick up the child, she drew back and left the room as suddenly as she had come in. She scurried back to the kitchen, her eyes wide open and with a look of shock and dismay upon her face.

The doctor had already left, hurriedly, after briefly shaking hands with the new father and grandparents, and assuring them that both the baby and mother were well. "Made it with flying colors. A girl, a healthy baby girl". He did his best to avert their eyes, and he grabbed his hat, and was quickly gone. "Must go, another baby due this morning down by the river." His hat had fallen off of his head, and he stepped on it as he leaped into his waiting carriage.

The news travelled among the house servants and then out to the field laborers at blazing speed, and everyone knew there would be trouble, for a most disturbing thing had happened when this new child was born. You see, as it happened, when Elizabeth came into this world, she was not completely white. Close, you might say, but no cigar. She was definitely not what the family expected. Her black hair was straight and not a bit silky, and her nose was small, like her mothers. But, and here was the problem, her skin had a slight, oh ever so slight tinge of brown. A lovely olive brown. And no, there was no denying it. She had some Negro blood. But where, and how did it, no, how could it have happened, that this child of Matthew and Juliet Springer could possibly have Negro blood. Juliet, perhaps one of the most, if not the most,

1

chaste woman in all of Charles Town, could simply not have had an affair with one of the field hands.

Margaret Springer, John Springer's wife and mother to the heretofore designated father of the child, was horrified when she heard the news, and the fathers, brothers, and other family members of the Springer side of the relationship and who were mulling about the parlor remained silent when the news arrived from the baby's grandmother. "Of course, you will have to get rid of this child in some manner", she spoke gently but firmly to Juliet. The girl, barely nineteen, was completely overwhelmed and, from her point of view, understandably confused. Matthew looked at her, then turned away, his stomach churning as he thought about his wife's infidelity. It was one thing for a man to sleep with a servant. He had done so himself, and even had two children by a black woman on one of the islands. But for a woman, for his wife, to have even considered sleeping with a negro servant, why – this was the ultimate act of disgrace.

"There's no alternative, my dear child", insisted Mrs. Springer. Mr. Springer senior nodded in assent. Mathew, who was immediately convinced of the infidelity of his wife, and who was unable to even entertain the thought of the child being raised in Charles Town, or Charlestown, as it was now being called in some circles, concurred. "We'll find a nice home for her, and of course provide a manner of support, but she will have to go. This is a matter of family honor, and this is the only solution. This is the only solution", he repeated. "Absolutely!" echoed Margaret Springer, who then slumped back upon the sofa, and collapsed.

CHAPTER TWO

I T FELL UPON Matthew Springer's father, the Honorable John B. Springer, alderman and owner of one of the largest ship building and trading companies in the New World, to come up with a solution. He had contacts with the mico of a Creek band far to the West, and he sent word that he wanted to do some trading. Eliza, as she was called, was four months old when the Creek trading party arrived, bringing with them a number of deerskin, beaver, and otter pelts. They also brought two Negroes who had family in Charleston, and who were being returned as unsatisfactory for the cotton plantations, a new industry that was beginning to take hold in Georgia.

"Amato, I have a problem and I need your help." The Indian smiled, and he knew he would get a good price for the two Negroes. "I want you to take this child back with you, and raise her. She is to be a free Negro, and I will send money from time to time to see she is well looked after. There is a Creek mission not far from where the river bends back North of your village. Take her there, and see that she is taken care of. For that, I will pay you well." He then took the child from Juliet's arms and handed her to a fat, copper skinned woman of about thirty. The woman wrapped the child in a woolen blanket, and scurried out to the wagon which had delivered the two African slaves to the Springer home. Before long the wagon was moving steadily along the deep rutted road leading South where the Altamaha River flowed to the ocean. From there, the canoes would take them upstream on the long journey to the Creek village.

"Mighty strange, this child", Amato finally spoke to the woman holding the sleeping infant. "The mother, she not like child to go, nor her father. But Springer, he run show. He the one with the power. He decide what best."

The Creek woman simply smiled. She was content. She liked the child right away, and wished she could suckle the baby, but she had no milk - only the warmth of her bosom and the softness of her body. Amato slowly moved

3

the canoe into the channel, and began to paddle with a deep, rhythmic stroke. He had spent a lot of time on the river, and knew his way. He placed the baby near the front of the canoe and handed the woman a paddle. A young brave sat in the middle, and they began to make speed. Amato began counting in his head the money he was carrying. Three hundred each for the two Negroes, plus three hundred for the care of the baby. Three hundred more for his trouble. Twelve hundred dollars. A hundred more for his part of the furs. He wished he had a safe place to keep the money. What would he do with it all? He wanted a horse. A tall, white horse. He had seen several in the white village by the river. He would buy a horse. The three hundred - he would have to give that to the white family he was to take the baby to. But maybe they would pay him to keep the baby. Then all of the money he was carrying would be his. He heard Mr. Springer say there would be more later. "What was it about this child?" he thought. "Why not just sell her and be done with it?"

It took two weeks to get the canoes back to his home at the Creek village on the Western bank of the river. Amato and his fat wife entered the village and heard about all the commotion surrounding the white settlement fifteen miles to the Northwest. There was talk that a large farm was in the works, and land was to be cleared and planted. Many slaves were to be brought in to work the fields, and a school was to be constructed. Plans to raise cattle and hogs were discussed. A school would be built, but not for white children - it would be for the Creek children. Children who were to be taught the white man's language, and instructed on the white man's religion. Benjamin Hawkins, an emissary of the great white chief, George Washington, was going to teach the Creek how to become farmers, and how to pray like the white man. Amato had to see this for himself, and he began to parley with himself about how best to approach the situation with Hawkins and the small package he had been entrusted to deliver.

The journey to the Hawkins encampment was only two days from his Creek home, and it was easy going along the well-travelled path which led to the banks of another river which was called the Flint by the white man. Amato, now considering himself unexpectedly wealthy, dressed his wife and the infant in their best outfits, with many beads and feathers, and he placed a large ceremonial tomahawk in his leather belt. The child's long, black hair was braided and strung with beads, and he mounted his new, white horse with great pride. His wife and the young child followed behind as he took to the path that ran alongside the river. The child was in a straw basket like enclosure and strapped to a wooden litter which contained, in addition to the baby, various weapons, food, and other necessities. His wife hauled it along with a strap which pulled from her forehead, and she strained to keep up with the horse, which led the way. Amato kept repeating to himself the name Hawkins, so that he would not forget the name of the man to whom he was to deliver the baby. The three hundred dollars was tucked away neatly inside his trousers.

CHAPTER THREE

L ATE IN THE afternoon of the second day the small party arrived at a clearing, not far from the river. A small wooden shelter had already been constructed, and the posts for a long fence were already in place. Various animals stood around or were tied to a tree or a post. Several stout black men were busy pulling a stump from a field, and the hacking of axes against the forest trees went on ceaselessly. People, it seemed, were everywhere, and a large black kettle was hovering precariously above a giant fire in the yard in front of the wooden shelter. Several heavyset Creek women sat about, shucking corn and making corn paste. The air smelled of food and sweat and, to some degree, merriment.

It seemed for a moment to Amato that no one even noticed them as they paraded about in front of the rudimentary shelter, in spite of the large white horse which pawed the ground and whinnied at the brown and white stallion tied to a tree down toward the river. Someone said "are ye looking for Mr. Hawkins?", and Amato nodded, and soon a tall, portly man of about forty appeared from the edge of the woods, carrying an axe and pointing here and there as people came and went about him.

Amato, taking the baby from the carrier, and trying to tidy it up the best he could, walked directly up to the man, and said in his best English "Are you Hawkins?"

The man nodded, and Amato continued, "Do ye know a Mr. Springer from Charleston?"

Hawkins smiled broadly, then said "John Springer? John Springer, the ship builder? Why yes, I do know the man? How do you know him, and why do you ask?"

"I am Amato, a tracker and trader of the Beaver clan. I trade down the river which reaches to the great ocean. He has sent me with a gift for you."

Amato reached forward with the baby and attempted to place it in the large man's hands, but Hawkins moved backward, avoiding the gift. Amato was so surprised that the baby slipped from his grasp, fell to the ground, and began to cry.

"What, what is this?" quizzed Benjamin, now reaching down and picking up the child. He saw the baby's beautiful, fair skin, and in the sun it was difficult to detect the brownish tone. "What is this", he said again, looking the child over. He then detected the olive complexion and concluded that the baby was a mulatto. "Whose baby is this?" he inquired. "And why has Mr. Springer sent you here with this child?"

"Why, this is the daughter of his son Mathew's wife and some field hand, I suppose. He has sent her here for you as a present, to raise as a free Negro. He has sent some money along with her for her keeping, and he says there will be more as the moons pass."

"What!" Benjamin exclaimed. "Why, I don't have time to raise a child that's not mine". But even as he spoke, he knew he could not offend the well-known and respected John Springer, and three hundred dollars, especially out in this wilderness, was quite a lot of money.

Amato detected the man's confusion and quickly jumped on the opportunity. "Why, my woman, she take care of child, for half of what Mr. Springer send. Why, she take care of him for you, and she make good gift. You see. You see that she make good gift. We take care".

The solution was too perfect, and Hawkins pointed to a large tree at the edge of the woods, about a hundred yards away. "See that big oak tree over yonder? Make a home there, and you can raise the child on the place and care for her." The more Hawkins considered the deal, the better he liked it. Amato had an immediate value to his new settlement, for he meant communication and trade all the way to Savannah and Charleston. And what was one more mouth to feed, when you had the money to do it with?

Amato had not planned on living in the white settlement. He had only imagined Hawkins being content to his raising of the child, and it seemed to him that splitting the money was a reasonable proposition. But with the offer of a plot of land to build a home, and acceptance into the settlement, the idea began to grow on him. And then it occurred to him that he could, from time to time, visit with the great John Springer, and tell him of the child's progress, and return with additional support, which might otherwise have been forgotten.

He sent for his other children, and his dogs, and the remainder of his money, which he had hidden carefully, and he was soon settled comfortably in the North corner of the Hawkins compound. It wasn't long before his two youngest children were attending the new school, and learning how to farm. His wife became enamored with the religion of the white man, and took the children each Sunday to a church which had been constructed where the path from the Creek village entered upon the settlement clearing. Life for the Creek trader was good.

CHAPTER FOUR

WHEN ELIZA WAS ten, her world suddenly changed. The Northern Creek clans, known as the Upper Creeks, resented the white man's efforts to incorporate them into their white society. They saw the disruption that was taking place in their way of life, and something as simple as a metal pan meant change in their habits and customs. A series of earthquakes that shook the entire region were seen as a sign that the white man was not good for the Creek people. He had to be destroyed, and driven back to the sea from whence he had come. The Lower Creeks in the South, many of which had settled in villages following the pattern set out by Benjamin Hawkins, wanted to continue the assimilation, and it wasn't long before Civil War broke out among the various clans of the Creek Nation - one fighting to preserve their past, one fighting for what they saw as their only chance for a future. Amato, whose family was well fed, content, and now prosperous, had three large fields planted, and were the proud owners of six Negro slaves. They were planting cotton, and the land was good for cotton. Amato had his eye on buying a cotton gin, which were being made by a white man in a fast growing town across the river to the East as fast as he could put them together. With the gin, he could make enough cotton to have regular shipments down to the burgeoning cotton markets. There was much at stake, and he implored the mico of his tribe to resist the Red Sticks, as the Northern clans were now known, and to side with the whites.

Hawkins, who had been living with a Creek woman and now had three children by her, was crushed by the development, and he reached out to the political forces in Washington for help. A victory by the Red Sticks would spell disaster for the noble experiment he had undertaken with the Creek. All of his hard work at bringing the Creek into the fold, so to speak, was at risk of being destroyed. The frontier was in complete turmoil, and the whites,

9

now with a growing town only miles East of the main Creek village, were increasingly fearful of the sudden rebellion. The Red Sticks began attacking white settlements indiscriminately along the frontier. It wasn't long before the general consensus among the white settlers was that all Creeks were to be feared. For Amato, that meant his trips down the river were much more dangerous, even though he had the full support and letter of safe passage from his friend and business partner, Benjamin Hawkins.

The news of the rebellion spread rapidly North and South. The Northern states considered it a local problem, one which the militias of Tennessee and the Carolina's would have to deal with. Trade along the river by the Creek was halted with the establishment of a fort, armed with cannon and in clear sight of oncoming river traffic. Amato's cotton was going to rot before he could get it to market. In a panic, he looked for help among the white planters.

"What have you got for sale?" inquired the portly gentlemen from the porch of his wood framed home. You can sell me the Negroes. Fifty dollars a head. The cotton I'll give you five cents."

"Five cents? Why you know that cotton is going up. Sky high. Why you can get 20 cents in Savannah. 20 cents."

"Five cents. Take it or leave it."

Five cents, thought Amato. White gold they called it. It might as well be yellow pee. It was selling for four times that in Savannah. He was ruined. The Negroes were worth ten times what he was offering. "What about a girl. I got a girl, now about 10. She can work the field, good as any man. What about her?"

"I've seen that girl. She's a pretty little thing. 'Bout as white as them niggers come. Tell you what", replied the planter, "you throw in the girl, I'll give you Five Hundred Dollars in cash. Five Hundred. You better take it, cause the wars gonna be the ruin of you Indians, and what you got will just be took here, sooner 'n later. Sooner 'n later, you gonna have nuthin' but a field of turned dirt and dead sticks. And now you got Five Hundred Dollars."

Amato could not believe his change of fortune. He knew the girl was not his to sell, but Hawkins had more than he could handle, and would not even notice she was missing for months. By then, the world might not even look the same. No one was going to get to Savannah to tell the Springers, and the money for the child had stopped coming when the war started. No one had ever come out to see the girl, and what did they care. What could they care?

"She think she free", said Amato.

"Well, we'll fix that", replied the planter. "That ain't no problem. Couple of months out in that field, and she'll be just like the rest. You let me and my Ole Barney take care of that little problem. Bet she will be throwing more cotton than a man 'fore she turn 12. Lessen of course I can make a mistress of her down the road. Can't rule that out", he laughed out loud, and his face taking on a broad, ugly look that was difficult to describe, it was so despicable.

Amato shook on the deal, and headed home. Eliza knew she was considered a free black, but she did not know the story of her birth, or the money that the Springer's had been sending over the years up the river with Amato for her care. Amato wondered how he was going to tell his wife that he had sold the Springer child. His wife had been attached to her since they brought her home with them ten years ago. She had been assimilated into the Creek nation, and was accepted as a member. If his wife appealed to the mico, his decision could be overturned.

Eliza's Creek name was Running Deer, and it was no secret in the Clan that she was a free Negro who had some relationship with Benjamin Hawkins, but no one seemed to know exactly what the relationship was. The Clan, however, was at war, and this was a war like no other in their history, for this was a war amongst themselves. The matriarchal nature of the Clans made this very complicated, for upon marriage the children of the marriage belonged to the Clan of their mother, and Amato's wife was from the Bear Clan. She had agreed to live among Amato's people, and this was particularly troublesome now because the Bear Clan had joined the Red Sticks. Children now were at war with their uncles and fathers with their sons. When the planter came for Eliza, her adoptive mother had warned her and put her in a canoe on the Flint, and, along with her cousin Long Foot, they headed upriver for a Red Stick meeting place. Close behind was the planter, but his flat bottomed boat, loaded with his dogs and two of his neighbors, were no match for the swift canoe. The deeper into the creek estuaries of the river they went, the more dangerous the odds became, until, even with their more advanced weapons, they were forced to turn back and scurry downstream. "I'll catch her one of these days", he promised himself, as he worked the boat back into the main channel of the Flint. "She'll be mine. She belongs to me!".

"Three hundred dollars, not a penny more" the planter told Amato, upon returning empty handled. His disappointment was readily apparent, for he had especially wanted the near-white girl. Amato beat his wife for her disloyalty,

CHAPTER FIVE

ELIZABETH, ALSO KNOWN as Eliza and to the Creek, Running Deer, was never so happy as when she joined up with the Bear Clan and its war against the whites. It wasn't that she liked war, for she found it repugnant and in her way of thinking, ignorant. But there was something special about the camaraderie and excitement that met her every morning. She particularly loved the family nature of the Clan, which was wanting in the Hawkins compound with its new ways which looked to abandon the past. Amato had been a good provider, but with him there was no emotional attachment, no feeling of love. With the Bear Clan, everyone her age was a brother or a sister, and she felt at home for the first time.

While the air was pierced with danger and uncertainty, there was a general feeling that this was a war for survival of their way of life, and there was a magic that permeated the atmosphere and made it almost surreal. Raised among the Creek, she could hardly fathom her clan mother's warning that her Creek father had sold her to the whites to become a plantation slave. The enormity of the betrayal by Amato, who had essentially been her father, was beyond her comprehension. But she had seen the negroes out in the field picking cotton, and she had seen the despair in their faces, and she knew she didn't want to be one of them.

When the whites entered the war on the side of the White Sticks (the Creeks who had fought for assimilation into white society) the victories against the ill organized and isolated bands of Red Sticks took a new turn. Andrew Jackson and an army of Tennessee Volunteers marched south and scored victory after victory. The Clans moved West into Alabama and further South into Florida in an effort to evade being destroyed by their pursuers. At last, following a ferocious battle on the Tallapoosa River, the defeated Creeks surrendered much of their ancestral lands. Running Deer moved south into

Florida where many of the Clans were joining with the Seminole tribes who had been armed by the British during the War of 1812 and who offered a sort of refuge, at least temporarily, to the retreating Creek. She was staying at a fort, ironically called "the Negro Fort", which had been abandoned by the British, when a powder keg exploded killing nearly everyone within its walls. Fortunately for Running Deer, she was outside the fort, gathering water, when the explosion occurred. The year was 1816. She was now 13. Everyone she was close to in the Bear Clan and who had made it this far into Florida with her was now dead. Unbeknownst to her, Benjamin Hawkins, having finally married his Creek wife, was also now dead and buried.

The fortunes of the Red Sticks went from bad to worse. A surprisingly large assembly of over 1000 White Sticks marched south with Andrew Jackson and pushed the remaining Red Creeks in Florida into virtual submission. After the battle at Pensacola, Running Deer found herself wandering Eastwardly, chased by slavers from the White Sticks, and finding the Seminole encampments cold and frightening. She learned of the Gullas, a group of black runaways from Georgia and the Carolinas nestled in the Florida panhandle, and found a large village occupied by them and which was remarkably prosperous. Well-armed and willing to fight to the end, the Gullas were impressed by the young girl's knowledge of warfare she had learned from living with the Red Sticks, and she soon became known and accepted in the Gulla settlement. She was a guerrilla among guerrillas, and they were well suited for each other. Before long she was fluent in Gulla, English, Mikasuki, Creek, and a smattering of Seminole. Surrounded on all sides, hounded by slavers, Creeks, American settlers and sometimes by the English, the Gulla lived lives of constant vigilance. Organized and disciplined, they were willing to do the extra things necessary to avoid being overcome and certainly enslaved. But in spite of the dangers and obvious conflicts, Running Deer missed the camaraderie of her Creek Clan, and she yearned for her lost family. The Gullas called her by her Christian name of Eliza, but in her heart she was Running Deer.

The Gullas practiced a form of Christianity, and Eliza had a lot of trouble with the teachings of the religion. She found it easy to accept and understand the Great Father of the Creek, but the Great Father of the Christians was something else. He had a child who he allowed to be killed by his own people. Eliza thought what Benjamin Hawkins would have done to someone who killed his son. Or Amato. Revenge was such a human emotion. But then to allow it.

To plan it, to approve of it. To sacrifice one's own kin. It was not something she could understand. And how could one have a child that was made by a god and a woman. It was not easy for her to comprehend this. Why would the Great Father need a son, anyway? Was he going to die someday, and need an heir? And this was a jealous God. Would not he also be jealous of his son? A son who was worshipped more than he was? She preferred the simplicity of the Great Father who made the world, and who watched over all his people. A belief that didn't threaten you with damnation. A belief that was simply there, there to give you hope, and understanding, and courage. It was a good thing she didn't join the White Sticks, she thought.

Chapter Six

ELIZA HAD REACHED puberty in stride. She was strong, limber and could run as fast as a man. Life among the Gullas was unlike anything she had experienced before. She took up living in a cabin close to the village gate. The entrance into the village was made up of sort of a narrow path bordered with tall poles about ten feet high, so that only two or three people at most could enter abreast. This was designed to slow down any direct assault into the settlement. The entire village was surrounded by these tall poles, so it was somewhat of a fort. Living in the cabin with her were several other slave women who had run away from Charleston and an old man named Poot. Poot had a grey beard and walked with a limp, but he knew how to make all sorts of good things to eat and was in constant demand.

Poot had a woman named MayMay, who he considered to be his wife and who was a conjurer. She was very active in the village's religious activities, and she set about to convert this poor, what she called the white girl, from her Creek upbringing to the religious mixture that was created when the Creole incorporated the Christian teachings of the white man into the African religious practices taught to her as a child. She would sometimes go off into a trance, and when she would return she would talk about conversations she had with people long dead - people who lived hundreds of years before she was born. She talked about these things in such a casual way and with such sincerity that no one doubted that what she said was true, and she had a large following that would come to her for remedies and cures for a vast variety of ailments, troubles and physical discomforts.

"Chil, you ain gonn make no evlastin liv wid that thot in yu min. You gid wid me, and I tach yu."

Eliza became fond of Poot, who had become her protector of sorts as she ventured into adulthood, and she allowed MayMay to become her spiritual

16

advisor. She would follow her out into the woods, where MayMay would gather various roots, herbs and other things for her mysterious concoctions, potients, and remedies. On several occasions a large following would go with her out into a clearing by a nearby stream, and a large fire would be built. MayMay would kill a chicken or another small animal, and lay the animal on a huge stone in the center of the clearing, and say all sorts of things over the dead animal, much to the delight and fascination of those around her. Poot would not attend these rituals, but he had a certain fascination and love for MayMay, and he tolerated her excesses and taught her to write letters on the stone.

Poot, who had lived in a large house in Charleston as a child and had been the property of a wealthy trader, had learned to read from his owner's wife, even though it was against the law for her to teach him. He set about to teach the art to Eliza. The only problem was that there were no books or papers or anything else to read, so the progress was slow and, because of the Gullah dialect, it was difficult for Eliza to make much sense out of it all. She did, however, see the wonder and importance of it, and she longed for an English book which was closer to the language she had learned from Amato's wife, who had learned it from her children who attended the white school started by Mr. Hawkins. One day a trader came to the village, and she got MayMay to trade some of her sweet smelling perfumes for an English Bible. MayMay would listen, and try to understand the words, then she would tell the stories as she understood them out in the circle as the fire stretched high into the star studded night sky. As the wood would crackle and the sparks exploded in and around the smoke rising to the heavens, she conjured up images of saints and demons, and as MayMay spoke, the story of Jedus, as MayMay pronounced it, seemed to come alive. This new religion offered Eliza a new perspective on things, as she liked the saintly images and the inspiration they provided. She began to struggle with her identity as a Creek, and began to see herself in a new light.

CHAPTER SEVEN

T HE DAYS SEEMED to roll by and the relationship of the Gullah's and the Seminole tribes became intertwined. Each developed a dependence and appreciation of the other. The Seminole, who detested slavery, welcomed the escaping slaves from the North, and the English soldiers who had come to the area even offered them promises of freedom in exchange for their cooperation. But as the English influence waned and then disappeared, the Gullah's had to become even more vigilant to protect their members from the marauding white and Creek slavers who ventured into the area searching for slaves who had escaped from the rice, sugar and cotton plantations further North. Some escaped South by canoe as far as the Bahamas in the West Indies. Others went further into Florida, into the Everglades. The remainder organized, militarized, and prepared for yet another war.

For Eliza, it was hardly a time to fall in love, but she was young and her youth reigned supreme. The lucky man was an escaped slave from a cotton plantation near Savannah. He arrived in the Gullah village half starved, ragged, and grateful to the Gullah patrol which had found him by a swamp, close to death. His name was Jonah, and he explained his escape this way. His mother, a mulatto who had worked in the fields all of her life, was being sold. The reason was unknown, but it tore at him so that, as the day came for her to leave, he could not restrain himself. As he watched her slowly walk away from the only home she had ever known, her destination an unknown, he completely lost control. He tore out at the overseer of the plantation, striking him with his fist. The owner of the plantation, wanting to set an example, and after having him severely whipped, decided to sell him to a slaver who was taking a train of shackled slaves down to New Orleans. He knew what that meant - near certain death working in the hot sugar plantations. Dark, angry and strong as an ox, he managed to escape his shackles, and bolted for the river. Fortunately for him, the river was swollen from two days of hard rain, and there was plenty of debris to grab onto. In a matter of days he arrived at the mighty delta, which opened into the sea. Traveling mostly at night, he walked hurriedly along the shore. Without any food for five days, he took a chance and entered an old Spanish mission, which looked abandoned to him. As he lit a lantern sitting on a table, he saw an old man curled up on a straw bed in the corner of the room. It was a Spanish priest.

The priest was weak and thin, but he understood immediately the plight of the poor shivering black man who stood next to the table, holding the lantern above him. He was not afraid, but he recognized the fear in his visitor, and he spoke to calm him.

"Ah, my amigo, do not worry. I am not your enemy."

This was not the first runaway this old priest had seen, and his only intentions were to help. To do so was against the law, but that did not bother the priest. He fed and clothed the stranger, who then curled up and fell asleep in the middle of the floor. When Jonah awoke, the priest drew him a map, leading to the general area where the escaped Gullahs had formed their camp. With a small sack of deer meat and his feet wrapped from their many cuts and bruises, Jonah set out, making it to the swamp where he was found by the Gullah patrol. Eliza saw him as he was carried past her cabin and had an immediate attraction, which she did not understand. She found herself watching the man as he gradually gained his strength, and she spied on him as the elders of the camp took him to the fields and trained him in the art of warfare. He was a quick study. And he spoke English. She found herself talking to MayMay about him.

"Gut yu lik em. Gut yu go, give self to em. Fore too lat."

Eliza did not known exactly what she meant by giving herself to a man, and she had vague memories that haunted her from her early childhood and her treatment at the hands of Amato. Strange, troubling memories. Being touched, touching, unnatural and horrific memories that would try to surface and then be buried deep into her subconscious. MayMay told her to watch her and Poot that night, but after a while Eliza became embarrassed and told herself she would never behave in such a manner. She did however, the next day, approach Jonah as he was walking back from the field, a long barreled rifle over his shoulder, and the sun gleaming off his strong chest. She felt an urge to do something, but she was not sure of what. These feelings were new, and strange. Stranger than the feelings she felt as she watched MayMay slaughter a deer on the great stone.

Jonah thought she was a white woman, and he didn't know what to do. He had been taught from birth that he could not touch a white woman, that to do so would result in immediate retribution, even death. When he returned to the village he asked MayMay about her. "Why, she negro. Look close. She raised by Creek. She no have man. Look close."

Jonah was intrigued, and they started up a relationship. They would talk about everything, and their time together was like a delicious stew, mixing the two minds until they began to think as one, and their bodies, too, became mixed, entwined, and the excitement, passion and love was overwhelming. MayMay became excited just watching them, and before long she became engrossed with the idea of creating a potion that would bind them together for eternity. Poot would take them with him to the creek, where he taught Jonah to fish, and Eliza to cook. When MayMay finalized her concoction, she took the two lovers alone one night to the great stone alter. There, she cut each of their wrists and drained blood into a goblet. In the goblet was her mixture, which when mixed with the blood, she urged them to drink.

"Ye nevr part, evn tho ye di. Ye liv like star in ski fo al tim as one."

Poot watched from the woods, afraid of his wife at moments like this, and tightened his grip around his spear as he listened to the sounds of the forest around them. In some ways he wished he, too, could drink of the spell, but for some reason the idea of being irrevocably connected to MayMay for eternity did not move him to action, and he stayed hidden until the ritual was completed, and the small party had returned to the camp.

CHAPTER EIGHT

T HE NEXT DAY Eliza awoke to find Jonah gone. At first she just figured that he had some sentry or other duty to perform, but when he didn't return by noon, she began to fret. "MayMay", she implored, "where could he be?" The long afternoon began to fade and her concerns now turned to worry, followed by fear, and then more worry. No one seemed to have seen him, or to know what had become of him. She checked his things, and nothing seemed to be missing. When Poot returned at dark, her anxiety had turned to panic. Poot was not much help, but he had seen what he thought was a campfire across the river the night before. He was reluctant to say anything, for fear MayMay would be mad at him for spying on her hoodoo conjuring the night before, which had put him in a bad state of mind, and he had spent the day down by the river, fishing.

"He no show tonight, I take you tomorrow where fire was."

Eliza spent a fitful night and long before first light she was shaking Poot, urging him to get ready and take her across the river. They followed the path in the darkness and arrived at the riverbank upon first light. Poot located a small canoe, and the two were soon on the opposite bank. Before long, Poot had located the still warm embers of a small fire, and began to search for evidence of whose it could have been. He saw the hoof prints of three horses, and a fourth, of what appeared to be a mule. The mule, he figured, was being used as a pack animal, but the prints were not very deep, so they, whoever they were, were traveling fairly light. Tracks led down to the bank, and it appeared that at some point they had crossed the river in the direction of the Gullah town. Eliza recognized the footprints as most likely Creek. 'Slavers!" exclaimed Poot, as if that was all that was needed to be said.

The trail out and away from the camp had followed the trail in, and they walked several miles Northward, when the trail turned East toward an old

Indian path that was used by the Seminole trading parties. Poot turned to Eliza: "Most likely headed to Savan. Mos likely Savan. Three men on horse. Two men walking. Mos likley Jonah wid 'em. Mos likely."

The successful kidnapping of Jonah by the slavers caused a great deal of concern in the camp. Due to their numbers, their close relationship with the Seminole, and their militaristic philosophy, they felt they had been violated as much as anything else. As a group, the Gullah camp had been lulled into a false sense of security, and they were shocked at their vulnerability. They would have to move the camp - that was obvious. All of their hard work in laying out the fields, planting and harvesting their crops, tending their large herd of pigs and sheep, building their homes - all of this would have to give way to the need for secrecy. Fifteen warriors were selected to track the slavers and kill them. The security of the settlement seemed to depend on their success.

Eliza went to Poot and obtained Jonah's long rifle. Poot showed her how it was fired, and she gathered the things she would need for light travel and hurried to join the party which had left to search for the slavers. No one prevented her, but MayMay tried to discourage her from going. "Bones say no. Bones never wrong. Stay", she begged.

A Yuchi Indian who had migrated South and who went by the name of Billy was picked to lead the search party. Billy was considered a member of the Creek nation, and he had fought with the Red Sticks in the rebellion. Now he wandered, seeking refuge in the various Seminole camps along the panhandle, and when he entered the Gullah camp, Eliza recognized him from a camp meeting many years ago, when she was still in Georgia. Billy was a known tracker, and if anyone could find the slavers, Billy could. But the trail was leading Northeast, and they would need to catch up with them before they got too close to Savannah, if that was where they were headed.

CHAPTER NINE

T O ELIZA, EACH step seemed a torment. With each step she thought about Jonah, and their relationship, and how much she wanted and needed him. They had shared so much in such a short time. They had shared their dreams, their hopes, their innermost secrets and desires. She had tried to open herself up to Jonah, but she found herself struggling at the most intimate moments with strange thoughts and her mind, suppressing those unwanted thoughts and memories, seemed to drift away at the most passionate moments, so much so that she was unable to enjoy the full physicality of the moment. Jonah, on the other hand, suffered from no such mental restrictions, and he would become frustrated with her sudden coldness during their intimacy. He was kind and loving, however, even at these moments, and she never felt threatened or rejected by him. Nevertheless, his frustrations were obvious and Eliza, while deeply wanting to please Jonah, found herself grateful when the passion had subsided and her mind was no longer ravaged by the mental journey she found herself taking during these periods of sexual intimacy.

Jonah too had a lot of mental difficulties he had to deal with. Especially difficult were the images of his mother being led away in shackles, and he being powerless to stop it. He had been raised as a Christian by his family, and the religious experiences were a lot like the Gullah, except for the hoodoo, which he found both fascinating and frightening at the same time. Like Poot, he had a lot of reservations about MayMay's conjuring, but was fascinated by Eliza's descriptions of the things she had seen and observed while watching MayMay as she carried out her many rituals and religious services. Listening to Eliza read from the Bible she had acquired, MayMay would invent stories to go along with the stories in the Bible, and she would create tales of magic about the characters in the Bible, characters who became saints, but saints of a mystical and secretive nature. As the stories would unfold, she would cast spells and

23

invent concoctions to go along with them. At times, she would seem to go into a trance, and those around her would report that she seemed as if she was talking to people who lived many years ago. Conversations that seemed as real and as meaningful as if the dead were indeed alive and talking freely to the living. Tales of woe, tales of love. Tales of creation itself. It seemed as if MayMay's mind, as it travelled down these trance like paths, had no limit as to time, and her thoughts could wander back as far as time itself. When she would come back to the present, she seemed to grow stronger and more committed to her beliefs, and her ability to understand the meaning of things and the purpose of things was powerful and alive.

MayMay had warned Eliza that something might happen to Jonah, long before it actually did. "But if she could envision the future, why couldn't she have prevented his capture or warned him of what was going to happen?" she asked herself. These thoughts, and many others, followed her every step as the party moved silently along the old Indian trail.

At the end of the fourth day, Billy turned to the group. 'We have failed." They have put the prisoners on one of the horses, and are now traveling faster than we can ever catch them on foot. It is useless to continue. They will be in Savannah before we can ever hope to catch up". Reluctantly, the party realized the truthfulness of his words, and before long they turned around and began the long trip back. Eliza's mind began to spin, unable to accept what turning back would mean.

The hunting party struck for their village at a fast pace, but when they arrived, the Gullah village had vanished. Billy had been told before they had left the general direction that the village would move to if the leaders felt it necessary. Apparantly that had become the decision. They had selected a small spit of land surrounded by water and not too far from the great Gulf waters. There was only one way in without crossing a swamp, and sentries were posted so plenty of warning would be provided if any strangers came anywhere near. Little had been unpacked when Billy led the group into their new home. It wasn't long before MayMay and Poot were busy constructing a small cabin, again near the entrance. Fortifications were already underway. MayMay was ecstatic when she saw Eliza. "Yu have com back! My bones tell trut. Jonah in whal, lost to sea."

"Yes", said Eliza, but I'm not giving up. I'm going to find him. No matter what. You must help me, MayMay. There must be something you can do."

"I help yu", said MayMay, "but bones not happy".

For days MayMay would go out into the woods alone, taking with her many of her jars of dead toads, snails, and other items she would use in her recipes. "No thin wuk. No thin".

The days turned into weeks and the weeks months, and Eliza's desperation became too much for her. "I'm going after him. I don't care what happens to me."

"Waat, waat," MayMay implored her. "I clos. I clos. I fin some ting".

The next day MayMay took Eliza way out into the swamp. Long beasts, as long as the canoe they were riding in, swam by the boat. Beasts with long bristling teeth, and huge jaws. Jaws that could engulf an animal or a man. They would watch as the long monsters would hide in the swamp waters, and then appear as if out of nowhere on the bank, trapping a deer or a beaver. They would drag their pray into the water, where they would take it down to the bottom of the pond or stream. From there they were in complete control.

Before too long MayMay pointed to a piece of dry land which contained a clearing. In the center of the clearing Eliza could make out a small stone alter and lying next to it were several of MayMay's jars containing various concoctions and other things, living and dead. Laying in the center of the altar was a leather bag about the size of a small pumpkin, and it was made from the skin of the giant lizards which had swum by the boat. "I have ide fo yu. Make yu wite".

As she talked, she opened the leather bag and withdrew a large jar. Inside the jar was a paste, which she drew out and rubbed on Eliza's skin. Then a seemingly miracle happened. Her skin, already near white, seemed to become milky, and then, to her amazement, the skin seemed to turn white. Her arm, it seemed, belonged to a white woman. "Yu go luk for whale, yu pass fo wite."

The idea immediately amazed and enchanted Eliza, who, after giving it due reflection, realized the brilliance of MayMay's scheme. If she was to find Jonah, she would have to travel to Savannah. And to travel to Savannah, she could not go looking like a black woman. But she could go looking like a white woman. All she needed was some money and some white woman's clothes. But where, and how? "Nev'r yu worry bout that. Road always provide. Saints be wid yu." Eliza was amazed. The old woman seemed to be able to read her mind.

CHAPTER TEN

U PON RETURNING TO the village, the plan began to take shape. There was a lot of discussion among the village members as to the merits of the plan, and the likelihood of its success. Some were opposed outright on the idea of passing as white, which they felt was an abandonment of her identity as a black person, and which, according to the law and custom, was clearly the case. One drop of Negro blood, it was said, was enough in the eyes of the law to make you a Negro. The idea of becoming white, or passing for white, was something that entered the minds of many mulattos, especially those whose skin color and tone were genetically close to white. There was resentment, and even a hierarchy created by many where the whiter the skin the more ostracized the person was in the black community. But the mulattos, especially those like Eliza whose bronze tone was close to white, were torn between their loyalty to the black race and their desire to be free of the many chains their darker skin color imposed upon them. A person's first loyalty, MayMay reminded her, was to themselves. "Do what yu must, but see fust to yur own need."

MayMay was delighted with her invention, but it was not without imperfections. Among these, it could not change bone structure, and Eliza was fortunate in this regard because she had a European nose and high cheekbones. The paste too had its limitations. Over time it lost its whiteness, and of course you could not get it wet, for it would wash away and soon the effect would be gone. You had to reapply it every few days, and she could only carry so much with her on her journey. The plan would be for her to wear long dresses and stockings, which, along with gloves, would only leave the area from her neck up where the cosmetics would have to be applied. She would need to try to stay out of the sun and avoid sweating as much as possible, and she would have to change her clothes in private. Many were simply amazed at the effect of the concoction on her skin, however, and there was enough acceptance of her transformation to encourage both her and MayMay that the plan could work. Of course, what she could do when and if she found Jonah was beyond their ability to invent, and that would be left up to chance and the opportunities, if any, of the moment.

The plan was for Billy to guide her, as his slave, along the trails to the outskirts of Savannah. There she would need money and clothes to carry out her transformation as a white woman, and at that point Billy would become her Creek escort, sent by her wealthy family along for protection. It was, of course, a crazy scheme, long on hope and short on certainty, but Billy was game and excited by the idea, and so supplies for the journey were collected and made ready. Eliza avoided the sun and this added to the whiteness of her skin.

On the night before the day scheduled for the departure, MayMay took Eliza back into the swamp. Traveling at night, with only the stars and the moon for light, was dangerous, but MayMay knew the way and they were soon at the site of the makeshift altar. "I give yu", she said, "to mak mo". There, in the moonlight, Eliza showed her how she had made the powder which was the base of the formula. "This com frum Billy. He giv. It mad wuk." In her hand was a small bag of a white powder. In the firelight, it seemed to glitter as the sun, even in the darkness. Eliza thought it must contain great magic. Taking each item one by one, MayMay carefully demonstrated how to make the powder, teaching Eliza certain sayings that, she said, had to be muttered at exactly the right moment in order for the mixture to work. Over and over they went with the making of the formula until MayMay was satisfied that Eliza had it down. Then they extinguished the fire, and left, returning to the village as the first light broke upon the dawn.

CHAPTER ELEVEN

MAYMAY BROUGHT THE small map that Jonah had carried with him, drawn by the aging Spanish priest near the Eastern coast, and handed it to Billy. Billy studied it carefully and handed it back to May May. "I know the way", he said, recognizing many of the same trails he had followed earlier. "Map lead to sea. Whale in Savan, not in sea. But we find priest first. Maybe he can help."

Eliza looked around at the many friends she had made over the past few years. The entire village had come out to the path leading to the river, which they would first cross on their journey east. With her head covered to protect it from the sun, she carried a pack nestled neatly upon the top of her head, and she carried a long walking stick, but no other weapons.

Billy was dressed in his finest buckskins, with Jonah's long rifle slung across his shoulder, and his long black hair braided and hanging wildly about his shoulders. Eliza had made a pouch which she had strapped about her waist. Inside she had carefully placed the alligator bag containing the magic powder and a wig which one of the women of the village had made for her, made from the finest chestnut hair, and which radiated ever so beautifully when it was struck by the sun. If hope could have been captured and put in a jar, it would have been full on that early morning. It was likely that not one person shared exactly the same thought as the small party made it to the river and Billy and Eliza entered the birch canoe, but there was unity in the desire that Eliza find her lover, and that the gods would smile on this undertaking. Poot joined them in the canoe in order to bring it back when they reached the opposite shore. As she stepped out of the canoe, Poot handed her a charm which he wore around his neck on a leather rope chain. "Bring luk", he said with a smile. Eliza clutched it in her outstretched hand, and tears began to form and drip down her cheek. On adventures of this sort one never knows if they will return, if their parting words with people close to them will be their last. Would she ever return to this wonderful little community of run-a-way slaves and desperadoes, she wondered. Her heart was swollen with a feeling of love for this place, and with each step along the path she could feel a sense of loss and hopelessness.

But, once across the river, Billy was quick to pick up the trail they had taken as they followed the three horses toward Savannah. A sense of escitement took over Eliza's being, and she felt those same feelings when she ventured forth as a Red Stick in the early days of that war. The trail took them to the swamp where Jonah had first been found. There the trail headed East, toward the sea. With dismay, Billy realized that the trail of Jonah's captors was following the map imbedded in his head, and was heading directly towards the old Spanish mission. Eliza had no problem keeping up, and Billy admired the agility and physical strength of the woman accompanying him. They passed the time sharing stories of the Red Stick war, and the changes that the whites were imposing on their way of life - a history going back 10,000 years. "They want Creek to be farmer and worship their God", said Billy. "Become farmer. Go school. This life no good for Creek. Creek hunt, share family. All one. Life of white settler not good for Creek."

Eliza shared many of Billy's ideas, although she found herself fighting a personal battle within herself as to what kind of life she wanted for herself. She saw a sadness, an emptiness that was building inside the White Creek settlements as they tried to adopt to the white ways. But who and what was she? And what, if anything, did she really stand for?

Like a tsunami overpowering a coastal town, the white man had moved in and over the Creek, the Cherokee, the Huron and the hundreds of other tribes which lived and died for thousands of years in the Americas, hardly leaving a trace upon the land, blending at death back into the ground, the rivers and the mountains like the deer, otter and beaver, who too were rapidly disappearing from the streams and rivulets flowing so peacefully to the sea.

"Cherokee defeat Creek. Take land. Move Creek South. War part of life."

"Yes, and so is your practice of slavery. How can you tolerate enslaving another person".

"Better than killing person. What so wrong with it?"

"What is wrong?", Eliza shouted. "Tell that to Jonah! What did he ever do? What right do these slavers have to come and take him from me? What right did they have to take his mother from him?"

CHAPTER TWELVE

THE SPANISH MISSION looked eerily quiet in the dark night. Billy told Eliza to wait in the bushes outside the entrance. As he entered the small room inside the walls, he saw a lantern sitting upon a table in the center of the room. When he lit the lantern, a figure rose from the straw filled cot. It was a young woman. She was terrified at the sight of Billy, and let out a scream. Eliza rushed in, and before long she had calmed the young woman down. There was dried blood covering the walls and the table.

"What matter?" he said matter of factly, disregarding her obvious state of panic. "Where priest?"

"Dead. Slavers came many days ago and made him tell where the slave village was located. He resisted, but they tortured him for three days. Eventually he broke, and drew them a map. Then they murdered him. He is buried on the hill, overlooking the mission. He was a good man". The young woman then began to cry, softly at first, and then the tears came in torrents. Gathering herself, she motioned to the hill. "I'll show you the grave when light comes", she said in Spanish.

As the dawn broke the small party went to the top of the small hill and saw the freshly dug grave of the priest. Eliza had brought her Bible with her, and she read over the grave from the Book, and then added a few words MayMay had taught her to say over the dead. "You mus invok saint", she could hear MayMay saying. "Saint bring dead to Jedus." Billy waited patiently until Eliza had finished. "No put me in ground", he said to Eliza. "Burn body. Go to Great Father."

Slowly they walked away from the cemetery and back towards the mission. The young woman brought them some warm soup, and their spirits were lifted.

"Do you know the way to the ocean?" asked Eliza.

"Yes, the ocean can be seen from hill where the priest's grave is. The path is easy to follow."

"Rest here today", piped in Billy. "Leave in morning."

It wasn't long before the Yucchi had curled up in the corner of the room, exhausted from their journey, and was soon asleep. The two women began to talk, and before long they struck up a friendship. Eliza told her the story of how Jonah had been befriended by the priest, and how he had drawn Jonah the map, and how he had been found by the village scouts. She told her about MayMay, and showed her the alligator bag and the magical powder. She shared her plan to find Jonah, traveling as a white woman on her way to Savannah. The young Spanish woman told of how her father had been an important soldier in the Spanish army, and how he and her mother had been killed in an Indian raid near the coast, and she had been taken in by the priest, who had raised her since she was a small child. Then Eliza shared with her something that no one else knew. She was pregnant.

"Come", said the young Spanish woman. "I show you something".

The woman led Eliza to the mission church. The door had been broken down, and the church was musty and damp. She lit a candle and took her to a small door behind the altar, which opened into a small room. A priest's frock hung from the wall. The floor was covered with a heavy rug, and she pulled the rug up, revealing a trap door. It was heavy, and it required the strength of both girls to lift it. Beneath, in a big hole cut out of the ground, lay the treasures of the church. They were not much. Some silver candlesticks, a pouch containing several gold coins, and various religious robes. She withdrew the gold coins and gave them to Eliza. "You take", she said. "They for God's work. I believe that your finding Jonah is God's work. The priest, I'm sure he would approve if he was here with us."

The small hiding place also contained a wooden trunk. The young woman pulled against the lid. Inside were the most beautiful women's clothes Eliza had ever seen. "They belonged to my mother", said the girl. "Take what you want."

When Billy awoke the next morning he could not believe the transformation standing in front of him. "Well, Billy, what do you think?"

Standing in front of Billy was the most beautiful woman he had ever seen. She looked Spanish, with a white-olive complexion, and long Chestnut hair. She was wearing a sleeveless jacket, cut to the waist, covering a white billowing blouse, with sleeves down to the wrist. A flowing dark green skirt went to the ankles, where they were met with beautiful green leather boots, the tops of which were hidden by the long skirt. The long chestnut hair was pulled high on her head and held in place by a curved wooden comb which looked like a tortoise shell. A large scarf dropped from the comb down to the shoulders. In her ears were large, round gold earrings, and in her hands were a pair of riding gloves. The blouse was decorated with jeweled buttons and stitched with interlacing gold and silver thread. The effect was stunning.

Eliza turned toward Billy. "Here", she said, "try these on. But first, you must have a bath?"

"A what!" Billy exclaimed.

"Yes, you smell like a dog lost in the woods."

CHAPTER THIRTEEN

T HE YOUNG SPANISH girl, having given her most precious treasures to the two adventurers, then gave them one more gift, a donkey. She placed a wooden riding saddle on its back. "For the baby", she whispered softly into Eliza's ear.

Riding side-saddle, the Spanish lady and her appropriately attired escort left the hilltop containing the small cemetery and followed the narrow trail towards the sea. "What she mean, the baby?" said Billy as they reached the bottom of the hill. You could smell the salt water and feel the dryness of the air. It was late spring, and the perspiration was beginning to bead on Billy's brow as he led the donkey along the old Indian trail northward toward Savannah "Oh, nothing", replied Eliza. "I'm sure she meant nothing by it. She thinks I'm such a big baby".

For two weeks they travelled, mostly in the early mornings and then late evenings. The trail took them far inland, and avoided the many waterways and inlets along the coast. By the end of the second week, Billy and Eliza could see smoke rising through the trees. They were hungry and tired, and felt it was time to try out their subterfuge. The trail turned into a rutted dirt road, and they were soon at the outskirts of a small village. A tavern was located at the opposite end of the village, and smoke was rising from its chimney. The tavern was built of logs, and was two stories tall. Eliza turned to Billy and motioned him forward. There would be rooms to rent, and food.

Billy went inside and inquired as to directions to Savannah. He explained that he was escorting the daughter of a deceased Spanish military officer, and that he had been entrusted to deliver her to her aunt, a schoolmistress. They had travelled a great distance, and were in need of a room and shelter.

"The woman can stay inside. No Indians. You can sleep in the barn with the donkey".

"But I'm her Spanish escort", replied Billy, "and she is under my protection". Indeed Billy was dressed in the style of a Spanish man, but his features were clearly those of Indian origin, and, to the barkeep, there would be no exceptions.

"There will be no such discrimination", replied a most beautiful woman as she entered the smoke filled room. "He must be accommodated in a room next to me, for my safety."

The woman's sudden presence in the room had an almost magical spell on all those who saw her. Without thinking of the consequences, the proprietor agreed, and the pair were escorted to a room on the second floor of the establishment. "I shall require a meal for me and my servant", she insisted, and the proprietor, who had led them to their room, replied simply, "Right away".

"Well, so far so good", she said, turning to Billy.

"Yes", replied Billy, looking about the room. A single bed rested against a small window, and a wooden table was against the opposite wall. On the table was a water pitcher and a bowl. Behind it was a small mirror. Eliza walked to the table, and looked at her image. She could see the person in the reflection, but she did not recognize her. She could not even believe that the person in the mirror was her. She only knew that she had passed her first test as a non-black - as a person entitled to freedom. And it felt good. Very good.

When Billy had gone to the room next door, and she was left alone, she opened the small window and took in the night air. A sweet breeze was blowing in from the ocean, and it was warm and comforting. She laid her head upon the bed. Then she remembered what MayMay had said about the magic potent. She raised up, and began to scrub her face. The make-up washed away, and the true color of her skin re-appeared. It was not much different, really, but it was not white, and she could not pass for the Spanish mistress as she now looked. She could only pass for another poor woman of the South, a woman without privilege, without freedom, and without hope. She laughed to herself about the way the proprietor had reacted when she insisted that Billy have a room for himself. Like a Queen, she thought, they had treated her like a Queen.

CHAPTER FOURTEEN

THE NEXT MORNING Billy arrived, banging on the door, and with good news. "They have a carriage which will take us all the way in to Savannah", he almost shouted. "It leaves in an hour. Get ready". Eliza leaned out the window. She felt nauseous, almost dizzy. "Lord give me the courage to face this day", she prayed in a hurry.

Eliza hurriedly put on her face, pressed her clothes, brushed the trail dust from her shoes, and went downstairs. There, in the barroom, were several men gathered and waiting for the carriage. They looked at Eliza with awe, impressed with her obvious good looks, and nodded to one another as if they were a bunch of teenagers at a school. "Ma'am", said one, "may I assist you with your things?" The others were obviously jealous they hadn't thought of it first, and when she said yes, why you could see the young man who had made the offer burst with pride as he hurried to take the woman's few things out to the road. Eliza handed the proprietor one of the gold pieces, and stepped out into the morning air. Billy was already there with the donkey. "I'll keep up", he said, as the carriage pulled from the water trough and headed out into the road leading to Savannah.

"Two day's ride", said the man sitting across from Eliza as the carriage passed over a bridge crossing a wide river. "Altamaha", said the man. Goes way up North. Much trade. Do you mind if I inquire where you will be staying in Savan?" he said with a broad smile.

Eliza had not thought that far, and her mind was caught up in the excitement of finding Jonah and seeing him again. "Ma'am", said the gentleman again, "I am in the shipping business, and I would be honored to have you stay with my family in our home in the city. We have many Spanish friends with whom we do business in the Southern islands, and we can make you feel quite at home".

"What about my servant?", she inquired.

36

"Oh, he will be more than welcome", the man replied, "but you will have no need of an escort when you are in our company. You will be quite safe."

"I would not have the means to pay you, I'm afraid", she said.

"Oh, don't be ridiculous", replied the man. "You will be our guest."

The carriage made its way slowly along the road, having to stop many times to deal with the deep ruts from a recent rain. The donkey had no problem keeping up, but Billy was worried with all of the attention that Eliza was drawing. He had thought that they would sort of sneak into Savannah unnoticed, and go about their business. Eliza, attracting men like bees to a flower, was clearly not going about this as he would have liked. He also didn't like the way he had suddenly become her "servant", but the ruse was working, and she did seem to be pulling it off with style.

Chapter Fifteen

THE LARGE HOUSE of Conrad Wilson sat on a hill overlooking the growing city. As the carriage pulled up to the entrance, several black servants came out to meet it. "Hello", Masta Wilson", was the greeting as he got out and then turned to help the beautiful Spanish lady accompanying him.

"Tell Mrs. Wilson that we have a house guest", he directed the servant opening the door to the carriage.

Eliza entered the large, spacious home and could hardly believe her eyes. She had never seen such a place. There was a patio and veranda in the back, filled with plants and flowers, the likes of which she had never seen. Her head began to feel dizzy and she almost passed out before regaining her senses, just as a young man approached.

"Uh, ma'am", said the man, a young man about her age, who was rather lavishly dressed and who seemed to be staring at her somewhat incredulously. "Father asked that I show you to your room."

They ascended a staircase, and she was led to a large bright room overlooking the veranda. The yard was not large, but is was beautifully detailed - every inch had been attended to. She could see out into the bay, and for the first time saw the large white sails of a ship on the horizon. So many sights and sounds were new to her, but the sight of the magnificient ship took the breath right out of her body. The sky was a beautiful blue, with a few white, billowing clouds. A warm Southerly breeze came in, and she seemed hypnotized. Her trance was broken by a loud scream, coming from somewhere towards the city's wharf.

"Don't be alarmed," cautioned the young Spaniard. It's auction day" The man had followed her into the room and was checking to make sure everything had been arrangead for her comfort, following his father's orders. "They should hold those auctions somewhere else so we don't have to hear the infernal hollering and goings on. Dinner is at six. I'll have some clothes brought up. Those you've been wearing need a good cleaning."

"Can you have my servant Billy brought to the veranda? she inquired.

"Yes miss, right away", he replied.

Eliza made her way to the veranda, and soon Billy appeared, escorted by one of the house servants. When they were alone, Billy expressed his concern that she was overplaying her hand. Eliza reassured him. "Do you have a better plan?" she inquired. "There is an auction house where they sell Africans. You could start there, and see what you can find out."

Billy had been housed in the carriage house, and was left pretty much alone, with no duties, and no one paying any particular attention to him, so he was free to come and go as he pleased. That evening, when the sun went down, he dressed in his old buckskin shirt and pants and headed to town to find the auction house. Down by the wharf he found a tavern that allowed Indians to come in and drink, as long as they had money, and he soon was drinking and carrying on with one of the barmaids. He was becoming worried about Eliza, as she was beginning to get big about the waist, and before long her condition would be known. One thing was for sure - their time in Savannah was limited.

After about a week plying the local bars, Billie found what he was looking for. A free mulatto by the name of Jim Olsen had been drinking quite heavily and began bragging about having found a large black village of runaways deep into Florida. They had snatched one of them, he reported, and they had returned by horseback. Afraid of him running off again, and unable to change his ways after several floggings, the owner had decided to sell him to an Indian trader who was coming down the river by canoe. He would be there in a fortnight. "It had to be Jonah", Billy mused.

When he arrived back at the Wilson home it was very late. He was let in through the kitchen by one of the servants, and made his way upstairs to Eliza's room. When she heard the news, she became ecstatic, an emotion followed shortly by worry and fear. "So, where is he now? Where will the sale take place? Where do they plan to take him?" A million questions, and no answers. But he was alive. He was in Savannah. And if they could only find out when he was to be sold, they could find him at last. "You must go to the auction house this week by the wharf. They must know something about when a sale like this would take place."

Eliza followed Billy out of the Wilson house and down to his quarters in the carriage house. When she returned, her room had been ransacked. There, on the bed, was the alligator pouch. It had been turned upside down and emptied. The powder was gone.

She hurried back down to the carriage house.

"No more!" Eliza wanted to scream. She looked at Billy pleadingly, but he was helpless. "No more! What shall I do? What shall we do?" Eliza by now was in a complete panic. They had come so far. They were so close to finding Jonah.

When her panic began to subside she considered her options. She couldn't reveal her condition to the Wilsons. Out of the question. She would soon have to be seen in public. They would know. They would see for themselves. The auction was a good two weeks away. She couldn't hide in her room that long.

"But what shall we do? I can't make it fourteen days. They'll see. They'll see what I am." There was no alternative. There was no choice. She would have to disappear, vanish. Just as she had so mysteriously appeared on the scene, and stolen the hearts of both the elder Wilson and his son, she would have to vanish, like a thief in the night – she would have to disappear. But where would she go?

She would head South, back down to the river and hide out until the sale. If the Indian trader was coming by canoe, then he would more than likely be coming down the Altamaha, likely from Milledgeville or thereabouts. He would almost certainly pass the bridge they had crossed in the carriage weeks earlier on their way into Savannah. But what would he look like? How many would be with him? How would they stand a chance against the trader? They will have to sleep, she thought. We will snatch him in their sleep. But how? Billy followed her to the outskirts of town. "Go back, visit the auction house. Find out what you can about when the sale is to take place." Traveling again in his buckskins, Billy returned to the city, blending into the back alleys, hiding among the shadows, looking for somebody who would know when Jonah would come upon the auction block for sale.

And then, one cold late night, he saw it, on a pole next to the large Methodist church by the square, an advertisement, an auction advertisement, and a picture, a picture of Jonah, right in the middle of the poster. Jonah, inside the belly of the whale.

Chapter Sixteen

THE STORY OF Jonah's capture out of the Gullah's very heart had just the ingredients of intrigue necessary to put the tale into every tavern within 100 miles. It seemed everyone had heard about it, and wondered who this slave was and how many more were to be found in the Gullah camp. The story of the fate of the Spanish priest was also circulating, not that there was a lot of sympathy for the old priest, but there were those who had known of his expoits in helping the runaways and outcasts of society, and who, secretly, admired him and who were saddened by this death.

On the day selected for the captured slave's auction a large crowd slowly made their way to the old auction house next to the church. The building was filled with the curious as well as the serious buyers and it was hot. The ceiling was low in the large room, and the trading was taking place near the center of the room where a raised platform had been placed. It looked almost like a boxing ring as the onlookers, buyers, sellers and auctioneer gathered around. Fifty slaves were on the list to be sold. Near the bottom of the second page was the name Jonah, belonging to a Mr. Graves, of Charleston. Billy had it on good authority that Mr. Graves intended on selling the slave to a trader from up-river, who was going to take him to the plantation up the Altamaha where the slave's mother had been sold. He was of the opinion that this was the only way to keep him from running again, and if he continued to run, they would just have to sell him off to a train of shackled slaves going to New Orleans, at half price. It really was the only sensible thing to do.

In some ways this humanitarian gesture on the part of Mr. Graves seemed to appeal to Billy, and he longed to tell Eliza the good news and that maybe she could just follow the buyer up river, and try to make the best of things when he reached his new home. The trading went slow, and the room moved and swayed with the sales as families, mothers, children, fathers, all - went hither and yon as the auction gavel rose and fell.

Page two was reached, and a stately gentleman entered the room and worked his way to the stage near the auctioneer. "This next item is Jonah, a strong and healthy negra with a good mind and who can count. He can be a fine asset, one day, and can also carpenter. Could build a wagon, or any other item you could be needing. Maybe even rise as high as an overseer. Who will give me $500.00?", and the bidding started. One heckler from the back hollered out "Yes, and he can run good, too!", and the crowd laughed and jeered. The stately gentleman, now directly across from the auctioneer and so close he could reach him with his cane, raised his hand, offering the $500.00 as if it were a kind gesture which surely would end the bidding, and turned and smiled broadly at the crowd behind him.

"Six hundred", came a voice from across the room. The crowd turned with sudden interest, and saw a well-dressed Indian, accompanied by several other braves of various ages, moving gingerly toward the auction block.

"Six-hundred and fifty", said the gentleman.

"Seven hundred", replied the Indian.

The gentleman, not expecting this turn of events, reached in his pocket and pulled out a large was of paper money. He had only brought a thousand dollars, as he had expected to get this deal done quickly and cheaply. "Eight hundred", he said.

"Eleven hundred", was the reply from the Indian, now standing next to the auctioneer, and holding his money high in his hand. "Eleven hundred", he said again.

The auctioneer looked at the gentleman from Charleston. He would have offered credit if asked, but the man looked over at Jonah, then back at the Indian, and saw the determination facing him. "Yours", he said simply, and turned, spun about, and walked out of the room, the anger rising in his face and his ears now a bright shade of red. As he left the room, perturbed and visibly annoyed, he muttered for all who cared to hear, "Damn Creek traders, they should be run out of the county."

Just then, as the Indian who had been awarded the prize stepped upon the stage to inspect his purchase, a loud scream erupted from the corner of the room. The voice came from a nicely dressed young lady way back in the corner. The crowd turned, and as the air from her scream swirled about the room, she collapsed, and lay in a clump among the wooden chairs, some of which had scattered and upturned as she fell. Her chestnut hair was covering her face, which had perspired heavily, leaving tracks of white powder flowing like rivulets down her light brown face.

CHAPTER SEVENTEEN

IT WAS, OF course, Eliza. Unable to contain herself any longer, she had worked her way along the road, arriving in town on the day of the auction. She had managed to duplicate the formula given to her by MayMay, being careful to use all of the chants and phrases MayMay had taught her as best as she could, and she worried to excess when she couldn't find a small flower similar to one MayMay had used in Florida as part of the paste. To her credit, for the most part what she had come up with worked just about as well.

Changing into one of the dresses given to her by the Wilsons, she had found her way to the auction house and nestled in among the crowd, yearning for a look at Jonah. When she saw him brought in, with chains around his ankles and a look of deep sorrow upon his face, she wanted to rush up to him and put her arms around him. It seemed an eternity before his name was called up, and she strained to get a better look. She knew he would not recognize her, with her chestnut hair and her powdered face, but that didn't matter. There he was. Somewhat worse for wear, but alive and well, nevertheless. She watched the auctioneer. She had seen the older gentleman when he had entered the room, and she was sure that he would soon be headed north into Georgia with her man. And she would follow somehow, and they would be together. She heard the first offer, and then, to her great surprise, the second. But the crown was standing, and she couldn't make out the second bidder. When the sale was consummated, and the older gentleman turned around to leave, she could see the Indian and his entourage move forward to claim the chained man. It was Amato. Amato! It was more than she could bear. She screamed in agony, and fell out onto the floor.

Amato, on the other hand, could not believe his good luck. He had the slave Jonah, who, along with two other young men he had purchased, was just what the plantation owner who had financed this venture to Savannah had asked for. And with fate itself sealing the deal, he had, and at no extra cost,

44

recovered Eliza. No amount of make-up or other disguise could hide the child whom he had raised. It was Eliza all right. All he had to do now was to claim her as a runaway slave, and she would be his once again. He immediately informed the local magistrate that the woman, who clearly had negro blood, was his own escaped slave from the Hawkins encampment.

The Sheriff, taken up in the furor now created over the discovery of the negro girl, dressed as a white aristocrat, and confronted with the positive identification and explanation of her escape from the Indian trader, readily handed her over to him with little fanfare. The girl was too weak to put up much of a resistance, and her claim of being a free negro was one not taken seriously. "Where were her papers", he asked. "Where are his?" she responded. In the end, of course, the Sheriff relented to the Creek slave trader's demands. "Had she not tried to hide her identity?" said one. "Yes", said another, "and she had hidden her color." "She must be a runaway", said a third. Before the legality of the matter could be taken up further, the Indians had disappeared down the dusty road heading South to the river with their property. But they would not remain on the Altamaha. No, they would take the Western bend, and their paddles would pull toward Macon, and the Flint.

Amato set the pace for the four canoes, each containing a slave settled more or less in the middle, and shackled about the feet, with their arms loose in order to be free to oar. There were no rapids in the direction they were traveling, and the dryness of the late Spring slowed the current. He had placed the woman in the canoe with him. Jonah he put in the canoe behind him, and showed him his pistol. "This will be your reward", he explained, "If yu run on me", and he cocked the gun and placed it at Jonah's temple. He turned his head and spit tobacco from his mouth, and laughed out loud, firing the pistol aimlessly in the air. "We're headed for cotton country, and yu better pull your worth or the only cotton you'll ever see will be at the bottom of this here river when one of them black snakes with the cotton mouths wraps it 'round your sorry neck!" Jonah, who couldn't swim, was sufficiently convinced.

Eliza, on the other hand, felt neither the coldness of the iron about her ankles or the fatigue of her oar, for her mind was enveloped in a state of euphoria with the knowledge that, not only was Jonah alive, but they were headed in the same direction and apparently to the same location. Slave or free, they were together again. With each pull of the oar she would strain her neck backwards to try to catch a glance of her Jonah. And Jonah, watching for snakes, would strain back, with a smile for her from ear to ear.

Chapter Eighteen

W HATEVER DREAMS AND illusions the two of them shared as they paddled upstream were soon dashed as the reality of their circumstances became evident. Amato made it clear that it was his intention on bringing the three men he had purchased back to the plantation owner who had financed the trip. It was the same plantation owner who had wanted Eliza years ago, and who Amato had promised to sell her to. For the men, he would get his commission. For the woman, however, the money from her sale would be all his.

"What would she bring?" he wondered. The plantation owner, who had given up all hope of ever seeing the light skinned Eliza again, was overjoyed. "Name your price! Name your price!" he said excitedly to Amato when news of the precious cargo reached the tavern where he was drinking.

"Oh, not so fast", replied Amato, remembering the manner he had been treated in the past by the unscrupulous man now standing in front of him. "Who ever said she was for sale. She's my daughter, you know. I might just keep her for myself".

"Your daughter", replied the man. "Your daughter! Ha! That's a good one. Why, she's no more your daughter than she is mine. Tell you what. I'll give you a thousand dollars for her. In cash. One thousand dollars. You'll not get that sum of money for her anywhere around here. And I'll have you your money by tomorrow evening. What do you say?"

"Not a chance", replied Amato, sensing a windfall. "We'll just see what she will bring in Macon. We'll just see what the market will bring. Why, I can take her to Milledgeville and get more than that for her. There's a demand for her kind, and I intend to get top dollar. You'll not cheat me again, Mr. Winthrop, not again!"

Retreating out the door, Amato was certain the fish had taken the hook, and it was only a matter of time before he could begin to reel him in. Out in the road circling the courthouse square stood the four chained travelers, each holding a small bag containing their meagre possessions. The woman was now in the rear, and Jonah was in front. Amato reached to pick up the lead chain when he heard Winthrop holler out. "Twelve hundred. Fifteen!"

"Not a chance. We're to Macon!" he insisted.

"Fifteen hundred!" cried Winthrop! You'll never see the likes."

Amato thought to himself. A new record for these parts. Winthrop must definitely be too drunk to think straight. Winthrop, definitely under the influence and now aroused to action, felt for the pistol on his belt. He would not let this damn Creek get the best of him. "I'll have her", he belted out, "or no one will!"

The pistol let forth, and the ball whizzed by the head of Eliza and struck a tree. Splinters flew in all directions. Had he been sober, Winthrop would not have missed.

Amato turned in horror. He had not expected this. His valuable property was subject to being destroyed or seriously damaged. "Wait!" he hollered. "Ok. You can have her for Fifteen hundred."

Winthrop turned, looking out at the street where the woman lay, now up on all fours, and vomiting into a rut in the muddy road. "Hey, what's the matter with her? Is she sick? I'll not pay if she's not healthy. What's the matter here?"

Amato rushed to the woman, who was pale and moaning as she tried to pick herself up. "What's this?" he said. Then, as he watched her rise up, he could see the stretched belly. He had seen this before. "Why, the damn negro is pregnant!" he hollered. "She's damn pregnant!"

"Pregnant?" yelled Winthrop. "Why, I'll not pay that kind of money for a pregnant negro. Why, I wanted her for a concubine. Someone I could take to Kentuck. Now she's good for nothing but a field hand. The deal is off".

"A thousand, then", replied Amato. "But I keep the baby. What do you say?"

Winthrop was having nothing of it. How could he take her to Kentucky with him? All of the other men would be talking about the baby, and whose was it? It definitely wasn't his. What good was this woman at this point? He turned, disgusted, and retreated toward the bar. As he reached the door, he turned and looked again at the poor woman, still hunched over, sweat pouring down her face and chest. She was still beautiful, he thought, even as she stood. He still desired her. "Ok, then. One thousand, and you can have the baby."

Amato, who was standing next to Eliza, and trying to figure what he could sell the baby for when it arrived, didn't notice the shadow stealing up behind him. Suddenly, a large arm wrapped around his neck, like a boa constrictor, and the two men fell to the ground, kicking and rolling in the mud. Winthrop reached for a second pistol, one which he kept in his boot, and raced toward the two men. Jonah had the clear advantage, and the Indian was no longer breathing. He placed the small pistol next to the man's temple, and pulled the trigger. Jonah fell over, as parts of brain and bone splattered the ground.

"You can just take that off your commission", he said to Amato. "I ain't payin' for no dead negro."

CHAPTER NINETEEN

IF IT WASN'T for the baby growing inside of her, Eliza would have been at Winthrop, begging for a similar end as had just met her precious Jonah. Amato, somehow sensitive to the situation, punched her in the face, knocking her out, and ordered the two black men chained to her to carry her to Winthrop's plantation, where she was placed on a mattress in one of the slave cabins behind the main house. There she lay, for two weeks, unable to move.

"She gonna lose dat babe", said Louisa, a house negro, calmly. "She get no better, she gonna lose it, no questin." Louisa was the senior occupant of the small cabin, which was shared by three women, two men and four children. Her opinion was held in considerable esteem, and several of the others in the room nodded in agreement. Eliza heard them talking, and began to stir. "Nothing's going to happen to my baby", she stated matter of factly, and sat up and looked about the room. "Nothing, you hear me! Nothing. I'm having this child, and nothing will keep me from having this child".

"Chil belong to dat Indian, Mato, what brot yu here from Savan, Miss Eliza. Chil not yours to raise. Don' you know dat?"

"We'll see, we'll see about that", replied Eliza. We'll just see about that."

"Mas Winthrop, he don give the chil to Mato in da deal fo yu", piped in Louisa. "Mas Winthrop say he take you to Kentuck, be his woman. Take you wid de odder men up to Kentuck. You lik it dere, not have to wuk. Jus lay 'bout, doin' nothin'. You lucky."

"Well, if you think sleeping with that pig is lucky, you have a funny sense of luck. No, my luck ran out when Winthrop killed my Jonah. He'll pay for that. He'll never have me, if I have to kill him and go to hell for it. If there is a hell. I don't see how Winthrop and I could both end up in the same place. And he for sure is going straight to hell. So I'll go somewhere else, somewhere safe from the likes of him. I'll go to the Indian place. They have no Winthrops there."

"Well, soon as that baby yur carrin' gats here, why you'll see what's what", added Cain, who was about the same age as Louisa. "Soons dat babe comes out yo belly, why Mato be dere to snatch it fo' it hit de flow. If not den, den someday. You know someda he come fo' dat babe."

Eliza lay back down on the straw bed. It was May. The baby would be here in the Fall. She had all summer to plan what to do. "Plenty of time", she said to herself, and rolled over, returning to the comatose state from which she had recently emerged. Except now her choices were clear. Only the method remained hidden from her understanding.

CHAPTER TWENTY

MRS. MARTHA JOHNSTON, formerly of Montgomery, Alabama, and now a prominent resident of Jonesboro, Georgia, had a lot to be thankful for, considering what had happened to her husband. They had married in Montgomery, right after it became incorporated as a town, and her father, of the Moore family, had been quite successful in setting up a cotton plantation. Franklin Pitts Johnston, who had fought in the war for independence from the British in the Carolinas, and who had moved to Jonestown following his appointment as the new Circuit Judge, was in need of a wife, and his connections in Savannah had told him of the Moores. They had seven daughters, and it was felt that one of them would certainly meet Mr. Johnston's needs, and Martha did. The stage line from Milledgeville to Montgomery was not yet in operation, and so they had travelled by wagon back to Jonestown after the wedding.

Moore then built a large home, two stories high, only a short way from the courthouse, and was planning a family when he came down sick. The town's doctor was out tending to a broken leg in the next county, and by the time he returned, Franklin was dead of pneumonia.

Martha, who had fallen in love with Jonestown and her beautiful home, didn't want to go back to Alabama. So she stayed. She put in a garden. She added pigs, chicken, goats and cows. She put in fruit orchards and her own dairy, and before long her cooking was known far and wide. She put in table-board for the single men in the town, and when gold was discovered in the northern part of the state, she raised her prices. Board was ten dollars a month, payable in arrears, in gold, on the 1st day of the year.

The discovery of gold was by no means a minor event in the State of Georgia. It was a long and wide seam, running a hundred or more miles in longitude, and extending from the Carolina border completely across the state and into Alabama. Speculators and miners flooded the Northern counties of the State, and the Cherokee, who had possessed the land since winning the war against the Creek, were now in danger of being dispossessed themselves. Pressure was mounting in Washington, and Tennessee was running for President none other than the fiercest opponent of the Indians in the South, a man who promised to move the Cherokee and the Creek Westward, out of the hearts and minds of the expanding Western civilization riding high on cotton and now gold as well.

For Jonestown, it was a time of change, and for the time being, there was abundance and prosperity. It wasn't until the railroad came and was routed East of Jonestown that the burgeoning county seat began to lose its glory. But for now, the gold in and on the ground in the area of the vast seam was so prevalent that it was said in one of the Northeastern Georgia towns that "its streets were paved with gold", right out of the Bible. It lay in beds beneath the earth, and it lay upon the ground, in streams, creeks, and along the mountain trails. It was everywhere.

The lure of gold was something that Winthrop could not resist. The best beds started about 150 miles north of Jonestown, which was the closest town to his plantation. He forgot about everything else. With a long string of mules, ten of his best cotton slaves, his two sons, and four women who worked in the house, he set forth, even with the weather starting to turn cool and the October wind whistling through the trees late at night, signaling the end of Fall. They followed the old Indian trail Northeast. Winthrop had hardly given Eliza any thought, and when he did, it was about Kentucky in the summer. But that would be next summer. "She ain't no good to yu now, with the babe jest here, and her in covery", Cain reminded him.

Winthrop's travels to the gold fields was good news to Eliza, who had visited the woods on more than one occasion to try to conjure up some potion which she could use to bring down the monster. Her efforts had been futile. As much as she wanted to poison his tea or stab him with a knife, she somehow couldn't bring herself to commit the act itself. And now the baby was here. With Winthrop absorbed with his new obsession, she was left with only one enemy to contend with, at least for the time being, and that was Amato. She knew that it was only a matter of time until Amato came for her child.

Eliza's fortunes were vastly improved a few weeks after the Winthrop cavalcade departed. Apparently, as the party reached the foothills of the high mountains, a lone Indian approached their encampment. He seemed friendly enough, and after borrowing a few strips of deer meat, he had left. Then, as the party was moving out the next morning, Winthrop, riding atop his tall brown horse, was struck by an arrow which pierced his heart. No one saw where it came from, and there was no trail for them to follow. The general consensus was that it was the Indian who had come into the camp the previous evening. No one understood a motive. Cain had not seen the indian before, but he recognized the arrow. It was Yucchi.

The sale of Mr. Winthrop's effects was scheduled for the first day of the new year. It was expected that there would be a good crowd in town, and that this would be a good chance to get the best price. All sorts of goods were assembled for the sale, and twenty of the slaves were to be auctioned off. Martha Johnston, armed with the $1,200.00 in gold dust she had just collected from her ten table-boarders, was intent on bringing home one of the slaves to help her with managing her growing estate. When she saw Eliza, she knew that was who she wanted.

Coming home that afternoon, she prepared a sumptuous meal to celebrate the New Year and her increasing bounty. With all of the young men standing around the dining table, Martha explained that she had purchased a new house servant and she had cost her every bit of the $1,200.00 she had taken to the auction. "They'll be no mistreatin' of this here niggra", she said firmly, then adding and with a bit of a smile, "lessen its by me". I 'spect all of you young men to treat her civilly. And there'll be no foolin' around. Is that understood?" she inquired. Martha opened the kitchen door and called for Eliza. "Here she is. Eliza, meet the boys." Eliza entered the room, as beautiful as ever, but with her head bowed and little more than a faint smile upon her face. She was dressed in a bright cotton dress Martha had given her. Beyond the door leading to the kitchen, one of the men thought he could hear a small child crying.

"Gold Dust! exclaimed a tall Irish man from the corner of the room. "We'll call her Gold Dust! Why, she's pretty as a picture." There was much general agreement, and a bottle of Irish whiskey appeared, with drinks all around.

PART TWO

1603 - OFF THE CAROLINA COAST

CHAPTER TWENTY-ONE

THE SKY WAS still dark as the ship approached the large outer island near the sound. There was an inlet, according to his map, and the hastily concocted plan was to put in, take on water and whatever available food presented itself, and get back out to sea as quickly as possible. Much had been lost in the gale. All hope of completing the ship's mission of delivering its large cargo of black slaves to a Brazilian port near modern day Rio de Janeiro had been lost when the main mast of the ship split in two, killing one of the best seamen, and rendering the ship practically unmanageable, if not outright unseaworthy. Difficult to control, the ship had drifted as much as it had sailed, until if found itself in the Atlantic Gulf Stream, where it began to move Northwestwardly up the coast of North America. Much depended on getting the vessel back to a European port in one piece, where she could be repaired in, as the ship's captain described it, an honest way. Antao Gonsello was the Captain of the vessel, The Barcelona, and he was leery of the reefs. He took great pains to make sure he stayed far enough outside of the inlet until daylight arrived. It would be dangerous enough in daylight.

As the dawn broke, the Captain aimed the ship inland. Just as he arrived at a place he thought he could safely put in, a small boat appeared out of a narrow opening along the entrance to the sound. Antao grabbed his spyglass and peered at the object as it bounced along. Two strong men were working the oars, and a third, dressed as a soldier, appeared to be standing, with one hand on the rudder, and the other holding a large weapon which looked like a long wooden stick which had suddenly exploded at one end. The metal of his armor glistened in the sun. "Ahoy", shouted the soldier. "Ahoy! Ye've come to rescue us! Thank the Lord in Heaven!"

Antao could not hear what was said next by the soldier, but by the looks of the boats occupants they were in desperate straits. Finally he was able to make out the call to "Follow us!" yelled by all as if in unison. Gonsello noted what appeared to be what was left of a large sloop, broken apart by the rocks and laying on its side at the shoreline. A fast ship, he thought, but fast no longer. Instantly, he ordered all sails furled and the anchor dropped. A boat was lowered, and Ant, as he was known to his crew due to his work ethic, went ashore with five of his best men. There, he was met by a young officer, covered in sweat, and breathing heavily. "You're just in time, he explained - we're in a delicate condition here. The natives have us surrounded, and are slowly starving us out. Our ship broke on the reef, and we tried to befriend the natives, but things went sour, and fighting broke out. We went inland and found their chief. He wasn't one to listen to reason, and in the disagreement we ended up cutting off his poor head. We thought that would frighten them off, but instead it just made them madder, and we fear for our lives, sure enough!"

"What are you doing here?", the Captain inquired. "By what right are you in these waters?"

"On the Queens own command", the officer replied. "We've been ordered to make a hide-a-way for our privateers, so that we can better pirate the Spanish gold. I think it best if I not say more. We were well armed, well provisioned, and had two cannon, but lost everything but a few pistols, a blunderbuss, and the swords - we managed to salvage most of the swords. But our provisions, our food, water, everything else was lost. At first the Indians were friendly and offered us food, but something went wrong. The Captain and four of our men were killed in the first attack. Six more have been killed since, and three are wounded. They are picking us off. There are about thirty of us left, plus the wounded. Our luck had run out - at least until you came along."

"On the Queens command, say you. English then. I think ye should be better served if you referred to the Kings command. It's King James now that rules these waters what's not governed by King Phillip of Spain. And the waters afloat with rumors that peace is on the horizon. Poor James has had his fill, and this privateering is about to end. Or so they say. Me, I thinks the waters will always have the pirate, lawful and crime-hearted. Sadly, he responded to the plea. "Well, I can't help ye", replied the Captain. "I'm near out of supplies myself, and I've got a hundred Negroes in the hole, and not enough food to feed them. You'll just have to fend for yourselves."

"Leave them, leave them!" begged the Lieutenant. "It's them or us, you must leave them!"

Gonsello knew as he said it that he couldn't abandon the English expedition to such a fate. Rumors of a peace conference between the two countries were abundant, and the English King would not easily forgive the abandonment of soldiers in these desperate straits if there was any hope of rescuing them, and word of such conduct could be taken the wrong way. "It could end the war!" he mused to himself. There was much political gain to be made in the rescue of this band of desperadoes. Much more than would be gained in trying to return the black cargo to Portugal. And besides, these English sailors were men, not property, and their priority when it came to survival could not be questioned. He searched the eyes of the desperate crew, which by now had formed somewhat of a semi-circle around him, and knew what he had to do. "Bring the Negroes ashore!", he ordered.

The black horde did not need to be chained. They were exhausted, sick, hungry, many with sores on their bodies, and in no position to put up any resistance. There were about 20 women in the crew - the rest men. No small children - most were between twelve and thirty years of age. A leader emerged from amongst them. He spoke some broken Dutch and spotty Portuguese.

"Name?" demanded Gonsello, speaking through a translator.

"Cahlib" was the reply.

"Well, Cahlib, I am going to have to leave you and your fellow passengers here for awhile. There is a native tribe about five miles inland. There is a small boat you can use to take yourselves from this island to the mainland. I must warn you, the natives are hostile. They may simply kill all of you. On the other hand, they may not."

Cahlib looked puzzled, although he clearly understood the situation. They were being abandoned on the island. With little water, and less food. The natives were laying in wait to massacre the white sailors. He looked about him. He saw there was no hope of resistance - no one was in condition to fight. It would be enough of a challenge to get them all from the island to the mainland. "I understand", he replied in his broken Dutch. A few casks of water were brought from The Barcelona, along with a little food. Nothing else.

Gonsello began the laborious task of taking the English crewmen on board his ship and stripping the small island of whatever food and water he could put his hands on. The English party was obviously relieved at this most fortunate turn of events. The gale which had crushed their sloop against the reefs had also brought The Barcelona to their rescue, albeit by accident or the grace of

CHAPTER TWENTY-TWO

C AHLIB WAS THE son of a chief. He, along with about ten of his tribesmen, were ambushed as they were returning from a hunt. Captured by slave traders from the Hindula tribe, the next thing they knew they were chained, beaten, and forced to march many miles to a seaport, where they were imprisoned inside a large castle built many years earlier to foster the gold trade along a strip of the African continent known as the Gold Coast. Those who had survived the forced march and the imprisonment in the castle were herded into the Portuguese ship Barcelona, destined for the slave market in Brazil. Chained to their bunks, they were crammed in the lower decks of the ship, much like sardines in a can. With little water and food, many had perished even before the gale split the main mast in two. He was one of the first from his tribe who were sought by the traders because of his tribal region's knowledge of farming and fishing, and their ability to survive the tropical heat and misery associated with working in the South American sugar plantations. "Black gold", they were called in the trade. Black gold, a commodity, much like any other commodity. Prized for its scarcity and usefulness.

As the son of a leader among his own people, Cahlib considered himself destined for greatness. In the weeks and months that passed following his capture, he tried to comprehend what had happened to him and what the future lay in store. Tales of the capture and sale of African slaves was not something he had been ignorant of, but it seemed just a distant possibility until it actually happened to him. "It happened so fast", he mused to himself, "and the men knew exactly what they were doing." He was a strong, healthy warrior, and yet here he was, half-starved, naked, moved a huge distance from his homeland - all in a matter of weeks. How would he ever get back? His mother, his father, his brothers and sisters. All gone from his existence.

And the seasickness. He never thought he would be able to hold down a meal again. He saw friends, captured along with him, perish from malnutrition, and he realized that he had to control his dizziness and eat if he was going to get off the ship alive. The tropical heat had become stifling as the journey progressed, but after the gale the ship seemed to stray into cooler waters. Then, a second gale. The ship seemed to pull and tear at every seam. "Shore", someone yelled, and suddenly his spirits jumped skyward.

It seemed an intolerable amount of time between hearing the cry of "land ho" and the arrival of the Sergeant at Arms, yelling with each step, ordering the slaves unshackled and brought topside. Getting off of the ship, for whatever reason, was no doubt going to be a joyous occasion. But as he passed the body of one of his tribesmen, limp and motionless in the ragged hammock near the passageway to the top deck of the ship, he thought that, perhaps, his fallen comrade was the lucky one, and an uncertainty began to gnaw at his gut.

When Captain Gonsello approached him and told him of the situation and the fact that they were essentially going to be abandoned on the island, surrounded by what seemed to be thousands of hostile natives, his joy, which had turned to anxiety, now turned to stark fear. As the Barcelona sailed out of view, he looked about his fellow passengers and realized there was indeed no hope of resistance. Few could even walk a straight line. The strongest would have to man the boat, the same one the three seamen of the beached schooner had rowed out to meet the Barcelona as she entered the bay. "Well", he said trying to humor himself, "at least I'm free!"

He looked about the island. There was plenty of fish, but nothing to catch them in. There was small game, but no spears, bows or arrows to shoot them with. The captain had not left enough food for them to last three days, and the water would soon be gone. They must move inland, and take their chances with the native inhabitants.

The task of transporting a hundred men and women, in ill health and hungry, thirsty, scared and bewildered, was not easy. The boat was small, and could only hold about twelve people, including the rowers, and it took the better part of an hour to make a round trip. That turned into about ten trips, and when they landed on the fifth trip, word reached him that a group of wildly painted natives armed with long bows were gathering on the edge of the woods surrounding their new encampment.

There was nothing Cahlib could do. If the natives killed them, then so be it. There was no purpose in fighting, they had nothing to fight with, and so he kept himself to the task at hand of getting everyone from the outer island to the mainland. Those in the worst shape were saved for last, as they were the most helpless. But really, no one was in much of a position to fight. They would have to throw themselves on the mercy of their hosts.

Deep in the woods, the Indian leader, Ootonabaugh, watched from the limb of a tall hickory tree as the small boat went back and forth. He had sent word to the tribe mico that the white invaders had developed black skin, and it was considered magic of some kind. Clearly the white invaders were to be killed. But these men had changed their skins, and the situation would have to be handled very carefully. This demanded a leader greater than he to make the decision as to what to do.

Several days passed. Word finally came that the Powhatan, the Chieftain of a family of more than thirty indigenous tribes, and known as the Powhatan Confederation, was coming himself to decide the matter. Ootonabaugh had had the black tribe carefully counted. There were many more than the thirty or so whites they had counted originally. Not only could they change the color of their skin, they could also multiply. This was great magic, indeed. If they were armed with the same firesticks that they had seen the white men carry, they would be a formidable force to reckon with.

Powhatan arrived with his half-brother, Opechancanough, who was more the warrior and less the statesman than Powhatan. Opechancanough lobbied for an immediate slaughter. Whoever they were, and with whatever armament they had, they had invaded their country, and it was not good medicine to let them live. Powhatan, whose Indian name was Wahunsenacawh, had travelled widely throughout the Southeastern part of North America, and was rumored to have even been to Spain itself. He had heard of a similar group of black men who had been abandoned by the Spanish. They had been traded as slaves, and brought a generous bounty. Powhatan saw no reason to pass up the opportunity, and he sent word to send in a peace mission and try to locate their leader, if any. He would talk to him and see if they could be persuaded to surrender peacefully. Dead, they were worth nothing.

The meeting was finally arranged, and Cahlib and three of his former tribesmen were escorted to the Confederation encampment. Powhatan recognized the black skin - he had seen it long ago. There was no magic here. When he learned they were unarmed and had no guns, and had been abandoned by the white invaders, the outcome was obvious. "Surrender or die", he said to Cahlib. "We will treat you well, and sell you to the Cherokee."

"Who are the Cherokee?", asked Cahlib.

"A mighty tribe from the North who are moving South along the great mountains to the West. They are in need of slaves, and they are not bad masters. They may even allow you to work and buy your freedom."

Cahlib was a man without options. They were out of food. They had no weapons. He surrendered his band of black Africans to the Powhatan, and his brief tenure of freedom came to an end.

CHAPTER TWENTY-THREE

CAHLIB WAS NOT unhappy with his decision to surrender peacefully. Resistance was futile, and the loss of freedom at the time meant little to his small band, abandoned in a strange land in ill health and with no means of survival. They now had food, and as they were marched Northward they began to regain some of the strength which the long voyage had deprived them. Finally they came to a mighty river which opened into the ocean at a great bay. There a temporary shelter was created, and their wounds were treated by one of the tribal medicine men. The trip had not been the forced march that they had experienced in the Gold Coast, and most everyone had made it safely to the main encampment of the Chief.

Word of the sale of the black prisoners travelled quickly, and a trade meeting was finally arranged. The sale was to be conducted inland, near the great mountains that had been described to Cahlib by the leader Powhatan. This trip would take several weeks, and it was clear to him that his little band was being fattened up, healed and made ready for market. "A life of slavery is a life of slavery", he thought to himself, even though it was held out to be better than the one he had evaded by the fortunate gale that deterred the Portuguese ship from its sugar plantation destination in Brazil.

As the days grew closer to the great trade council Cahlib noticed that his band of black compatriots was being placed into smaller and smaller groups, each isolated from the others. Some were sent to other villages. The women were separated. Some of the women were taken out and sent to the home of the Chief. These would not be sold, at least not for now. The weakest, deemed unfit for sale, were placed in a hut. No food was brought to them, and their outcome carefully predicted. Finally, as the day of the beginning of the journey to the trade expedition arrived, each of the black slaves that were to be sold was bound by the wrists, and a rope chain was wrapped around each neck. The slaves were then assigned to a keeper, and the keeper led its prisoner as you would an animal out onto the path leading to the forest. The long train set out with much merriment and excitement among the Indian braves, who looked forward to the adventure and the excitement of meeting a new tribe. Many had not seen a Cherokee, and they were curious to see what they looked like. It was rumored that they possessed a firestick like the ones the white invaders possessed.

The excitement continued among the warriors, but as the days wore on, the trail became rockier, with many roots across the path. Streams had to be crossed, and the foothills of the vast mountain chain were mostly uncharted, so the trail, such as it was, would disappear and then re-emerge miles further along. The guards became increasingly insensitive to the troubles of their captors, who had to travel without shoes and whose feet were often bleeding as they marched along. "Let the Cherokee make them shoes" was the common sentiment. The guard assigned to Cahlib had grown weary with his task, and would often jerk the chain about Cahlib's neck out of amusement, and he seemed to relish in the anguish of his captive. "Would it be like this with the Cherokee?" Cahlib wondered.

Finally the mountains appeared. Cahlib had never seen anything like it. They were magnificent. They seemed to stretch forever in each direction - tall and fierce. It was the fall of the year, and the brilliant yellows, oranges and browns of the leaves painted a glorious scene. Like a mighty river, Cahlib thought, these mountains must have a mighty soul. He wanted to be free, like the mountain, and the rope chain about his neck seemed to dig a little deeper with each step.

The trade counsel was to be conducted in a valley between two of the mountain peaks. It was necessary to cross the first mountain, and Cahlib could hear the warriors talking about setting up a camp before the counsel the following morning. Opechancanough was leading the Federation at the counsel, so there was always the possibility that things could turn sour and fighting break out. As they reached the peak of the first mountain, Cahlib's keeper had taken the lead and was pulling Cahlib along. His feet slipped, and the rope tore into Cahlib's throat, choking him until he almost blacked out. Instead of helping him up, his keeper began to beat him with a wooden war club. Cahlib felt the blows, but was unable to fend them off. A tooth flew from his mouth, and he watched almost as if in a dream as the slave next to him reached down and picked him up and put him on his back. When the group reached the peak, they stopped, and the slave released his burden down to the ground. Bloodied, Cahlib saw something glistening in the rocks at his feet. He reached for it. It was a piece of flint, sharp as a razor blade. It must have fallen from one of the warrior quivers. He placed it carefully in his mouth. The keeper of the slave who had carried him was laughing with Cahlib's keeper about what had happened going up the mountain.

Each night on the trip to the mountains the keepers would untie the rope around their charges' neck and tie their feet together, so that they would have to sleep on their stomachs with their hands behind their backs, and then their feet and hands would be tied. This made it almost impossible for anyone to escape. On the night before the counsel, however, the keepers were to participate in a tribal ceremony, so all of the slaves were herded into a makeshift corral. Each slave was tied to a stake, and the corral was guarded by four braves carefully chosen among the best warriors in the expedition.

As the revelry reached its crest, Cahlib took the flint from his mouth and spit it into the palm of his hand. Carefully he sawed the rope which held him to the stake. Two of the guards were arguing, and a third had fallen asleep. He cut the rope about his wrists. He grabbed a bag of dried venison that had been carelessly left by the fourth guard, who was checking the rear of the enclosure. He slithered along the grass until he could see a trail leading into the valley where the counsel was to take place. Then he jumped up and began to run.

The moon was new and was giving very little light. What seemed like a million stars shone overhead, and Cahlib could make out the Cherokee encampment near the base of the second mountain. He ran directly towards it, then veered off and headed straight up the mountain. The initial ascent was sloped and easy, but the path was his own and it was unfamiliar ground. He was sure he had been spotted by the guards, but then he didn't hear them behind him. Maybe, in the excitement, they had taken him for a deer. He stopped and listened for the sound of a pursuer. Nothing. Tearing at the limbs and underbrush, he picked his way along the rim until he finally arrived at the crest. Then he heard the cry of the guard. A long, horrible scream, and he knew it meant they had realized he had escaped. The clouds had moved beyond the new moon, giving some light, and the stars from the top of the mountain seemed to have their own glow. He ran.

Cahlib had come from a tribe that was used to running, and running was something he could do well. The biggest problem was he had no idea where he was going, and who or what lay ahead of him. Faster and faster he travelled, all through the night, without stopping. As the sun began to break on the horizon, he could make out the valley below to his left. He was traveling South. For three days he ran, stopping only for water from a stream, or to chew on a piece of the venison. He was afraid to stop, and from time to time would find himself asleep, standing up, or curled in a ball upon the ground. When the venison gave out, he grabbed berries. Some people are born with special abilities, and Cahlib was blessed with the ability to read and understand the environment around him. He watched the birds, and saw where they fed. They would often lead him to a patch of berries or other fruit. He had a knack for being able to tell what was edible and what was not. He watched the fish and saw where they pooled. He made a small spear, and soon had his first trout. He could read the trails of the beaver and the otter, and was amazed at the size of the bear which roamed the mountain, also looking for food. Deer were everywhere, but he could not get close enough with his small spear to kill one. With every mile he made a new discovery. The mountain laurel seemed to make the landscape almost surreal, it was so beautiful, and he began to imagine that he was traveling through paradise.

At the end of the third day he collapsed, his body completely exhausted. If he had left a trail that could be followed, then he would just have to be caught. Nothing seemed to work. His legs would not move, even as he talked to them, ordering them to pick up his weary torso. But his legs, his arms, his feet and hands, they simply would no longer do his bidding. He collapsed into a heap, his head spinning, and his body fell to the ground.

When he awoke, he was laying by a brisk mountain stream. Birds were singing overhead, and the sun was shining on his chest, warming him. A slight breeze moved across his face, and he seemed to himself to be returning from the dead. In his collapsed state he had begun to dream. He had dreamed that he was being taken up to a great house where he was bathed and fed. He was offered drink from a golden cup. The drink was strong and thick, black as tar but sweet. It altered his consciousness, and he could see and understand all of life, all of its secrets, all of its mysteries. Its perfection, and its enigma. All of it was revealed, and then it disappeared from his mind, leaving only the memory that, at one time, he possessed such knowledge. It gave him a sort of peace, which followed him all of his days. In his old age, he came to believe in the soul of the mountains, and in the spirit people, the Nunnehi as the Creek called them, who lived in the spirit world but who would travel to visit with humans, especially in their time of need, and nurture them, and sometimes bring them back to life. A spirit people, they were known as "The People Who Lived Anywhere", and they were thought to live in great townhouses in the highlands. It was the Nunnehi, he believed, which had placed him beside the running water of the stream, warmed by the sun, feeling refreshed, and able to go forward into the morning light. For the second time in his travels, he was free.

CHAPTER TWENTY-FOUR

CAHLIB CONTINUED ALONG the mountain range, always heading Southwestwardly. He had travelled several weeks in this manner, and had not seen another human being. He trapped a squirrel, lit a fire, and had made a stew, and was congratulating himself on his accomplishment, when suddenly he realized he was not alone. He could feel their presence before he could see them. From the corner of his eye, he could see strange forms moving in his direction. Three warriors, dressed in warpaint and carrying large wooden warclubs, and they definitely had him in their sights. Then, to his left, he saw the children, two walking and an infant, and a woman carrying a large bundle of sticks above her head, which she sat down as she gathered the children about her. The three men came within about ten feet of Cahlib, and then began to discuss something among themselves. He was outnumbered, and he figured these strange people were the Cherokee, and that he had been foolish to think they had not followed him this far, and he should never have taken the time to trap the squirrel. But the three men made no further move in his direction, and continued talking among themselves. It was a dialogue he had never heard before, and the warriors were not dressed like the men of the Powhatan. It seemed like they were taken aback by this stranger, and they seemed to be arguing amongst themselves about what they had just seen.

Later, when he understood their dialogue, he learned what they were discussing. Word had travelled quickly across the valley floor and along the mountain range about the black man who had escaped the Powhatan. The Cherokee had given their best mountain trackers the task the morning after the escape of finding the escaped slave. They had come up empty handed, and their failure had almost led Opechancanough to declare war on them, but by this time he had been so infatuated with the firestick that the Cherokee had brought with them that he eventually lost interest in everything else. The strange Indians who now hovered around him were not the Cherokee, nor were they a band loyal to the Powhatan. No, these were members of the Bear Clan of the mighty Creek Indian Nation, and they were on a hunting and fishing expedition up the streams running off the beginnings of a huge mountain range. They were traveling in hastily made birch bark canoes, and most of the canoes were filled with game or fish. The debate, it seems, was in how to offer this embattled hero, who had escaped their old and distrusted neighbors, the Powhatan, and their new and even more distrusted neighbors, the Cherokee, a ride.

Finally, a canoe was brought up and a large buck was quickly sliced into small pieces and distributed among several other canoes which were gathering along the shore at the news of the black man's discovery. Before long, Cahlib found himself traveling downstream, not as a black slave of the Cherokee, but as the free, and somewhat heroic, newly adopted member of the Creek Nation.

Now the Creek are an old people. Their stories go back to a time when the earth was covered in water, and there was only one piece of dry land. This story, which had its roots in folklore since the time of man, somehow had managed to travel, like the Creek themselves, down the rivers and streams of the planet, until its story tellers found themselves, in the Sixteen hundredth year of the white man's Lord, to be the inhabitants of an enchanted land known today as the State of Georgia.

The Creek were not big believers in blood. Blood alone could make you a member of their tribe, but it was not a prerequisite of membership. The Nation itself was divided into various Clans, and the Clans maintained their identity through a process by which each person belonged to the Clan of his or her mother, who belonged to the clan of her mother. So if you got married, your children belonged to the Clan of your wife. In that way, the Creek women maintained a great deal of power within the family structure. The children were often raised by the brother of the child's mother, and this seemed to keep things in some kind of order. During the advent of slavery in North America, the Creek owned and traded in slaves as well as most all colors of people did, and it became such a strong part of their society that the white settlers in the Carolinas even made them buy permits to engage in the slave trade. It may have been from the matrilineal nature of their culture that slavery itself developed the practice of determining a person's slave or free status by going by the mother's status. If the mother was a slave, then so was the child.

Blood not being a requirement of membership, the adoption of Cahlib into the Bear Clan was an easy thing to do. He simply belonged. Slowly he learned the language and the customs of the clan and the larger tribe beyond. But he was lonely, and the nature of the culture was to promise the women as young girls, so most of the women were having children of their own by the time they were physically able to bear them. In the Bear Clan, all of the available women were taken. Cahlib would have to wait until one of the warriors was killed in battle, succumbed to some fatal illness, or had a tragic accident. And then, it would not be a matter of picking a wife, it would be "wife by default".

In addition to many other attributes, Cahlib was blessed with one of those endearing personalities that soon made him a welcome member in most every hut in the Clan. Everyone was in agreement that he should have a wife, but there was just no one was willing to give up their own, and some of the younger braves were themselves looking.

Just when it seemed as though Cahlib would never find a bride, a strange thing happened. A war party, seeking revenge on the Monacans, a neighboring tribe who had killed one of their Clansmen, stumbled across a white woman who had been captured as a child and who was being held by them as a slave. The woman cried out as they left the Monacan village and ran after them. They tried to run her off, but she would not leave them, and, as she was able to keep up with them as they returned home, she entered the village and sought the help of the mico – the tribe's leader. The mico looked at the woman with pity, as a large part of her nose had been ripped off by the jealous women in the Monacan village, envious of her natural beauty when they learned the tribal leader was developing an interest in her. The mico was concerned she would not find a mate, and was about to expel her from the village or sell her back to the Monacan. Cahlib had heard of the woman, and entered the hut of the mico while her fate was being discussed.

"I will take her!" he exclaimed from the back of the room. The crowd parted as he came forward to claim his bride. It was only then that he saw her disfigured condition. The mico, seeing the reaction on Cahlib's face as he saw the tortured woman, offered him an out, and was prepared to banish her, when Cahlib turned and faced the crowd. "I will take her, I said, and I will".

Chapter Twenty-Five

THE MARRIAGE OF Cahlib and the disfigured white woman of the Monacan's was not an event that went unnoticed by the tribe. Many thought that Cahlib had become desperate, and that his marriage was an act of that desperation. But that was not the case at all. Cahlib's own mother had been savagely scarred by a neighboring tribe as a child, and he had always admired his father for marrying her. Never once did his father mention or make fun of the jagged scar which stretched from his mother's brow, down her cheek, and across her other cheek. Her right ear had been cut in two, and the scars were thick as there had been no medicine or knowledge available on how to treat such wounds. When he saw the Monacan woman, huddled in the corner of the mico's large hut, the image of his own mother engulfed him, and he acted instantly to protect her from the Clan's humiliation.

Her Christian name was Mary. The Monacan had given her the name Antheka, which meant "woman of spirit", and she did live up to her name. Mary made it clear from the beginning that she didn't want any pity from Cahlib due to her looks. She would cook and do all of the things the women were expected to do. And she had no illusions about leaving or going back to the white man. For one thing, she was developing a love for the Creek way of life. She loved the feeling of belonging which the Clan shared with everyone, even these adopted creatures who stood out so at the Clan's gatherings. She loved their simple religion, their belief in an afterlife, and their sense of justice. She admired Cahlib, and thought of his heroic escape from the Powhatan as just that - heroic. She did not see him as a black man. She saw him as a man. A man who she could love, and who seemed to love her. A man who rescued her from humiliation, and who saved her from abandonment to the wilderness, or worse, being sold back to the Monacan. On their wedding night, she came to him and opened her body to him. He responded. There was no sense of shame or misgiving. She felt every bit the woman, and she felt safe and wanted.

Mary bore Cahlib three children. The first one was named Hopping Turtle. She was a delight. Every time Cahlib saw her, he could not help but smile. She made his heart seem lighter and his mood stayed upbeat whenever he was around her. There was just something about her, something happy. A happy child, and a happy poppa.

The second child they called Mary, after her mother, and her Creek name was Running Deer. She was the athlete. She competed with the men as they ran after the deer in the hunt, and she learned to shoot a bow and arrow as straight as any man in the tribe. The women looked at her as an aberration, and they put up with her. The men seemed to be attracted to her, even with her tomboyish ways, and Cahlib was assured he would have no trouble marrying her off, and he would get a good dowry for her.

The third child, Adam, was trouble from the start. In the first place, he was born completely white. Not brown, or a shade of black, or a brown, or a brownish white, or even a very light colored brown. No, Adam was completely white. Cahlib was certain that Mary had not been unfaithful, as there were no other white men anywhere around. No, he was the father, and his son was white. "Well", he thought, "it must mean that the white men are supposed to possess this land as well as the black men and the red men." Other members of his Creek family were not so certain. "How can this be?" they would say. Neither Adam nor Mary had any explanation for the aberration. To them, it really didn't matter, as Adam was a son, and Cahlib wanted a son very badly. As Adam began to grow from childhood to manhood, Cahlib saw in him a strength and will that he had seen in his father, and he could not have been more proud. "He has the heart of lion!" he would tell Mary. "Strong, good heart. Make us much proud. Black man heart. White man soul. Good mix. Just too white. But ok."

Mary, too, was unconcerned with her son's skin color. She thought he looked like her brother, but it pained her to think of the past and her family. All she would speak of was a sister, Sarah, whom she was apparently very close to. She would put the matter out of her thoughts, as it only brought her pain to remember those days - the days before her capture by the Monacans. Was she ever not an Indian? She buried the past as one would bury a favorite dog. She would live for the moment. And her moments were good with Cahlib.

Mary and Cahlib were happy with the Creek, and they prospered. They were frugal and were able to accumulate a bit of wealth. Mary, who knew English, taught it to Cahlib, who seemed eager to learn it, as is came easier to him than his native tongue came to Mary. Their children grew up learning a combination of Creek and English, and Mary insisted that only English be spoken in their home. It was a difficult language, and much more complicated than the Creek, but the family honored her wishes. From time to time a white trader would visit the village, and Mary would be called by the mico as an interpreter. Knowledge of English gave the Clan a certain advantage in trade circles, and word spread that the Bear Clan could speak English, and that brought the status of the family up, as things go.

As Adam grew into manhood, thoughts about his family, on both sides, began to haunt him. He was looked on with some sense of distrust by his fellow tribesmen, who had heard bad things about the white settlers who had established a colony where the James River met the ocean. As the colony prospered, word travelled throughout the region of their desire to take more and more land. Stories of war and massacres, on both sides, drifted back to the Creek villages. The Cherokee, too, were becoming more and more of a problem as a never ending tide of Cherokee families began to populate the Appalachian Mountain range, taking more and more of the Creek hunting land from them. There were less beaver in the streams. Fewer otter. The Cherokee were beginning to trade deer skins with the white man, and that made if possible for them to buy guns. With guns, they made a formidable enemy to the Creek, and this forced the Creek to find new ways to compete and survive.

Then, one day, following the visit of a white trader, calamity struck the village. Many of the villagers began to develop large sores all over their bodies. Mary became very sick. The medicine doctor was summoned, but her illness was beyond his powers. It was smallpox, but of course the people of the village had no name for it, and no cure. Many of the whites had developed an immunity to the disease, but Mary was not so fortunate. The medicine man said it was a ghost left behind by the trader, a ghost who brought this great misery upon the Clan. For days she languished, and in her fever she would cry out for Sarah. "Sarah! I'm coming Sarah!" she would scream. Cahlib grew despondent, and the girls too. Then, as she lay dying, she looked at Adam and smiled. Her pain was passing, and she was calm and thoughtful. "Adam", she said, "find my sister". And with that, her life left her.

Chapter Twenty-Six

WHEN MARY SPOKE those dying words about finding her sister, Sarah, Cahlib became distressed. He desired to keep his family together, and it had never occurred to him that one of his children might leave the village, or the Clan. Adam's mother had taught him some English, but as he had no one but her and his sisters to share it with, it was broken and uneven. Adam himself was frightened at first at the prospect of leaving the village and going on his mother's quest. These new people, they would wonder who he was, and where he had come from. They would make fun of him. He didn't know their ways. He was raised a Creek, and a Creek he would remain. Running Bear, on the other hand, thought it would be a great adventure, and Hopping Turtle was so busy raising a family of her own that the thought of her brother leaving the village seemed only a distant reality. She really didn't think he would go. Where would he go to look, anyway? The chances of finding her Aunt after all these years was catastrophically remote. Could he just walk into the white village and start asking around for some white person that had a sister who disappeared some fifty years ago by the name of Mary? Highly unlikely.

The tribal council had their own ideas. They seemed to like the idea of Adam going to the white settlement. He could find out about their intentions, and learn about their notorious weapon - the firestick. He would make a great spy.

Cahlib thought the whole thing foolhardy. "In the first place", he said, "you will probably get killed. If not by the white men, then by the Powhatan. No one will know whose side you are on. If you tell them that you are a Creek, they will laugh at you, because you most certainly don't look like a Creek. If you tell them you are a white man, they will want to know where you were born, and who your parents were, and what you are doing here in the middle of the Powhatan Nation with no history and no past. They won't believe or trust you, and your chances of finding out anything of importance for the tribe are practically non-existent. And speaking of non-existent, your chances of finding Mary's sister are completely non-existent, if you ask me. Your mother remembered very little of her childhood, and she was only six when captured by the Monacan. You will never find her. The trip is not only a waste of time, it is also a mistake. A bad mistake, if you ask me."

Adam loved his father. He loved his sisters, and he loved his Clan. The only thing he loved more was his mother, and he was not about to fail her. He realized there was no convincing Cahlib. He would have to make his arrangements and slip out of the village at night when his father was sleeping. But Cahlib could read the language of his son's face, and he knew what he was planning before Adam put back his first stash of deer meet. "Here", he said, pulling out an old leather pouch. "I borrowed this from the Powhatan. It is one of theirs. I'm sure they didn't miss it as much as I needed it. Now you can have it. It will bring you good luck. Take Hopping Turtle's oldest son with you. He's fourteen now, and can help you carry the canoe over the rapids. You will need to make one, if you're going to find the white ones. I've drawn a map of the trail as best as I remember it. The mico will know the path to the river. I have some things that you can use to make a good canoe. Come, we'll figure it out."

Big Toe, the oldest son of Hopping Turtle, didn't have to be persuaded. He already had a bow and a quiver full of arrows. He had made his own knife, and had a new pair of moccasins. He was old for his age, and quite up for the adventure. "Toe", his uncle warned him, "this is a long journey. We may be gone a long time. Can you live without your family for such a long time?"

Big Toe thought about it for a moment, and reached for his bow.

The mico had planned a route, just in case. The senior tribal leaders, the micalgi, knew the trail Northeast, along the mountains - much the same trail that Cahlib had taken years ago. Don't go too far, they warned. When you get to the Moratuc, you must take it. Build a canoe on the creek near the mountain, and it will lead you to the Moratuc. Take the Moratuc, and it will take you many miles to a giant lake by the great sea. There, you can go North, up the black waters, to the white settlement. The trip to the sea we have taken. The trip from the sea to the white settlement we don't know. If you stay too long on the mountain trail, you will be in the lands of the Monacan. There you are in grave danger of being captured or killed because you are white. They don't like the white man, and you cannot trust them.

The Monacan people, unlike the Powhatan, were afraid of and hence distrusted whites generally and stayed clear of them, so it was unusual for them to have one like Mary in their midst. They, like the Cherokee after them, had moved South and settled. They believed that mankind came from four women, and was divided into four tribes. They were all of different colors, and their names were Sagoones, Occaneechis, Tutelos and Tuscaroras. The Monacan were from Tuscaroras, and they liked the Africans, but had no use for the whites, and didn't know the yellows. An oracle had told them to move to the land where they now lived some four hundred years earlier. They buried their dead in large mounds, which were sacred to them. Their main god, the Michabo, also known as The Great Hare, was shared by a number of the other red tribes. Michabo was responsible for their condition, as he created the earth, and all of the misery and merriment that went along with it. Their Easternmost encampment was near the white settlement, but it was up the river and beyond the great fall line. The fall line was marked by a magnificent waterfall, which stopped all river traffic and limited greatly the size of any water going vessels to those that could be carried up or down the trails on each side of the falls.

It would have been better if Adam had been all black as far as the Monacans were concerned. It was rumored that they had participated in the Powhatan slave trade with the Cherokee, and many had intermarried with the Africans. It was even said that many blacks had come from the Spanish explorers as well. As a result, many of the Monacan were of a rich copper color, with high cheek bones and long, straight black hair. Very handsome and fierce warriors, warriors who had no love for the white invaders. At one time it was said that the white man had stolen their chief. They had never gotten over it.

"Remember what they did to your mother", the mico warned. "When you reach the great sea, look for the Chowanocks. They know the path through the black waters. The travel is dangerous - there are many swamps, and it is easy to get lost."

The Chowanocks were reputed to trade in the largest pearls ever seen, and in order to get pearls, you must have access to the sea. The Chowanocks were known to trade with the Powhatan, so their outlet to the sea must be somewhat near the Powhatan Confederation. It was also common knowledge that the former leader of the Powhatan Confederacy, Chief Powhatan, had been dead many years, and the Confederation was being controlled by his half-brother, Opechancanough, whose reputation for diplomacy, treachery, and warfare was well known. Opechancanough had brokered a shaky peace with the white man several years before, and the whole area was in a state of high anxiety. Indians, regardless of their tribal affiliation, may be seen as the enemy, and killed on sight. To make matters worse, the Moratuc was sometimes referred to as the River of Death, because in the Spring, if the winters had been harsh, the water would rush down from the mountains and flood the river valleys, taking out entire villages in its path. With that, Adam and his nephew set out. In the Spring, of course.

CHAPTER TWENTY-SEVEN

THE CANOE WAS strong and held out the rushing water of the Moratuc. The lessons and the materials given to him by his father were put to good use. As they travelled, they discussed what they would do if attacked by a hostile war party or settler band. If it was a white party, Adam would say Big Toe was his guide, and could be trusted. If it was a Powhatan war party, Big Toe would say Adam was his prisoner, and he was taking him to the Spanish at the mouth of the River. If it was the Spanish, they would say they were working for the Dutch, and if it was the English, they would say they were a secret trading party looking for the French. They made up so many scenarios that their own logic often became confused, but it amused them and helped to pass the time. The reputation of the River proved to be correct, as the villages along the River which were hospitable confirmed that the River was prone to flood, and there were many stories of loved ones who had been washed away, many never to be seen again. When they reached the firsts rapids, every survival skill they knew had been put to the test.

The wildlife changed as they became closer to the sea, and they began to see long necked crane and frogs of every description. They found the fish plentiful, and there were huge striped trout, herring and pike. Lakes became common. One of the trout actually jumped into the canoe with them, and made an easy and tasty meal.

Big Toe proved invaluable. He was mature for his age, and he was strong and a natural woodsman. He had inherited many of the traits from his father, and his brown skin and green eyes already made him stand out. The women found him very appealing and at times his ego was more than a soul could bear. As they travelled, he was careful to mark the trail so that they could find their way on the return home trip. He would identify bends and turns in the River. Where it divided, he would remember the proper fork which would take them back to the main river channel. With a piece of charcoal, he would mark the inlets along the insides of the canoe until it looked like a giant map. He was so attune to the river and the maneuverings of the canoe that Adam would catch himself wondering who was the captain and who was the crew.

The water became brackish and they could smell the salt air. On the bank to their right they saw two boys fishing. Adam thought they appeared to be natives, maybe part of a Chowanocks fishing expedition. They approached them cautiously.

"I'll do the talking", said Big Toe. "You wait and let's see what they think of the white man."

The two boys, about ten or so, got up as if to run, then realized the two men in the canoe did not seem to mean them any harm, and they gathered up their bait and watched as the birch canoe made the shore. Adam grabbed a tree branch and pulled the canoe next to the bank, and Big Toe stepped out. The two boys were perplexed, but soon the two parties figured out a way to communicate. The boys knew a spattering of the Creek dialect, and they all developed a kind of sign language. It soon became clear that Adam was right about the boys being Chowanocks. They had come with about thirty of their tribe, who were in the out-waters fishing for shellfish and pearls. They had left the boys behind to watch their encampment, and there were several women in the camp preparing a meal as Adam and Big Toe wandered in.

"Men back when sun go down", was the interpretation of what one of the women offered. Adam and Big Toe looked at each other, trying to decide if they wanted to take a chance on waiting for the returning party.

"Let's take our chances and see if we can get some information on where the white settlement is", suggested Big Toe.

Adam was uncertain, but he remembered the advice of the mico, and the smell of the meal coming from the fires overtook him and all he could think of was his stomach. "Ok, we'll wait".

Right on time, as the sun began to dip to the West, the sound of the fishing party could be heard as their canoes banged and bounced along the river bank. A large, heavily tattooed man was in the lead as they walked into the camp. They had seen the strange canoe on the shore, and the leader had his war club in his hand and his other was clutched at his belt around his hatchet. He saw the two strange men sitting close to the fire, talking to one of the women, and as there did not appear to be any cause for alarm, his hand eased back from the hatchet, and he swung the war club back over his shoulder, where it hung from a leather strap. The strangers, he concluded, appeared peaceful.

Big Toe explained that they were members of the Bear Clan of the mighty Creek Nation and that his uncle was in search of a white woman who was the sister of Adam's mother. The Chowanock who had lead the band into the camp became the spokesman. The conversation, in broken sign language, Creek and a little Cherokee thrown in, went something like this:

"You look for white woman? How old?"

"She would be about sixty years old. Her mother was captured by the Monacan when she was six. She died last year when she was sixty-one years old, as a free member of the Creek Nation. She had a sister."

"No white women here. Only white woman in tribe is up river at main camp. Belong to Menatow. She not sixty. Maybe twenty years, no more".

Adam did the math. He was twenty-seven. It was possible this could be Sarah's child.

Before anything else could be said, the conversation was broken up by the sudden appearance of a young brave running into the camp. He hurried up to the tattooed leader. It was difficult to understand exactly what was said, but Adam did make out the name Opechancanough, and that war had been re-ignited between the whites and the Powhatan. Opechancanough had called on all of the tribes of the region to join with him in a great assault which was designed to drive the white man entirely from the continent. Suddenly, the white man had become persona non gratis throughout the region. While not all of the tribes agreed with Opechancanough, most all feared him and his methods. He was a man to be reckoned with, even at his advanced age. As long as he could walk or be carried to the battlefield, no white settler was safe. It was not a little ironic that the white translation of his name meant "the chief whose soul is white". The name may have come from the many diplomatic overtures that Opechancanough had made throughout the years, and the many treaties he had made, only to break with unprecedented viciousness and ferocity. It was no accident that he was sometimes referred to as the Hannibal of the Americas. But alive, a Hannibal is not a person to be ignored, and the Chowanocks were not about to get on his bad side. The problem now was they had befriended this white man sitting about their campfire, and it didn't seem quite right to just up and kill him.

As the discussion progressed, Adams white skin seemed to shine more and more in the moonlight. Big Tow tried to explain his heritage, and that his mother was white but his father was black, but that did not seem to satisfy anyone. He was obviously a white man. By his tattoos, he did bear semblance to a Creek, and he was certainly dressed as a Creek. But there was no mistaking the fact that he was white. And now, the whites were the enemies of the Chowanocks, at least as long as Opechancanough remained alive.

A council of the most senior leaders of the fishing party conducted a quick meeting. There were two things that the Chowanocks, as did many of the Indian tribes, considered to be of manifest importance. The first was that no favor, or good deed, was wasted. If you did a kindness, that was always remembered. The second was that no insult was ever forgiven, no matter how long ago the insult occurred. There had to be resolution of it. The tattooed man had been insulted at a gathering by one of Opechancanough's lieutenants. The sting of that insult still bore on his mind. After a brief discussion, the decision was made to let the white man go in peace. He had come in peace. There were no adult warriors in the camp when he arrived, and he did no harm to the women. The peace pipe was smoked.

A rough map of sorts was drawn, leading to the white settlement, many miles up the Chowanook River, a brackish estuary and river of momentous proportions. Two miles wide at its mouth, it was hard to believe it was even part of a river. Both the Chowanook and the Moratuc rivers fed out into the bay, forming a vast sound. Upstream, it was a good ten day trip in a canoe to the white village. The way was made particularly treacherous where the upper waters of the river turned into swamps, which made navigation difficult at best. Travel at night would be particularly difficult, because the water was dark, a deep tan color. The only good thing they heard said about it was the fishing was good, with striped bass, river herring, sunfish, bluegill, crappie, catfish and chain pickerel all in abundance. The Chowanook, anxious to return home in light of the recent news, agreed to guide the two men as far as their main village where the Wiccacon River met the Chowanook. From there they would be on their own - up the Blackwater River and into the Blackwater Swamp, and beyond. The path, they said, if followed correctly, would take them either to the doorstep of Powhatan or the doorstep of the great white settlement. Luck would have to guide them the final way.

Chapter Twenty-Eight

ADAM HAD TO make a decision. From this point, would it be safer to travel as a white man, or to travel as a Creek? Obviously, the Chowanocks had trouble accepting the fact that he was Creek. To them, he was a white man. His mother, while she was living, had sewn Adam a set of white men's clothes - why, it was never clear. But when he had put them on, it seemed to bring back something in her heart, something strong and powerful, and she hemmed and re-stitched until the clothes fit him perfectly. She had little memory of what the white people wore, but she made a shirt of cloth traded by the white traders, and she copied their leather shirt and shoes as best she could. All in all, she did a pretty good job of reproducing the dress of a white trader, and Adam had brought the clothes along with him in the canoe. When he had changed into the white trader dress, the warriors of the Chowanock were convinced that they had been duped about the story of his parentage, but the decision to let him go had been made and they were in a hurry to break camp and head upriver.

The next morning the camp broke and the canoes headed into the bay. The Chowanock knew the way well, and were soon entering the Chowanook River itself. They rowed all day before the River began to narrow to the point you could see clearly both sides at the same time. For two days they travelled in this fashion. On the third day, the tattooed warrior pointed to smoke rising from an inlet to the East of the River.

"We leave you here", he asserted. "Not safe for you to go further with us. We must part. Kill Opechancanough for us", he laughed. Gratefully, the two Creeks pushed their canoe to the opposite bank and sought a hiding place until nightfall. The river here was still wide, and the moon was full, and navigation was easy. As the days passed, the waters narrowed, and they finally found themselves in the marshes. This is where the going gets tricky, they were warned. Big Toe, who had carefully drawn the instructions on how to navigate the Blackwater Swamp, and staying in the front of the canoe, whispered instructions to his uncle, always looking for signs that had been foretold by the friendly Chowanock. And so the two men pushed forward, the one praying not to be shot by the whites, and the other, the reds.

The days passed. They could no longer travel by night. The waters were more like a creek now than a river, and the overhang from the trees and foliage, together with the blackness of the water, made travel by day essential. If they were to get lost, they may never find their way out, and if they did, they could be in the heart of one of the tribes loyal to Powhatan. But Big Toe was up to the task, and traveling at first light, they would get several hours in before the heat would overtake them, and they would find a narrow sliver to put in and hide the canoe. In the early morning Adam caught a sunfish, but they had to eat it raw, as a fire was out of the question. In the late afternoon, they put in again hoping to get about five hours of paddling in before it became too dark to travel.

Then one morning they heard a rifle shot. Quickly they beached the canoe and hugged the ground, listening for any movement. It was a white settler, and he had a small buck strapped across the front of his canoe as it headed down the stream in their direction. Adam rose from the ground as the canoe came even with where they were lying. The hunter was startled, and looked for his pistol when Adam called out in English. "I am white hunter", he said, "like you. We seek the great white settlement where the tall ships are."

The hunter, who thought he knew every white person within fifty miles of his small camp, was obviously having difficulty figuring out what this person was doing there. He seemed legitimate enough. "Yes, and who is that Indian there with you?" he asked.

Without thinking, Adam replied "my nephew, Big Toe".

"Yes, I know you call him your nephew, mon ami, but of what tribe is he?"

"Why, he's Creek", responded Adam.

"And what is a Creek doing in these waters?" asked the hunter.

"He's my guide up these black and foggy waterways. I've escaped from a Spanish fort below the Moratuc, and I'm looking for the great white settlement at the end of these waters. He was staying with the Chowanock,"

"You've taken a wrong turn, my friend" said the hunter. You're headed straight into a Moratuc encampment. "I, myself, am headed down stream to the big oak you see way down there to your left. I followed this buck this morning, and he led me too far West, and I was ready to give up on him, but he doubled back and came so near the creek that I chanced a shot. I'll not be dallying here. Best to follow me and stay close. They'll be out looking for who fired the shot, but they can't track much in these marshes without a boat, and I can keep ahead of them. Either you are lost, as you say, or a French spy. Come, and follow me. Do you trust the Creek there with you not to give us away?".

"Yes", replied Adam. "He's my nephew".

"Yes." said the hunter, with a confused look upon his face. "Just keep a close eye on him. "Looks just like a Negro to me. He's not Monacan, is he?"

"No, he's Creek."

"Well, you make sure he doesn't sell us out. Let's get out of here." And with that, the two canoes headed for the tall oak, where they turned East into a small inlet, one Big Toe hadn't even seen as they progressed upstream. The inlet turned into a wider creek about a hundred feet or so past the opening, and from there the men paddled hard for the remainder of the day, the white hunter showing no sign of fear of moving in the daylight. It was obvious as he maneuvered his canoe that he had travelled these waters many times. Big Toe looked at his drawing and could recognize nothing at this point. It was obvious to him that if he had continued on his own reckoning that he would have been completely lost by the end of the day, and perhaps hopelessly lost. It seems that the luck spoken of by the Chowanocks had been with them.

CHAPTER TWENTY-NINE

THE APPEARANCE OF Adam and his nephew, Big Toe, as they entered the white settlement, would have garnered more attention were it not for the fact that an English ship had just entered the harbor, and everyone was at the dock, curious as to what had been brought from home, what news there was, and what the demand would be for their tobacco, which they now grew in patches at every doorstep. To add to the confusion, the ship carried a number of indentured farmers who had bargained away as much as the next seven years of their lives in return for their passage to the New World, and many of them were milling around the fort, grateful to be off the ship.

"Our luck is continuing", Adam said to Big Toe. "They think we have come from the ship. Or at least I have. Where did you come from?"

"Quit joking, uncle", was Toe's reply. "This is serious. What are you going to tell them about me? Or you?"

"Well, let's just keep our story about my escaping from the Spanish fort for now. I'm sure I'm not the only white looking person who has wandered into this place."

"I wouldn't be so sure", replied Toe.

"Well, it's you I'm worried about. What will we say about you? There is a war on, and you look, well, you look Indian. Not any Indian they may have seen before, with your green eyes, but you do look Indian."

"I'm a Creek, uncle. And don't you forget it."

"Well, Creek or not, you are a stranger here, and a red stranger. The hunter in the white camp who led us here says you look Negro. You can be my Negro, and that should satisfy them. My Negro who was imprisoned along with me by the Spanish. It seems a reasonable enough story."

"So, does that mean I have to do what you say, as your Negro?" Big Toe laughed.

"It means I can sell you for enough money to buy a firestick", replied Adam, caught up in the joke.

Big Toe was deliberating on that thought when a man dressed in the strangest clothes they had ever seen came up to Adam and addressed him. "Captain Abraham Locke, captain of the Hopewell", said the bruising looking sailor, a pipe hanging from his mouth and with four fingers gone from his right hand. He grabbed Adam's hand by it anyway, and the size of the hand enveloped Adam's, even without the fingers. Thick, strong and powerful. "You can call me Captain, or Abe if you like. That is, unless you sign on. She's a beauty, isn't she?" pointing to the magnificent vessel at the dock.

The ship was now filled with every sort of person carrying and emptying the ship of its contents. One large stack contained what appeared to be firesticks. "What I would give for one of those", Adam said out loud, without thinking. Big Toe gave him a curious look, and punched him on the arm.

"Any sailing experience, my good friend?" said the Captain.

"Only by canoe", replied Adam.

"Well, I'll be taking her up the river to below the falls. Do you know those waters at all? I have some supplies for a settlement thereabouts, and a pot load of 'dentured servants, headed for work on the River up above the falls. Understand that country to be quite dangerous."

"Never been that way", replied Adam.

"Who's the Negro?"

"He's no Negro, why he's my nephew. He's Creek."

"Creek, is he? He looks to have Negro in him. Nephew you say?"

"Oh, yes, that's right", replied Adam. "He does have some Negro, and he belongs to me."

"Well that's more like it. So, how 'bout him. Does he know these waters?"

"We know the Moratuc, and the Chowanook. But we have no knowledge of these waters, and how to make the fall line."

"Well, that's a shame. Ever been on board a ship like the Hopewell?" said Abraham.

"First time I ever seen such a vessel", replied Adam.

"Well, it's a shame you have no experience. I have three sick crewmen, and I need someone to help repair my sails. Can you sew?"

"My mother taught me some. She made these clothes I am wearing."

"Well, yer hands seem strong. Yer need that to sew the sails. Tell you what. If ye want to consider it, I will take ye on to work with my sailmaker, and ye can be of value to me. Can't take the Negro, er, I mean the Creek. Unless you want to 'denture him, of course. I can use him with the cook."

"And just for how long would that be", inquired Adam.

"Well, as long as ye like, my friend. "I can buy him outright, or I can use him by the month. The choice is yours. Only, if he's on board when I sail for England, he's on until we land. There's no gettin' off at sea. Unless you Pirate. And of course, we'd have to hang you for that. Seems to be old enough to cabin. I could make him me cabin boy. Our cabin boy fell overboard in a storm. Mighty sad. Well, what say you?"

"Can't be of help to you, right now" replied Adam. "I'm looking for my Aunt. A white woman who disappeared some fifty or so years ago."

"Aye, from the colony that was lost, perhaps? replied the Captain. "Me own paw, who Captained this same here ship, looked for 'em his own self. Sailed South along the coast. Found where they left word they went to, but then nothing. Nothing was ever found but some buried chests and some writing. He figured they was all lost in a massacre, or sold by the Indians. Never heard from again, none of 'em. The father of one of 'em sailed with him, and when they give up, why his heart was just crushed, like a melon that's been stepped on. His own daughter and granddaughter was among them. Sad case, as they say. Well, if she was part of that group, you'll never find her, I'm afeared. Wasting your time, it seems to me. And so, where did you come from and how come ye to be here?"

Adam diverted the question, and the Captain resumed his tale about the lost colonists. "And so where would this be, this place they were last seen?" inquired Adam.

"It's easy to find. An outer island at the tip of a great barrier reef that wraps its way South. I've heared of the Moratuc, and I know that bay. It's near that. South of there, at it's tip, is where they was last rumored. Tell you what. You and that Negro there with you, you sail with me up to the fall line and back, and work on my sails. For that, I'll take you South along the Coast, as I'm headin' that way when I get done here, and I can drop ye off at the island where they was last seen. Can't pay ye none, but there's no good way to get there from here, lessen you want to travel the rivers South, and I hear the Indians are stirring things up, so nowhere's safe. What say you?"

Adam looked at Big Toe, and they both agreed, this was no time to be going back down the Blackwater. Too easy to get lost. "Ok, we'll sign on, but just for this little bit".

"Just this little deal it is." said the Captain. "Just this little deal. Good deal for both of us. Here, take you a sip of this hear liquor, and we'll seal this little deal right here and now. No need for paper. We sail in two days."

CHAPTER THIRTY

THE FIRST OFFICER of the Hopewell was a jovial little man who went by the name of Smitty. Lt. Smitty. That wasn't his last name, of course, but he didn't like formalities, and while the English navy would have severely frowned on his manner of addressing the crew, he cared little for the Admiralty, a fact which the captain admired and which put him in good stead with his boss. After depositing their 'dentures, as the Captain called them, and the rest of their supplies, they planned to leave the bay and head South, with a path drawn down to the Caribbean island of Nevis, their purpose being to supply and provide protection to an English settlement on the island and which seemed to be constantly needing help of some kind from the homeland. Sugar was the lure - the island was said to make the sweetest, best tasting sugar ever eaten by man or beast. Sugar - so good that only a few dissidents thought to grow tobacco. And of course, if a fat Spanish galleon, laden with gold, were to get in the way, well, that would be their bad luck now, wouldn't it. It was no surprise to Smitty, then, that no papers were presented when the new white sailor and his Negro companion strolled up the plank leading to the main deck of the ship.

"Captain gave me all the particulars, Mr., ah, what name was it?" asked the officer.

"White. Adam White".

"Well, Mr. White, and who is your friend here."

"That would be Big Toe. He's to work as a cabin boy."

"Don't need to be telling me, Mr. White", replied the officer. "Know all about it. This y'ere is Banson. He will show ye around and to yer quarters. Banson's our sailmaker, and he's also our carpenter, so ye'll be working with him I suppose. Don't know where we'll bed down that Negro of yours though.

Can't have him sleeping with the white sailors. We'll find a place for him in the hold. Glad ye can join us on this little expedition."

The ship spent the better part of two weeks traveling up the bay to the falls, and Adam's fingers were sore from the sewing. The Captain was not one to waste an opportunity, and before long he cancelled the cabin boy duties, and Big Toe was instructed to work on the sails along with his uncle. Two of the main sails had large tears in them, and the spare for the third mast had disappeared somehow before they ever set sail from England. Banson knew his job, and Adam was a fast learner. Adam searched the ship from bow to stern, fascinated at its construction. It was like a giant puzzle to him, and he wanted to know all of the pieces, and how they fit.

At the end of the bay, as the waters began to resemble more of a river than a bay, there was a small settlement, and the settlers there welcomed the firesticks more than anything else. Several of the passengers, who had signed on as indentured servants, were reluctant to depart, as it seemed so remote a location, and there was only a handful of what seemed to them to be fighting men at the makeshift dock. But de-board they did, and it wasn't long before the ship was sailing back to Jamestown. Once there, the Captain laid her over just long enough to fill the water barrels and take on a bit of tobacco. He was saving most of his hold space for his Southern exploits. As promised, once the ship cleared the outer bay and made open waters, she turned South, staying within telescope view of the shore as much as possible, and keeping as far East as they dared due to the reefs.

Adam and Big Toe, though separated in their living quarters, spent the majority of each day working together on the rigging and sewing a reserve sail. He watched as the ship wound its way South, tacking back and forth against the wind. Then, one afternoon, the ship dropped her anchor, and the Captain came to the foredeck and called for Banson.

"Where's the help?", he asked.

"They're just finishing up the last of the spare mainsail. Good job, too. That Negro is a fast learner. Just took to it, right away. The white man, well, he was slow and too meticulous. These are sails, not leggins. We ain't wearing 'em. We're hanging them from a pole!"

"Well, we'll just keep the Negro, and let the white man off here at the point. Set out the boat."

"But don't he own him, the Negro?" asked Banson.

"Well, he does, but there's no law out here at sea, other than me, and it doesn't seem to me he should mind too much. What's one more Indian, or Negro, or whatever he is. We'll give Master White a firestick for him. He'll need that as much as that Negro. Maybe more. And who can resist such a bargain?"

Adam reached the deck and saw the small boat as it was lowered down the side of the ship. He looked around for Big Toe, but he was nowhere to be seen. "Where's Big Toe", he asked.

"We think he would be happier here on the ship. He's good with the sails, and we can use another hand when we get to where we are going", replied Benson. "And of course, he would be good to work on the sugar."

The Captain appeared, holding a rusted blunderbuss in one hand, and a sack of ball, powder and flint in the other. "Got a trade for you, Mr. White", joined in the Captain. "A good deal. A real good deal. A good deal for both of us."

Adam was aghast. "You don't seem to understand. That is my nephew, Big Toe. He is not some piece of property you can do with as you wish."

"Your nephew?" sneered the captain. "He shore don't look like no nephew of you'n. Tell you what, you see this here pistol, pulling it out of his belt and pointing it at Adam's head, I will refrain from discharging this weapon if you will withdraw peacefully to that thar island yonder."

Adam found himself surrounded by seven or eight of the crew. Several had wooden clubs, and one carried a large knife. Smitty, along with the Captain, were armed with guns. "Not really a choice here, Master White. Now do ye go peacefully, or do ye jest go over the side, and swim fer it. Which way will ye choose?"

Adam turned to grab the flintlock from Smitty's hand, when a stanchion from the deck was laid across the right side of his skull, splitting open the skin and rendering him unconscious. "Take him to the skiff, and drop him on the island", piped in the Captain. "Oh, and give him the gun. He's gonna need it. Be quick about it. Benson, go below and put the Negro in irons until we get south of the reef."

CHAPTER THIRTY-ONE

ADAM AWOKE TO the shrill sound of the sea gulls fluttering along the beach. Next to him rested the rusty blunderbuss and a weapons kit, containing flint, ball and powder. Also lying next to the weapon was a small cask of water, a pouch containing three or four pieces of hardtack, and a hatchet. His head was spinning, and he couldn't comprehend what had just happened. He had caused these men no harm. And for what gain had they committed the most barbaric act that he could imagine. Big Toe. What would he tell Hopping Turtle? How would he explain this to his dad? This was all his own stupid idea. He didn't have to go on this quest, and he had endangered Big Toe, and now his nephew was lost. He searched the horizon, but there was no sign of the ship. He kept thinking back, back from the time they first set foot on the vessel. He remembered the crew talking about an island. What was the name? What was it? He racked his brain. Oh yes, Nevis, that was it. They were headed to Nevis. The Island of Nevis. His eyes returned to the sea and stared at the blue water for a very long time. Nevis. But where is Nevis?

He reached down and grabbed the keg. His throat was dry and burning. The small keg was practically empty. He had learned how to load and shoot the weapon from the hunter who had killed the deer and who had led him safely through the Blackwater. He primed the gun, and fired it. It was broken. Useless. He picked it up and threw it angrily into the surf. He grabbed the hatchet, and began to toss it, too, into the ocean, when his senses took over and stopped him. He reached for the pouch containing the hardtack, threw it over his shoulder, and headed inland. It was the pouch Cahlib had given him when they started the trip, the one Cahlib had taken from the Powhatan.

The island wasn't much more than a spit of land separating the mainland from the ocean. Mostly sand. Adam could see what appeared to be more land further West. He slung the pouch on his back and tied the hatchet to his waist, and ventured out into the water. He swam to the next bit of land, and then again and again until he reached a large island, some two miles wide. From there he could not see a shore, and he felt himself marooned.

He crossed the island and made camp on the Western shore. From there, he began to search the island for water. He saw footprints in the sand, and his heart stood still.

The footprints led to an area along the bank shaded by a small stand of trees and a long strip of scraggly underbrush. Underneath the brush was a long, hollowed out log, about fifteen feet long, Not much effort had been put into trying to hide the canoe, if that was what it was. Adam had never seen a canoe made in this fashion before, but it certainly looked seaworthy. He was about to shove it out into the water when he heard a sound coming from the Northern end of the island. Quickly, he jumped into the brush, and waited for what was next.

The sound was coming from two men, moving slowing down a path leading to the very place where Adam had elected to hide. The men paused within a few feet of him, then passed him and began to uncover the canoe. They were light skinned, not a copper but almost a very light almond color, with long straight blond hair that hung down their backs. They appeared to be about fifteen years old, and they were each armed with a bow and arrow. Each was bare above the waist, and you could see a large, black tattoo on each man somewhat resembling a lightning bolt, starting at the right shoulder and extending halfway down the back. They were carrying a basket of sorts, which had a loop on the top, and they had placed a long pole through the loop, and each carried one end. It was loosely put together, and appeared to be filled to the brim with some sort of shellfish. They were talking English. Adam couldn't believe it, as they certainly looked like Indians to him. Except for the blond hair. English. "How can this be?" he thought to himself. But then, he could speak English. Before he had time to think, he jumped up and hollered out "Hey, I need help!"

The two men, or boys, depending on your take, thought they had just seen a ghost or other apparition, and dropped the basket and began to run, loading their bows as they ran. "Wait, wait! I mean ye no harm", replied Adam at the top of his voice. The two men, stopped, looked at each other in bewilderment, and lowered their bows. "He speaks English!" exclaimed the first yellow haired warrior.

"Yes", replied the other. "Yes, and he's no ghost. Why, he's jest white."

PART THREE

1712 - CHARLES TOWN, SOUTH CAROLINA

CHAPTER THIRTY-TWO

"**G**ET HIM, GET him!" cried the old man from the rocking chair next to the fire. "Get him Margaret, get him. He's been into the chest again. And he's got the leather strip. Hurry before he tears it!"

Margaret wasted no time scurrying after the youngster, who had made it past his grandpa and was already jumping off the porch. It was such a curiosity, and it was so well protected, that it was a natural impulse which caused the child to seek it out, and this time he had been successful. He headed for his favorite hiding place down by the creek-bed, and would have remained hidden if it weren't for his curiosity getting the best of him, and the long, leather strip could be seen by Margaret sticking out from inside the little fort the boy had made from the rocks, logs and other debris floating downstream during the last rainstorm.

"Get your butt out of those bushes", she hollered.

"Aw, I was just wantin' to look at it. It's so old and pretty", he said meekly.

Back on the porch, Margaret handed the long piece of leather to her father, who had made it to the doorway, smiling broadly, but with a stern look for Adam as he rounded the corner.

"Alright", he said, "tonight I will tell you the story of my father, and what the symbols on the leather strap represent. But for now, young man, you will be chopping wood until sundown. Now git!"

The young boy rounded the large cabin and headed for the woodpile next to the back porch. He lifted the heavy ax, and with a broad smile, began to cut the hickory logs into kindling. He couldn't wait for the story to come, and he had outrun a whoopin', although for the life of him he couldn't figure out how.

The fire was crackling when Aunt Betty finally gathered up the evenings dishes from the table and the old man gathered himself in his favorite chair. The three children, their father Bill, and their mother, all gathered around, for when Poppa William told a story, which was a rare event, it was always a good one. The fire popped and Poppa William began.

"This story starts a long time ago, when my Father, Adam White - well, he wasn't a White when the story begins. He was a Creek, an Indian. A white Indian. And he had been marooned off the coast of Caroline by a band of cutthroats flying under an English flag."

"What, you mean we're Indians?", piped in Adam from his seat on the floor next to his Granddaddy. "But we don't look like Indians, and we don't live like Indians. And we don't think, at least most of the time, like Indians." The boy seemed perplexed, and he awaited the explanation anxiously.

"Now Adam", piped in his father, who was standing next to his wife in front of a large wooden table, smoking a pipe. "Let Poppa tell the story and don't interrupt. You will learn the answers to your questions in good time, I reckon". Hopefully, he thought to himself, as there were many questions that even he had running around in his head that wanted answers.

"Now, as I was saying", said the old man, drawing deeply on the slim narrow pipe, "us Injuns have a most interestin' history. My Daddy was a Creek, yes a Creek Indian, from the Bear Clan way up river, and deep into Country. But he was, like so many of the Creek people, a man of mystery. As the story goes, he came looking for his momma's family, and had with him a nephew, a boy who went by the name of Big Toe. Big Toe was part Creek, part mulatto, and he passed for Creek part of the time, and part of the time he was a black man. He had a scar across his chest, made by a sharp Navy cutlass, and he wore a patch over his left eye, which had been cut out by pirates down in the Carbean. That strap there, that strap tells the story, though there's parts to it which even I don't quite understand. But you, Bill, and maybe even you, little Adam, you may be the ones to unravel the secrets that it carries, that the strap has carried since the markings on it were made.

The fire spurted, and sparks flew like crazy up the narrow chimney. The children smiled but inched closer to the adults nearest by.

"Like I was sayin', his uncle Adam, he didn't go by White back then. In fact, he didn't have no white name, which is why, I believe, he picked White to be called by. All he had was Adam, and he also had a Creek name, but I don't know it. Adam, like I said, was looking for his momma's sister, who was English. His daddy, as the story goes, was a black man from Africa. An African slave. See the first picture on the strip. It's a man, and he's black, and next to him is a woman, and she, why she's white. And then there's three small children, and two of them are brown, and the third child, the youngest, and he's white, like the woman."

"The white woman as I said had a sister, and they was both English, and she and Adams's mother had been separated back when they were just children, and his momma had been captured by a cruel band of Indians who hated white people. What happened to her sister, she wondered all her life. So Adam went in search of her, and he was tricked by the Captain of a British ship, headed for the Carbean. He came ashore way North of here, up a creek black as pitch and infested with the darndest creatures you ever saw, long crawling lizards with long mouths and sharp teeth. Gators they is called by the whites, but the Spaniards, they call them "el Caiman", and they can eat a dog or child fast as anything. Well, Adam, he was brought in from the outer islands by two men of a local tribe. Those in that tribe, they was different somehow, and they stayed mostly to themselves. They was of mixed blood, with long blond hair and copper colored skin. They spoke a mixture of tongues, and could read the book. They took Adam in, and he became one of them".

It wasn't long before Adam shared with them what had happened to Big Toe, and his desire to find his nephew, at any cost. "The copper men, they were a curious bunch. They longed to go North and join the whites at the great bay, but the Confederates, that's what the large Indian band was called that was fighting the whites, they made it hard on anyone with Indian blood to go North. So they stayed here, in the deep forests back away from the Ocean, and they raised their kin. Some went and married Indians. Others went South and found white women and Spaniards. The Spaniards was brutal at times, but they could make some beautiful children. That is, for the most part. When Adam came into their group, he married your Grandma, and he called her Maria, after his own ma, and she was a pure white woman. So their children was white, and they was able to move South down here to Charles Town. But he was Indian too, and he loved telling about his childhood as a Creek brave."

"If you look on the leather strap, you will see him drawn next, from the top, in the corner. That stick figure is Adam, as a man. And next to him is a picture of the Ship that left him to die. Hope..., Hopew...., you can't hardly make it out. But the Ship was English, and the next picture is the picture of the English flag. And then next to it, the picture there, that's the picture of a pirate ship. A skull crossed by bones. My daddy said that that was what they had become - the men of that ship - pirates down in the Carrabean.

Little Adam, who was sitting on the floor, picked up a leather pouch from which he had earlier found the leather strap. "Careful, careful there with that pouch there boy. That pouch is the only thing that my daddy had when he was left ashore. He said they left him with a gun, but it didn't work, and he threw it out into the sea. The pouch, he said, came from his father, who, as the story goes, had stolen that pouch from the Powhatan, who planned to sell him to the Cherokee. The Cherokee was just then gettin' into slavery, and they were up to trading with the Powhatan. But my grandfather was too smart for them, and he made it to the land of the Creek, where he was made a part of a Clan living in the foothills of the great mountains."

"Anyway", he started again, "the next picture is a picture of an Island. According to my father, this is where the ship was heading when he was marooned on the outer banks. The pirates, that's what he called them, had taken Big Toe as something they could sell, and all that Dad had was the name, the name of the place they was headed – Nevis it was called. He had no idea of where it lay, or how in the Lord's will he could ever find her. But his mind stayed on it, and Big Toe was not to be forgotten, not by him. Of course, at the time, the task must have seemed impossible."

The fire popped loudly and little Adam was sent for more firewood. He separated the green wood he had cut earlier, and brought some good dry pieces, which he lay next to the stone hearth. Stoked well, the fire rose in the hearth, and everyone hunkered down for more of the tale.

"Now the white Indians, as I said, they kept mostly to themselves, and they had things hidden away, deep in a cave, which was things no other Indian tribe had ever seen. They had things that belonged to another people, things that, to them, were treasures. Treasures of their past. The book. Strange weapons. Metal. Copper. Things not seen in any other Indian camp. And among these hidden away treasures there was a map, a map of the Carbean. And one day, Adam saw it, and there, almost dead in the center of that map, was a square sort of island, and written next to the island was the word Nevis. It was like manna from heaven, he would say, and right then and there he knew what he had to do. The only question was how."

"There was also a log - a ship's log, and as Adam began to read it, he could tell that the Carbean lay just South of a long stretch of land that was inhabited mostly by Spaniards. These islands formed a semi-circle as they stretched their length to the slave capital of the Southern hemisphere - Brazil. Famous for its sugar production, and famous as the last destination for many a slave ship. Halfway down this semi-circle was the Nevis. Next to the island, drawn on the strap, was a British flag. And then another island was drawn, and on it was drawn a French flag."

Again the fire sizzled and popped, and the old man began again, almost in a whisper. Everyone in the room leaned in, not wanting to miss what was next. The leader of the tribe was a man named Thomas, he went on, and Thomas was drawn to Adam, mostly due to his color and the fact that he could speak English and read the book. He showed him a diary that the tribe had found on one of the outer islands in a shallow grave. It was the diary of a Spanish sailor, buried with him, and dug up by some hungry animal. No one could read it, as it was in a language no one understood. "Where?" Adam pleaded with Thomas, "Where can we find someone who can know the words?"

CHAPTER THIRTY-THREE

AS IT TURNED out the old Spanish diary proved as important to what happened next as the map and the ship's log, for having the map, while it provided a means by which Nevis could be located, was no motivation, in and of itself, for Thomas or anyone else to accompany Adam on a sea voyage to the far away island. But the diary, when it was finally deciphered into a language they could understand, told of a sea voyage, not to the Caribbean, but to the northern tip of South America in search of the cinchona tree. High in the Peruvian mountains the tree grows, with its pretty white flowers, tinted with red, and hidden within its deep red bark, the ingredients for a substance more valuable than the gold carried in holds of the caravans of ships sailing back to Spanish ports. Gold could make you wealthy, but cinchona could cure malaria. And malaria was rampant. The Spanish were protecting their discovery, and controlling its distribution.

"We have the same thing right here!" exclaimed Thomas, "but we don't have a fancy name for it. Some of the tribes call it fever-bark. But it will treat the fever they call malaria. It grows down by the coast, in the swamps, along the creek banks and in the estuaries."

"Then you could trade, Thomas, trade! You have something to sell. We can build a vessel, something that could make it to the Caribbean, and trade for most anything. Sugar, guns, you name it. I can build it. We'll put a sail on her, and sail her to the Caribbean. A canoe. A large canoe, with plenty of room to put the bark from the plants, and we can even take the polished beads. Can't you see it? They will love us. And you can become rich. And I can find Big Toe. You've got to do it, Thomas, you've just got to.'

Thomas weighed it over, talked to his wife, and got hooked. The voyage to Nevis was going to happen.

CHAPTER THIRTY-FOUR

T HE BIGGEST PROBLEM was figuring out how to mount a mast to the middle of a canoe in such a way that it could withstand a strong wind and not rip a hole in the bottom of the boat. The boat would be designed like an outrigger, with one mast and which could hold a six man crew along with cargo, food and water for the trip. Everyone from the tribe pitched in, whether it was hollowing out the main log for the canoe, making rope of all sizes, and working on the sail. From the cave emerged three strong cutlasses, but there was little likelihood of pirates wanting their meagre vessel. The bigger concern was cannibals. There, on the leather strip, was the picture of what Poppa Bill said was a picture of a Carib Indian, replete with headdress. The Spaniards had enslaved many Caribs because of their reputation as eating the parts of their captured enemies, and part of their treatment, besides the gallows, was to force them to dive for pearls off the Venezuelan coast. The life expectancy for that occupation was exceptionally brief, as the practice involved the diving into a deep bay carrying a large rock so the diver could go deeper faster, and of course that entailed considerable risk. But there was a large European market for pearls, as the Chowanocks had discovered further north.

Staying within sight of the mainland, and not worrying about the reefs so much with their short draft, the boat made good progress and could do 10 knots against the wind as it worked its way South. Following the map, the boat reached Southern Florida before it had to venture East, leaving the safety of the shoreline and relying on the stars to provide guidance as they made the hundred mile cross of the Atlantic to Cuba. On the third day after the crossing, and as they were working their way towards Puerto Rico, the weather turned very hot and still. It was early August. Thomas noticed a large number of fish visible beneath the clear surface of the water. The men were at their oars, as the wind had stopped and they were making little progress. No land was in sight. Then the sea began to seem to change, and large swells appeared, washing into the boat. Only the outriggers were keeping her afloat.

Bill picked up the wrinkled strap, and there, beneath a sketch of a canoe, was signs of a storm, with high swells and lightning bolts.

"Yes, continued the old man, "the sky darkened and the swells lifted the heavy canoe, thrusting it upward, and then downward, so there was no control whatsoever except by the storm itself. The wind was now at gale force and getting stronger. The six sailors had never seen anything like this, but had heard about such storms from the Indians from deep into Florida on hunts coming into the Carolina's. It was a hurricane, although no one in the outrigger had ever heard of one. There was no doubt among them, however, that they would have to find land or all would be lost."

Papa Bill leaned back in his chair and took a deep draw from his long pipe. "That's about a good place to stop for the night", he said sleepily, and he threw his arms out wide as he yawned and stared into the fire. Against the protestations of Adam, he called the story telling for the night to be at an end. "Well, you know they made it, or otherwise I wouldn't be here" he smiled broadly. "They had made it all the way to St. Thomas. And you know her reputation. Home of the pirate and the cannibal Carib."

The fire burst into what seemed like a hundred sparks as a piece of sap-soaked pine log exploded, and the old man turned toward his bed.

CHAPTER THIRTY-FIVE

IT WAS ONLY after several weeks of constant hounding by Adam that Papa Bill agreed to return to the story. There had been a hard rain and the creeks were swelling bad, and it only seemed appropriate, with the dead cow out in the field, drowned and of no value to anyone, that the story should continue. Everyone had been shaken to one degree or the other by the rising waters and the impassable roads and the possibility of flooding, and the fireplace was again the backdrop as Adam hurried to find Papa's long pipe. And the strap, of course.

"Well, the outrigger was torn to pieces, but as luck would have it, they were within sight of a Dutch island East of Puerto Rico. From what they heard, it was a good thing they missed Puerto Rico, because the storm had done its worst crossing the island from the East. Many lives had been lost. St. Thomas, however, had gotten a lot of high wind and rain, but the eye of the storm was too far North to do too much damage. The Carib, who had dealt with these storms for centuries, and who's long canoes were mostly pulled up along the coast and not battered about out in the ocean, had survived the storm with little incident, and their canoes were mostly intact. The deep water sanctuary which was a part of the Island, and which had attracted the pirate ships, was, however, a most dangerous place for a masted ship like a frigate or a sloop to be anchored during a major storm. Only one remained in the harbor, the rest had raced away in a panicked attempt to outrun the howling winds and high waves. There she lay, now amid the calm water, and while the horrific winds had done their best to beat about her, she had somehow held her own, and the meager crew aboard apparently had been too drunk to even take down her black flag flying from the mainmast. It was the Hopewell. She had never made the slightest effort to leave the harbor. The Hopewell, now a pirate vessel hiding in the relative safety of the port of St. Thomas. Safe but for the storm. But luck was with her, and she stood tall, quiet and serene now in the aftermath. The waters were thick with debris, brown and ugly. The temptation of Spanish Gold had been too much for the Captain and his English crew, and they had taken to a life of misadventure upon the Caribbean waters. Why share it with the King when you can keep it all!

So there she stood, proud and defiant, even her sails were intact, as nothing was even close to being unfurled in the rigging. The flag, of all things, had seemed to have gotten the worst of it. No one had thought to take it down, and it was little more than a ragged piece of cloth, drooping lazily from the mast. The Spanish they say, are the first to build a church when they colonize an island. The French, they build a fort. But the Dutch and the English, they build a tavern, and, as the storm rolled across the island, all but a skeleton crew was well entrenched inside the island's sturdiest building, The Blue Lagoon.

A mile away, on the Northern side of the island, the small crew of the forlorn trade expedition to Nevis lay exhausted on a small stretch of sandy beach, all alive, and only one seriously injured, and that a broken leg. "That looks pretty bad, Thomas", said Adam. The large bone was stretching the skin.

The canoe, with all its cargo, supplies, and food, was lost.

Adam agreed that someone would have to try to find help. He spoke no Dutch, but he did speak English. One of their crew, Peter, had married a Spanish woman, and she had made him learn the basics of the language, so he went along, and the two men set out across the island. As they left the beach, Adam noticed a long log laying longways away from the water. A canoe. A canoe that would hold maybe twelve or more men.

They proceeded in a Southern direction, and soon reached a tall ridge, covered in trees, with a narrow path leading upward. They took it. When they reached the top, they could see a scattering of lights in the valley below, and the ocean. There appeared to be a crescent shaped deep harbor, and a number of lights coming from various sources in a small village at the base of the ridge and protected from the ocean beyond. "Look", Adam whispered. "There's a ship down there. It's got two masts. Looks intact. Can you make her out?"

Peter knew a little about ships from tales of his wife, who was the child of a Spanish trader. He recognized it as a ship they called a sloop. "I'll have to get closer" replied Peter, and he edged his way down the hill towards the water's edge. The ship was anchored facing the harbor, and Peter had to swim out from one corner of the semi-circle until he could see her stern. He wished he had a pencil so he could draw the letters that were the ship's name. He tried to sound it out, but his English was not so good. He recognized the flag, however, as that of a pirate vessel, which even in its battered condition would get caught by the breeze and display what remained of the skull and crossbones dressed in black and white.

Smoke was rising from a fire burning inside the Blue Lagoon as Peter returned to the men's vantage point half way up a high hill forming the backdrop to the bay. "She's a pirate, Adam, and doesn't look much the worse for the beating she took from the storm." They had been in this position for only a few minutes when a tall figure emerged from the thick wooden door of the tavern. Adam recognized him immediately. It was, and he could recall the words he spoke and the manner of his speech, Yes Sir, he had a good deal for him, a real good deal. Thank you, Captain Locke.

CHAPTER THIRTY-SIX

I T WOULD FALL to Peter to enter the Blue Lagoon and investigate. Adam would surely be recognized by the captain or crew, and Peter could pass for a survivor of one of the vessels sunk by the storm and who had managed somehow to make it to dry land. He certainly looked the part, and would have no trouble recalling the horror of being tossed about the sea, trying to make land with little more than a wooden paddle for a life-vest. Adam described Big Toe to Peter, but it had been years now, and the boy was now a young man. "He has a tattoo across the back of his shoulder in the shape of a lightning bolt, and green eyes. Part Creek, part white, and part negro. You can't miss him", Adam smiled with a broad grin.

There was a natural distrust as Peter entered the tavern, and he made his way slowly to the bar and asked for some rum.

"Don't suppose ye'll be paying for it" replied the man behind the bar. "But a free drink for ye for mastering the storm. It was surely the rum which got us threw her worst." There was a good laugh all around, and the rum appeared in front of the ragged seaman, who drank it down with one gulp. "Another", he implored the barkeep, and another mug of rum appeared. The tavern was not concerned about a profit on a day like this. On a day like this, it was everyman's condition to thank the heavens for being above the ground and not lost in the watery grave which the sea had become to many a brave seaman only a short time ago.

"And what ship would it be that ye were about, and where did she go down?" asked the barkeep.

"A sloop out of St. Kitts. A French sloop, bound for Nevis she was. Down with all aboard except for me, I suppose", replied Peter. "Must have struck a reef. Tore plumb into. The water came in so fast that no one below had a chance to get above deck. Only those on top could get to the water, and the waves were taller than a dozen pine trees standing one on top of the other. Lord knows how I ever made it to shore. I walked the beach, but there was nothing, no one. Just me".

"Lucky yes you were", replied the tall sailor coming up beside him. "And lucky ye didn't run into the cannibals when you got to shore".

"Cannibals?" replied Peter.

"Yes, the Caribs. Will eat you for breakfast if they don't like your looks. Name's Locke, Abraham Locke, and I'm the captain of the Hopewell. A fine ship, a seaworthy ship, and she stands tall and secure in this here bay. You're welcome to come aboard, if you like. Of course, the invitation is voluntary, of course, but then if ye were to decline the nice offer, we would probably just have to kill you here and drink then to your sad story. Or hand you over to the Caribs. We always try to offer a choice, as it is. It would be such a shame."

Adam and Peter had discussed the situation beforehand and agreed this would probably be the Hopewell's offer of sanctuary. Pirate or die. It was an option frequently made to those lost at sea or finding their way into the bars and taverns of a faraway island. Peter of course, would have to accept and see where it would lead.

"Any skills, have you?" piped in the Captain.

"Just an able bodied seaman", replied Peter.

"Well, fine then. You can work in the rigging and work the mess, your choice. Pay, of course, depends on our good luck at sea. And of course you're free to do as you choose on land, but when we are in a fight, you take my orders or die on the spot. Can you work under those terms, Matey?"

"Looks like my best option", replied Peter.

"An excellent choice, and well-reasoned. And, of course, your only option." replied the Captain.

CHAPTER THIRTY-SEVEN

LITTLE ADAM RETURNED with more wood for the fire, some of it wet and a few dry pieces he found near the bottom of the pile. He picked up the leather strip and saw the words Thos. next to a large X, and assumed that represented St. Thomas where the marooned crew had washed ashore. The old man pulled out a knife from his pocket and began to whittle on a piece of the dry wood, and the chips, when he threw them into the fire, would catch fire immediately and sometimes dance up the chimney.

Adam, he continued, watched the door of the Blue Lagoon for several more hours, and, not hearing any ruckus, concluded that Peter had been successful in his meeting with the pirates. He climbed higher on the hill, trying to find a farmhouse in the valley on the back side of the large hillside. He saw some smoke coming from the treetops, and worked his way down and along a wide trail leading to a cabin neatly tucked into a tall stand of pine trees. There was a small boy chasing a three-legged dog in the yard. "Hey boy", he whispered. The boy, looking puzzled at the ragged seaman, concluded correctly that he had been a victim in some way of the storm, and wasn't afraid.

"What can I do for ya?'", he replied.

"I have a friend, a fellow seaman, and his leg was badly broken in the storm, and he needs a doctor real bad", replied Adam. "Is there anyone on this island that can do anything for him?" he asked.

"My pa, he's probably your best hope", replied the boy. "He can mend most anything. Only, if its got to come off, he won't' do that. You don't know, he might be able to set it."

"The bones broke clean in to, and looks like it's going to break through the skin", replied Adam.

"Well, where's he at?", replied the boy.

"I can take your pa' to him", said Adam. "It's the other side of the island. On the Northern end."

"There's Carib in that part. You never know where they might be hiding out. There are a lot of places to hide. Not safe for a white man to go at night, or any time, for that matter. Lest of course you're a pirate, and well-armed", replied the boy.

"I'll bring him here", replied Adam.

Adam turned and began to run in the direction of the beach where he had left his small crew. He had to warn them about the Carib, and somehow get Thomas to the cabin. But when he passed the long canoe and entered the beach, there was no one to be seen. Afraid to call out, he began to walk westward along the beach. Where the sandy beach met a rocky shore, he saw the light of a large fire. Around the fire were about 40 Indians.

CHAPTER THIRTY-EIGHT

R ETREATING TO THE high grass, Adam slithered along the dunes and then among the rocks until he could see the faces of the Indians clearly. There was Thomas, tied to a stake, along with his other crewmen. It appeared that something terrible was about to happen. Then, suddenly, all motion seemed to stop as a long canoe, much longer than the one he had seen earlier, came into sight and headed straight for the roaring fire. Running itself at full speed, the long boat ran up against the shore and beached itself. A tall, bronze Indian with long, black hair, braided down his back, and carrying a long spear, bounced effortlessly to the sandy beach. He seemed very much in charge, although somehow out of place. Adam could not believe his eyes. It was Big Toe.

As the canoe's leader stepped from the water to the shore, the group by the fire parted to allow him to make his way to the Chieftain, who was wearing a large headdress. He greeted the green eyed Indian warmly, and showed off his captives as they gazed back, certain now that their fate had been determined.

Thomas was brought first to the inner circle of the tribe's leadership, and cried out in pain as his leg was dragged across the rocks. Adam heard the English word pirate, and it became clear to him that the Indians thought that Thomas and his friends, even though they were, at least in part, Indian, were indeed pirates marooned from the hurricane. Thomas too recognized some English was being spoken, and he called out in a futile effort to explain who they were and why they were there, but it was to no avail.

"Big Toe", Adam screamed from his hiding place in the tall, rocky grass.

The bronzed Indian stopped in his tracks, looking into the darkness for the voice that had cried out his name - a name he had almost forgotten as he had struggled to survive following his abduction on the English ship. First, as a slave aboard the Hopewell. Then, sold to the planters to work the sugar fields in

Nevis. And finally, after being almost hung at the gallows at Jamestown on the Nevis shore, he had been saved when the Carib's savagely attacked the island, freeing all of their kinsmen who, like Big Toe, were about to be executed.

It was a joyous reunion. The Caribs stared in amazement at the two men, Adam and his nephew Big Toe, as they embraced.

CHAPTER THIRTY-NINE

OF THE TWO men, Big Toe had changed the most, both from a physical appearance standpoint - he was now four inches taller, almost six feet, bronzed by a life in the tropical sun, and now no longer the face of a boy, but a man. His face was etched with a large scar that ran across his left eye, which was covered with a black patch, and down across his lips and across his left cheek. But he was still quite handsome, and his smile was broad and grateful. It was just in his eyes, those beautiful green eyes, that, when Adam looked closely, he could see the change from one of joyful wonder to an anger created by the evil he had endured and witnessed, not only upon himself, but among the slaves in the sugar fields and, indeed, the Caribs and what they had suffered from their treatment by the Spaniards who controlled most of the Caribbean.

The Carib's had seen in him the essence of a leader and the spirit of a warrior. He had quickly risen to a leadership position, and commanded one of the larger of their war canoes. His chest and arms were heavily tattooed. Their only reservation was his refusal to share in the roasted heart of a Spanish Captain of a captured sugar drover off the Cayman Islands. But then, nobody was perfect.

It was perhaps Big Toe who was the most surprised to see the other on this isolated beach far from the worlds of their birth. To Big Toe, he was deeply touched by the loyalty shown by his uncle in coming to find him. And for Adam, it was relief from the guilt he had felt upon Big Toe's capture and his inability to save him from the barbaric acts of the Captain and crew of the Hopewell.

Adam explained their expedition, one of trade for the green eyed tribe from the Outer Banks, and also a relief expedition, even if poorly organized, for the salvation of Big Toe, who, to the travelers from America, now stood as the one providing the hope for salvation. He told them of their experience with the storm, and finding Captain Locke at the Blue Lagoon. But both men, as they surveyed their situation, realized that they could no more stay amidst the Caribs as they could with the pirates, and escape from the island was their only hope.

It was Big Toe who devised the solution. "We'll take the Hopewell!" he whispered to Adam in the Creek dialect.

"We'll what?" replied Adam.

"Take the Hopewell. We know how to sail her. They'll be charts aboard her. Four men and a good Captain. Why, we'll have her at sea before they can launch the first boat from the shore. But first, we'll need to find a way to free ourselves from the Carib", he said, smiling widely. "They looked like they were about to eat your friend with the broken leg".

The Carib chieftain was a bit dismayed at the situation as it was now developing. He agreed to release the prisoners, but kept two guards around them, and directed them to remain together until he could get a better feel for what should be done. The night sky was beginning to show signs of early morning when the Indians retreated inland to a wooden enclosure where they planned to spend the next two days, waiting on the pirates to exit the harbor. They had no desire to mix it up with them. It was far too dangerous for everyone involved.

The plan to take the Hopewell was hotly debated, but Big Toe explained that the Carib are an untrusting lot, and lost seamen, well, they would just be a handicap or something else to feed. The pirates, they too could become distrustful, and seeing the Indian blood, would likely want to sell the lot of them to the sugar plantations. So the plan was developed, and went as follows. Big Toe would tell the Chieftain that he and Adam would take Thomas to the farmhouse at the foot of the ridge overlooking the bay. There was a man there who had the knowledge necessary to properly set the leg, if it could be saved. He would have to be carried. Big Toe would return, alone, and move the canoe that lay across the path to the sea near to the Carib encampment. The following night they would make their escape, paddling the canoe around the island to the mouth of the harbor. From there, Adam and Thomas would join them, and they would paddle out to the Hopewell. There should only be a skeleton crew. Everything depended on Captain Locke not realizing their plan and putting out to the Hopewell in numbers sufficient to spoil the robbery.

CHAPTER FORTY

"**B**UT WHAT ABOUT Peter?" piped in little Adam from his spot close to the fire.

"All in good time", replied the old man. "All in good time. But first, you need to know what happened when Adam and Big Toe returned to the cabin at the foot of the big ridge." The boy, it seems, had told his father, who told his wife, and eventually the word of other survivors to the storm had made its way to the Blue Lagoon. Captain Locke had sent out several men to look for the survivors, and had begun to question the story of the stranger who had wandered in to the barroom with his tale of being the sole survivor of a French sloop. He posted one of his men at the cabin to see if the man returned. The island was large, but not so large as to hide a man for long.

Adam and Big Toe had made a litter for Thomas, and managed to make it to the cabin at the foot of the ridge. But as Adam entered the cabin, he was met by the member of the Hopewell's crew.

"And who might you be?" he said. Then, suddenly, Big Toe waked into the room. Upon seeing the large Indian, who he took for a Carib based on his dress and tattoos, the pirate ran from the cabin and headed up towards the crest of the ridge, and, from there, straight for the tavern.

The boy, along with his parents, were hiding in the loft of the cabin. Seeing the pirate run from the cabin, they emerged into the main room, and upon seeing Big Toe, also began to run away. Adam hollered out at them, and, seeing the litter with Thomas writhing in pain, they boy's father stopped and turned toward the men, unsure of what to do. The boy exclaimed "it's him, it's the one I told you about. And he's brought the sailor with the broken leg".

"Yes", replied Adam, "and this is my nephew. He's no Carib. He's here to help me."

The father turned to his wife. 'Get me some strong green sticks for a splint. Boy, get me some rope.'

The man felt about the leg, locating the bones. "I can put a splint on it, but only time will tell if the bones will heal or you will have to lose the leg." Thomas nodded, and the leg was stabilized. The boy handed Thomas a strong wooden pole which would have to do as a crutch, but the litter would still be the fastest mode of travel. The three men, given directions for the Eastern end of the harbor, hurried from the cabin, much to the relief of the small family.

Chapter Forty-One

CAPTAIN LOCKE WAS furious when he learned of not one, but at least three men in addition to Peter who had been roaming the island. And the fact that one of the men was thought to be a Carib made the situation even more irritating, as it could lead to a confrontation with the Indians. While Locke felt he could handle the Caribs, there was always danger of losing men in any scrape.

He turned to Peter. "Ye haven't been straight with me about the situation, now have ye, my French friend?"

Turning to his first mate, he ordered him to take Peter to the ship and put him under lock and key. "For safe keeping. Jest till we see what's this all about. Jest for this safety of us all, Mr. Frenchman." And then, to the rest of the men assembled about, he ordered: "Every man is to scour the island and find these scoundrels. Cap the rum!" he bellowed, as he gulped down what remained in his mug. "Cap the rum!"

The men spread out around the island, heading in all directions, which made the search parties little more than two or three men each. It was unclear how they expected to tackle the men they were looking for, but then most had been drinking for two weeks, not to mention that they had just outrun a hurricane, and they were not at their sharpest. They were, however, well-armed.

Big Toe said his goodbye's and headed back to where the Carib's were encamped. Following Adam's directions, he located the abandoned canoe, moved it quietly into the water, and then paddled to within sight of their small campfire which was the only light to be seen. The sun was beginning to rise, and there was a slight red glint coming from the East, making it easier for Big Toe to locate the hidden Carib encampment among a large stand of tall trees.

Adam, meanwhile, moved Eastwardly along the base of the ridge, hoping to find a way around it on their way to the harbor's edge. The litter, with only one person to pull it, had proved too cumbersome, and he hoisted Thomas on his back. The going was slow. It was a long way to the Eastern shore, and there was no way he was going to get Thomas either over the ridge or along the shoreline, which had become slippery among the rocks. Near the water's edge he found a small cave and decided the best course of action was to leave Thomas there and come for him later. Without Thomas to slow him down, he went straight up the ridge and, from the top, located the corner of the harbor's entrance. The sun was now breaking the horizon, and he could see the bay clearly. There he saw a small boat heading out toward the Hopewell which stood at anchor about a hundred yards from where he was hidden among the rocks. In the boat, which was coming from the center of the harbor, were two men at the oars, with Peter in the front, his hands tied behind him, and another man seated at the stern holding a cutlass. The man was hollering to the Hopewell, but no one was answering his call. Its flag hung lifelessly from the center mast.

When the small boat finally reached the ship a light appeared from the foremast, and a rope ladder was dropped over the side. Peter and two of the men went up the ladder, and within ten minutes or so one of the men came back, descended the ladder, and the small boat headed back, slowly, toward the shore.

"What a relief", sighed Adam to himself. He hadn't quite figure out how to retrieve Peter from the nest in the Blue Lagoon, and now he had just been handed over on a platter. If all went well with Big Toe, they should be there in the canoe before the break of the following day. Adam decided the safest place was to return to the cave. Thomas would need water, and there was no safety on the shoreline of the harbor during daylight.

CHAPTER FORTY-TWO

"**WHAT DO YOU** mean you can't find them!" screamed Locke to his first mate. The island is not that damn big. They are three men, and unless they are prisoners of the Caribs, or have taken to one of the outer islands, they are findable. Findable, do you hear!".

The first mate, Smitty, was understandably concerned for his own safety at times like these, and he looked about for a scapegoat to direct the anger of his Captain. Finding none, he promised better results, and scurried quickly out of the tavern and down the street of the village, determined to find out what he could from the boy or his father who had befriended the stragglers. He really didn't understand what the big deal was, as they were only three men, likely survivors of the hurricane, and to a degree at their mercy, as there was no other ship anywhere to be seen by which they could return to civilization, and of course the Caribs provided no option. But he had learned not to be in the line of fire of his Captain at moments like these, and he picked two of his best men to help him track the missing sailors.

Arriving at the cabin at the base of the ridge, they found it empty. "Aye, the family knows something", he ventured. But there was a track now clearly visible in the light of day, a track of what looked like two sticks being drug across the earth. "A litter!" he exclaimed, and the men found the tracks easy to follow. Two men. Pulling a litter. Then, as the trail moved Eastward along the island, they found the litter abandoned, and the tracks of one man going North, and the other continuing along the base of the ridge. His feet were making deeper indentions along their path. "He's carrying one of them. They should be easy to track".

The tracks led Eastwardly along the base of the ridge, but when he neared the shore, the way became rocky and the tracks disappeared. He was not about to return to Locke without success, and he feared the men might have been taken aboard a boat, or captured by the Carib. He decided to return and follow the tracks that lead Northwardly left by the other man, and before long they discovered a large canoe at the edge of a sandy beach, covered in brush. They decided to wait and see who came for it. The sun was beyond its peak by now, and, this far away from the angry Captain, Smitty felt safe, accompanied by the upper hand he held on whoever had taken pains to hide the canoe. The men broke open a bottle of rum one had brought along, and before long the three men were sound asleep, hidden in the high grass about fifteen yards from the canoe. They were armed with cutlasses and Smitty had a flintlock pistol which he had laid next to his side. One of the men carried an axe, and another, a wooden club. Well-armed, and lazy, and with one eye open for the Carib which might return for their precious little boat.

The moon was near full and the stars had begun to fill the sky when Big Toe slipped from the counsel enclosure and headed toward the area where the three light skinned Indians with the green eyes were gathered around a small fire. When the sun finally eclipsed the horizon, the area, surrounded by the tall stand of trees, became quite dark, and the men knew it was time to make their break. Big Toe talked briefly to the two Carib warriors who had been assigned to keep an eye on them. He told them there was a canoe about a hundred or so yards from there that he had spotted on his way in, a canoe that must have been lost in the storm. He was going to bring it along the shore line and Northward up the spit. "These men will need transportation, so they might as well be the ones to have to haul it to the camp." The warriors nodded, glad they didn't have to bother with pulling or paddling the heavy canoe in the darkness. Big Toe grabbed a long spear from one of the warriors. "Might need this", he whispered.

The five men crouched low and made their way toward the water. They could hear the surf hitting the shore and began to trot toward the beach where the canoe had been left by Big Toe. As they approached, Big Toe turned and pointed to where he had left the canoe. Smitty heard their footsteps, and rose from his hiding place in the high grass, but before he could pull the hammer to the pistol fully back, it exploded in its half-cocked position, temporarily blinding Smitty and frightening the other two men who were with him. One grabbed his axe and ran toward the first sailor, but Big Toe had anticipated the attack, and threw his spear at the man's midsection. The pirate fell back, dead. Seeing this, the third man, holding the club, grabbed Smitty by the arm and began to run back into the thicket behind the grassy area. Smitty had dropped the flintlock and his cutlass, and Big Toe quickly scooped them up. He then retrieved his spear from the dead man's chest. The sailors began to chase the two men as they hurried to escape. "Forget them", cried Big Toe, "and let's get this canoe out into the water."

The surf was strong and pushed against the canoe as they headed into deeper water and searched for a beacon of some sort to guide them around the island. The moon provided light against the blackness of the sea. The clear sky allowed Big Toe to navigate his way through the night toward the rendezvous with Adam and Thomas. It was near daylight when they reached the inlet to the massive harbor. They searched the rocks, and as the first sign of the morning sky appeared, casting its light on the horizon, Adam saw the canoe paddling furiously towards his direction. They saw his wave, and he waded out into the water and jumped into the small boat. He explained that he had to leave Thomas in the cave, and that if they were successful in getting the Hopewell out of the harbor, they could turn Northwestwardly around the island and pick him up.

Adam looked about the canoe. Five men to take the Hopewell. Five men, a cutlass, an axe, a spear, and a club. And, oh yes, a modern flintlock pistol, but no powder or ball.

CHAPTER FORTY-THREE

WITH THE SUN now welcoming in morning, it was not going to be easy to remain unseen as they paddled toward the ship in the canoe, but there was no other alternative. They decided to approach her from the rear, as most likely the lookout would be on the island side, watching for the return of the crew or anyone else approaching from the island. To do this they had to paddle out toward the middle of the inlet opening, and then turn toward the ship. Adam stared at the name written on her stern, and thought about the last time he had been aboard her. He grabbed the axe, ready to board her and get his revenge. Big Toe, who had travelled with and knew most of the crew, had saved his ill will for the Captain, whom he blamed for his captivity, treatment, and sale to a plantation owner on Nevis. "Let me be first aboard" he said to Adam.

The canoe was silent and made its way to the rear of the ship unnoticed. The rope ladder, which had been dropped in order to bring Peter on board, had been hoisted back on deck. Someone would have to climb the anchor rope. The tide was coming in and the ship was being pulled sideways, so the anchor hung a bit as the ship began to come about. Before Adam could say anything, Big Toe was in the water, swimming silently toward the side of the ship, with the cutlass strapped to his back and the flintlock between his teeth.

When Big Toe made the upper deck, he dropped the rope ladder down to the canoe, and the five remaining men climbed up and made it over the rail. The lookout was asleep next to the ship's wheel, and he was promptly bludgeoned with the club. There was no one else to be seen.

Adam led the group down the ship's stairway to the main deck and burst into the Captain's cabin. Two of Locke's crew, both of whom knew Big Toe and were aware he was now in league with the Carib Indians, reached for their cutlasses. The pirate closest to Big Toe slashed wildly, cutting a big swath across Toe's chest, but the wound was not deep enough to do any serious damage. Big Toe aimed the pistol at the man's head and pulled the hammer back as far as it would go. Both men stopped their resistance. "I'm taking command of this ship", bellowed Big Toe. "Are ye with me or are ye ready to die".

"With ye, declared both men in unison."

"And the man ye brought on board yesterday, where have ye put him" demanded Adam.

Big Toe knew at once the most likely place to find Peter. It would be the same place he had been imprisoned on the day Adams was abandoned off the Carolina coast. Down the hall, down to the lower deck, then forward to the lockers where the sails were stored. A small, windowless room, shut with a large wooden door and locked with a rope chain. Big Toe took the axe, and as he kicked open the door, there stood Peter, none the worse for wear, his eyes trying to adjust to the sudden light from the hall lantern.

"A full crew!" declared Big Toe, much to his delight. Adam and Big Toe, who knew the ships sails intimately, had no trouble directing the rest of the crew, four of whom had never been on a vessel anywhere near this size, and the two smaller sails on both masts were soon being unfurled. Adam took the axe, which was proving to be most valuable, and cut the heavy rope anchor. The ship began to glide silently out of the harbor. Captain Big Toe. He would have to change his name.

CHAPTER FORTY-FOUR

ADAMS'S ONLY REGRET at this point was not being able to see the face of Captain Locke when he realized his ship was no longer waiting patiently for him in the harbor. They took a small dingy from the rear of the ship and picked up Peter. They found navigation charts in the Captain's cabin. Adam decided the best bet was to head West and the try to find the coastline of Puerto Rico. They could continue west from there and work their way back up the Florida coast, eventually finding home. Adam, more than anything else, wanted to go home. He wanted to take Big Toe back to the Creek nation and deliver him all in one piece to his family, who by now had surely given them both up for dead. He wanted to rest his tortured soul from the guilt he had felt when Big Toe was enslaved aboard the Hopewell. He wanted peace. Big Toe had something else in mind.

Little Adam looked over at the old man, who had fallen asleep. The next item on the strap was another depiction of a ship like the one before it, only this time, below the ship, was a flag etched like that of a British warship. And the word Nevis.

The old man awoke, and was soon back in the tale.

"I'm taking her to Nevis", commanded Big Toe, sounding now every bit like the Captain of the ship. "The British will pay a handsome reward for her return and the whereabouts of the poor Captain Locke, who had violated his oath and took to pirating. At a time when he could make a handsome living just raiding the Spanish for the King. But the lure of gold seems to take on its own destiny, and drives a man beyond the point of sharin' to the point of wanting it all, and therein lies the evil of it. That's why God put it here for man. To show him his evil ways, and that he was helpless by himself to resist the devil's call. And I'll need you, Adam, to negotiate the deal. Because me, they're just as likely to try to hang me again, once they find out who I am. I've not been unnoticed in my years with the Carib. And the Carib, well, they can be a mighty fierce and cruel enemy."

And with the money from the sloop, thought Adam, he could buy a smaller vessel, something more seaworthy than the hapless outrigger, and the small Carolina trading company could have its first real ship. "Ok, Big Toe, you got a deal. Nevis it is."

CHAPTER FORTY-FIVE

THE GOVERNOR OF the island of Nevis was hospitable to the deal. He had seen the Hopewell from a distance on his second floor window overlooking the ocean. He had ordered an immediate call to arms and was putting on his boots when the commander of his small force entered the room. "She's flying a British flag. The Hopewell. She's under British command."

"It's a trick, my fine Cavalier" replied the Governor. "That's one of the oldest tricks in the pirate book. Sail her in under a friendly flag and hoist up your jolly roger when you're under her guns. She's come to raid us. At your post Lieutenant!"

But the ship dropped her sails and began to float aimlessly, well within sight of the shore, but out of cannon range, still sporting the British flag. A small dingy began to work its way towards the island, manned by two men and a third at the rudder in the stern. Not enough force to be much of a threat, intoned the Lieutenant. Still distrustful, the Governor remained with his hand on his cutlass until the three men had disembarked at the main dock. A handsome, although somewhat shabbily dressed, Adam White stepped forward, bowed profusely at the elaborately attired Governor, and made his case. "We've returned your Hopewell to his majesty's service, your Honor. I apologize for leaving her in such a condition, but our anchor has been cut and we've not had time to repair it. We are in a position to return her to you, assuming of course our kindness is rewarded in kind. My price - a sloop, not as big as the Hopewell, but something seaworthy, and a thousand pieces of gold. You'll find much more in the captain's cabin, and I think you'll find this a very good deal."

"And the Captain Locke, the pirate, an explanation if you please".

"Oh, yes. Well, she was put in at the harbor on an island held by the Dutch, east of Puerto Rico. A deep harbor, well protected from the storms, and a sanctuary for all sorts of riff raft, including pirates and your own island enemy, the Caribs. My nephew organized a party to take her, and there she is. Her crew is, at least for the time being, stranded and in need of a ship. I come from the Americas, and I have medicine to sell, and do business with this island, but I am in need of a ship, having lost my only vessel in a storm. And as for Locke, he is still on the island, stranded, and waiting for your Lordship to come and bring him to the hangman's point here at Nevis. But we want none of that, only a just reward for our efforts, and an invitation to return, and do business with ye."

"And explain this, this "medicine" of which you speak. What is it that is so valuable as to carry it this long distance, to these islands, and to trade, should I agree to your proposition?"

"Medicine, my Governor. Medicine, for the fever. Medicine much like the Spanish have and refuse to share. Medicine, for your gold taken from the Spanish. Medicine, from the Americas. It seems a fair exchange, all around. Let us have a ship, something with a large hold and that can withstand these ocean currents, and we'll be back. In fact, we'll use our reward to furnish her and to take much needed goods back to our homeland."

And so the deal was struck, the Governor gave them a single masted sloop, in need of minor repair, which had been captured from the French and was serving little purpose at the moment due to the condition of her sails. No gold, all gold on board the Hopewell would be given to the King, but in return, a generous supply of gunpowder, muskets, lead, hoes, ploughs, 6 pigs and 3 goats, nails, hand goods and various food supplies, including several tons of sugar. The best sugar in the world.

Thus began the development of the White Trading Company, in the shores of what would become the greatest shipping port on the Eastern Seaboard south of the Chesapeake, Charles Town, South Carolina. Adam White, proprietor. Big Toe journeyed to the mountains and his Creek family, only to return and captain the Just Reward, the trading company's able sloop and prize possession. A creek lodge, and then a one-masted ship, appeared near the end of the leather strip.

"And Maria, why Maria, she gave birth to twins, Thomas and Peter White." said the old man.

"And don't forget Poppa Bill, piped in young Adam", smiling widely at his father, who was putting out his pipe.

"I'll bet Big Toe and Adam had those sails fixed in record time". Little Adam followed his grandfather, who had gone out to the porch to stretch. It was late, and the boy's father was busy writing on the kitchen table. When he finished, Poppa Bill rolled the paper he had been writing on with the old leather strip, and put them both inside the leather pouch, which he then returned to the wooden chest at the foot of the old man's bed.

PART FOUR

1831 - JONESTOWN, GEORGIA

CHAPTER FORTY-SIX

T HE GOLD WAS everywhere. In the creek beds, along the road, in the mountainside, deep in the ground. The biggest problem was the Cherokee, who lived in the mountains and valleys where the gold was to be found, and it was essential for any politician wanting office to take a strong position on getting rid of them. The move was on to relocate the entire population to Oklahoma, and the Creek too at a convenient time, even though their nation had been moved southward into middle and lower Georgia after the great Cherokee-Creek war, and little if any gold was to be found on what was left of the old Creek nation.

There was talk of a land lottery. A lottery which would repopulate the state of Georgia with farmers, but the fact was as long as there was gold fever, the majority of the newcomers would be people looking to get rich off the gold. In spite of the fact that the Cherokee had, for the most part, bought into the new, American, white way of life, and had developed schools, a newspaper, farms, and an agricultural economy, they just had to go. The frontier was still afraid of them, the newcomers were in need of the land, and there was a conqueror mentality which prevailed in the Congress, both statewide and within the Federal government as well.

The tall Irishman, who had just shelled out $100.00 to Martha Johnston for a year's board, was excited about his prospects, and in spite of the winter weather which had moved in, he was anxious to spend what little money he had left to get back to the gold fields further North. Having paid for his board and lodging, he had a safe harbor where he could return from time to time as he ventured into gold country.

The Indian trail which led North to Lumpkin County was easy to follow and showed the signs of the heavier traffic which was now moving along its dirt path. Not wide enough for even a cart, the trail could, however, easily handle a horse and a mule loaded with supplies, tools and the other necessities for survival in a wilderness where stores were a thing of the future and health care little more than a concept. If you had a toothache, you had a serious problem. And everyone, from time to time, had a toothache.

There was a spring about fifty miles north of Jonesboro, and it could be easily made within a day's ride. Michael Downing, the Irishman, led his horse away from the waterhole and into a grassy area. He checked his gear, tightened his belt, wiped the days toil from his brow, and reached into his pack for a piece of apple pie, a gift from Mrs. Johnston as he headed out. It was sweet and sugar was something he would not find much of at the gold fields. He sat near a tall poplar and kicked his boots off, taking a long slurp of water from his canteen. His mind wandered back to Jonestown, and the beautiful woman he had seen in the bright cotton dress. It was a yellow dress, and the sunlight through the window seemed to sparkle in her dark chestnut hair. He could see his mouth on hers, melting into a long kiss, and he wondered where she had come from, and what type of life she had led. Her complexion was so light she could almost pass for white. The child, however, could not, and the child would define her in the eyes of the community. But to Michael, color really didn't matter, and he found himself thinking about her more and more.

His partner in the gold fields was a man by the name of Hank O'Malley. It would be putting it mildly to say he was a bit rough around the edges. His hands were large, his arms well-muscled, and his ruddy face covered in part with a short red beard, which gave away his Irish heritage. In fact, it was that heritage which had drawn the two men together in Savannah, where they had met, and when they ran into each other in the Kinship and Hutchins store across from the Jonestown courthouse, looking for mining pans, they both recognized the benefit in having someone to watch their back as they travelled north. Michael too had come from Ireland, fleeing the complete lack of opportunity and fear of famine, not to mention the political repression from England. Hank was from Northern Ireland, and was a Protestant. Michael was from the South, and Catholic. Neither liked the idea of being told what to think or believe, and for that reason they were attracted to the Mason lodge which had just opened on the opposite side of the town square, next to the Gibson hotel, where they had taken up temporary residence. At the tavern situated midway between the Hutchins store and the Gibson Hotel, over several pints of beer, they heard about the Johnston boarding house, and after their first trip to the gold territories they had the money to make more permanent arrangements such as the Johnston boarding house provided.

"You got that woman on your mind, I think", smiled Hank. "Very dangerous, that woman."

Michael reached back, yawned, and went over to their campfire and stirred the ashes, adding a log. Yes, he thought, she is dangerous. Dangerous because she is a mulatto. Dangerous because she can never be a wife. Legally. Not in Georgia. Never be anything, really, but a poor slave girl. "I'm just thinking about that gold we're going to find", he replied, trying to shake off his friend's inquiry.

"Yeah, right. And what will you do with all that gold", replied Hank. "Buy yourself a racehorse? Find yourself one of those Southern Belles? Raise a family? Buy that little filly from Mrs. Johnston?"

Michael looked at Hank, and realized he had no idea what he would do, and what he wanted or expected from life. He was just going to find some gold, and figure it out from there.

"Me, I'm going to buy me some land." Hank was someone who knew what he wanted. "Land. The riches of Georgia are in the land. And I wanna be rich. Money is the only thing that can save you in a time of want." Hank, at least, had a vision, even if it was somewhat clouded by an obvious lack of any formal education. There was little, if any, refinement in this man who found each day a challenge to overcome, and a willingness to do just about anything to get what he wanted. Independent, strong willed, and fully aware of his surroundings, he was a good match for Michael and they made a good team.

CHAPTER FORTY-SEVEN

HANK DID NOT understand a lot of things, but one thing he did understand was the value of land. The economy of Jonestown, like most of the newly formed counties of Georgia, was fairly simple. You had some stores, but here was little money and few jobs. You had farms, but there was little commerce. What set Jonestown apart, however, was its great entrepreneur, Benjamin Jones, for whom the town was named, and who had brought a new and marvelous industry to Georgia, as well as to the states surrounding her. He built a plant, although no one called it by that name, for the purpose of making the newly invented cotton gin. And with the cotton gin, the economy of Georgia, and indeed all of the South, was transformed. Along with the cotton gin came the cotton plantation, and with the cotton plantation came the need for more and more labor. And that labor, of course, was black labor. Slave labor. And with labor, and the cotton gin, one could become rich. Very rich. Other than the very few industrialists, and politicians, no one in the South could amass much wealth that didn't bring it from Europe except for those who invested in cotton, and of course, that required land – and people to work it.

And so, when the Georgia legislature began looking at ways to populate the vast territory they now held, the idea of a land lottery took strong hold. Hank saw the opportunity, and was ready to seize it. He headed to the state capital, in Milledgeville, and placed his name in the pot. Within six short months, he had 40 acres of land along the Ocmulgee River. The Ocmulgee flowed to Altamaha, and then on to Savannah, and from there to Nevis in the Caribbean, and from there to the ports of Europe and beyond. And the Ocmulgee would carry his cotton. Georgia was soon to be in cotton, high cotton, and his white gold would soon be making its way slowly down the lazy river.

Michael was opposed to slavery, but he was not one to see the world in rose colored glasses. Except, perhaps, when it came to the woman in the cotton dress. When Hank returned from Milledgeville, armed with his fancy land deed, and showed it to Michael, he told him of his plans to build a house on a high hill overlooking the river. "This land here, this will be where we'll build the road down to the river. Here's where the barns will go, and here we'll put the smoke house. We'll build cabins for the slaves right along this tree line." He had it all planned out. All he needed was the money to get started. Slaves, he had seen, were expensive. And you couldn't work a place like that without them. Not and remain competitive. He showed Michael on a crudely drawn map where he was going to acquire more and more land that surrounded his awarded plot. "Before long, I'll have the money to buy whatever I want."

By Spring the men had about two hundred dollars' worth of gold each, taken from the streams of Lumpkin County. A bit disappointing, given their dreams, but still a lot of money for the times. They were at the Gray Tavern, where they had met, sitting in the corner, when an Indian walked in and went directly to the bar. He was older, dressed well, and had a hatchet on his belt. His hair was braided, black and straight, and his shirt was a blue silk. Hank looked over at Michael, and thought he would be denied service, but the bartender welcomed the man, and poured him a drink.

"Back from the Savan", they could hear him say. "Good trip. Much trade." Michael did not understand the Creek dialect, which the man spoke along with a spattering of English. Enough English to understand the flow of the conversation. Apparently the man was well known, at least to the barkeeper, and no one was giving him any trouble. When the man had finished his drink, he turned and walked out, his back strong but slightly bowed with age. There was a fierceness about him, which spoke of his life in the wilderness. He was not a man you could take lightly.

"You know that Indian", inquired Hank of the barkeep.

"Yes, that's Amato, a Creek trader. You live around here for long, you will know about the Creek and their people. He trades mostly down the river to Savannah. He trades in guns and people. This is Creek land, and we've taken it from them. Most have gone West, some South to join with the Seminole. They'll all be gone one day. All but the ones that helped Jackson in the Red Stick War. President Jackson, I should say. President of the entire United States. And still carrying the bullet from his dueling days."

"So Amato sided with the White Sticks in the war? asked Hank.

CHAPTER FORTY-EIGHT

T HE HOUSEWORK WAS done, the kitchen cleaned, and the firewood was neatly stacked by the large stone hearth where the food was cooked and the water boiled. Mrs. Johnston had connected the kitchen building to the main house with a breezeway, and the floors were put in with large stones cut to fit. The chickens were getting so populous that a coop had to be build next to the well-house. Gold Dust, as she was now called, had a small room next to the kitchen, and it was there that she kept her young child, who was now about four years old, and a handful. A handful, but old enough to be given chores to do by Ms. Johnston, and it helped keep him occupied and out of mischief. Gold Dust was going to name him Jonah, after his father, but Jonah got swallowed by the whale, and for some reason, she just couldn't call him that. So she named him Daniel, another survivor, and she liked the fact that Daniel, the Bible Daniel, had tamed the lions. She was worried about Amato, but she knew Amato and figured he would not want to have to take care of Daniel until he was a little older and more valuable. Martha hadn't paid extra for the child, as the auctioneer said he was owned by a Creek warrior, and as long as the child stayed out of trouble and allowed her new purschase to do her job, she had no problem with the mother keeping the boy around.

The Spring had been wet, and that was a good and bad thing in the gold fields, where there was little protection from the elements and no roads to speak of in the mountainous terrain. Of the twelve that were there when Martha purchased Gold Dust, only ten remained. One had been snake bit on the trail and had died. Another had been shot over a claim, and his brother from Texas had showed up one day to pick up his meagre belongings.

It was Gold Dust's job to make sure the rooms were neat and tidy. Generally there were two to three men to a room, and there was an occasional spat over someone's missing tobacco or woolen shirt. But for the most part the boarders got along, and they enjoyed the fact that the place was kept up and looking clean with everything in order. And they had minded, so far, Mrs. Johnston's warning not to mistreat the help. Hank and Michael shared a room on the third floor of house. The third floor was more of a converted attic, and only had two rooms, and it had housed five boarders. The man who had been snake bit lived up there, and so now it was only four.

August came, and with it un unbearably hot sun with little relief, expecially in the late afternoons. The windows of the boarding house were all open, but there was no breeze. Between them, Hank and Michael now had almost Five hundred dollars each, and they had staked a claim on the back of a large mountain which had a beautiful narrow stream running down its side, and they had set up a panning operation and were pretty happy with their situation. The biggest problem was taking trips away from their stake, since there was no registration of claims up in the mountains, and the minute you left there would be someone there trying to take your stake over. So on this occasion, Hank had remained to work and guard things, and Michael had traveled back to their oasis near the Ocmulgee for a well-earned R&R.

There was no respite from the heat, and Michael got his horse from the corral and headed to a lake about a mile or so from town. He had a favorite spot where some boys had tied a rope from a big maple tree branch overhanging the water, and he stripped down and his naked body swung way out and dropped into the water. The lake was hardly more than a hundred feet across at that point, and when he surfaced, he heard a giggle coming from the bank on the other side of the lake. He looked up to see two women running up the bank and behind a tree on the opposite side. He didn't know what to do - which side should he swim to? So he decided to swim back, where his horse was tied, and ride to where the creek creating the lake had been dammed, get around to the other side of the lake, and from there investigate the situation more closely.

The girls, or women, whoever they were, had certainly seen him ride off from the opposite shore, and he wasn't really into spying on them, but he was a man and these women were attractive, so his curious side got the best of him and he continued on around the lake until he could hear them laughing playfully out in the water. From his vantage point on top of his horse he could make out the girl, maybe thirteen or so, and she was jumping up and down in the water. The other person, a woman, appeared to be in her twenties, and she was circling the other girl, laughing, and they were talking about something funny but he couldn't make out what. Suddenly the older woman saw him on his horse, and she quickly swam to the shore and hid, again, behind the tree. The younger girl followed her. Michael turned the horse. He had seen enough. She was as beautiful as the first time he had seen her, in the calico dress.

Chapter Forty-Nine

—⁂—

"THE SOUL. IT'S so old"

They were talking. Down by the river. Michael was due to return to the gold fields. It had been several weeks since they had discovered each other at the lake. And now they were back, at the lake, together. They lay, both with their backs to a giant oak tree whose large branches swung out in all directions. Watching the water, the fish, the ripples in the water as they came and went. They were exploring each other, examining. What and who they were. Lovers, at this moment, seemed to share everything. They could talk for hours about nothing, everything. Their dreams, their hopes, their desires. Gold Dust told Michael about Jonah, and how he had fled the horrid slave life, only to be caught back up in it, and when he was, he didn't really care, as long as he had Eliza to share his existence with. And Eliza, she had been so in love. She told him about Daniel, and what she wanted for him. She knew he was born to do something great, but, in rural Georgia, in the height of the slave era, what future could he have? He was a slave, even at birth, and his measure was taken in dollar bills, and his worth was in what he could produce for someone else. But she didn't dwell on it, it was the reality of the times, and her own worth, as a person, was just the same. She likewise had no control over her own destiny. Her greatest fear was losing Daniel, and she told Michael about Amato. What could she do? Where could she turn?

"There are old souls, and there are new souls", she told him. "I am a new soul. I don't understand my place, what life wants of me. I don't see the future and work to plan for it. I am in the moment, all the time, and tomorrow is always guaranteed, at least for now, and I don't think about the time that will come when I won't be anymore. I have so much to learn. So much to feel. And, but for Daniel, nothing to die for. It is good to have something to die for. Something that doesn't change with the morning weather."

Michael thought about his home in Ireland. His mother and father. His brothers and sisters. How he would probably never see them again. But he could, if need be and circumstances permitted. He was free to do so. She was not.

He tried to imagine how he would deal with Amato. How could he stop him from taking the child when he came for him? Would he have to kill him? Could he do that? Would he do that for Gold Dust? Risk everything? So many questions.

Their hands touched, and they slid their fingers together. They kissed. Some kisses are remembered, and most forgotten. There are kisses, however, which never vanish from the memory - they are so complete. The two pairs of lips melt into one another, and everything, for the moment, is forgotten.

The fish pulled on the string, and the pole began to slide into the water. Michael reached over to grab it, but it was too late, and the pole was out in the water about six feet from shore. He would have to jump in to get it. The cold water on the hot August day awoke him to his surroundings and he quickly found the fishing pole, just as the fish was beginning to pull it down toward the bottom of the lake. His feet searched for the bottom and, finding it, he began to fight the fish. The hook had set, and he pulled it to shore. A good size. It would make a good meal.

Gold Dust began to gather sticks for a fire, and Michael went to his saddle bags and found some spices, a bit of sugar, and some real butter. He had a flat iron skillet, small but effective, and gutted the speckled fish, laying back the flesh and making two big steaks. The air began to smell with the smell of something good to eat, and both mouths began to water. Michael looked over at the woman by the fire. He saw the tips of her breasts impressed against her thin dress. Her long, slender legs. Her swollen lips. Desire overcame his hunger, and the two fell back into the grass and made love. The fish would have to wait.

CHAPTER FIFTY

"WELL, THAT'S A damn fine pickle you have got yourself in", said Hank after Michael had revealed to him his infatuation with Gold Dust, and her similar feelings for him. "Damn foolish situation, and it can never be any good for either of you. I don't have to tell you that this relationship is never going to work out. She just a slave girl, Michael. It's aginst the law for the two of you to get married in Georgia. And when you get old and she gets old and you die off, well then she'll just be sold to the highest bidder by the Executor of your estate. Assuming you have an estate. Same thing for that young'un. Yep, you have just bought yourself a mess. Not to mention what you are going to run into when that Indian comes for the baby. You'll either have to have a ton of money at that point, or you'll have to kill him. Now you might get away with killing that Creek Injun, that is, with the whites, but from what I seen of him that is not going to be that easy to do, and you know, killing for a woman is bad business. It's just bad business and that's all there is to it. You need to just let that one go, and move on to some nice white woman with a rich daddy, and get yourself fixed. That's what a smart man would do in your shoes. And then, if you're lucky, and you have the money put back, you can buy that Gold Dust and have her for a mistress. Take her to Kentucky with the other rich plantation owners, Best of both worlds. Hell, there's another lottery coming up, and I've got enough money put back to buy another 60 acres next to my spread, and I'll have over 100 acres before long. 100 acres makes a lot of cotton. And I've heard that old man Jones will let you take one of those cotton gin machines, if you have the acreage, and pay him from the profits. He's got to be one of the smartest darn people in this whole damn state. Why, in a couple years' time, I might just buy that Gold Dust and take her to my spread for myself.

Hank didn't see the fist as it landed with full force on his jaw. Michael could handle his fists, and he had held back to keep from breaking the jaw, but his anger had taken the best of him and there was plenty of blood coming from the inside of Hank's mouth. Hank started to swing back, but he held up and looked at his friend. "Didn't know you felt that way about her." And then, trying to smile in the midst of all the blood, said to Michael, unsure if he was about to swing again: "What can I do to help."

"Make me a partner." was the reply.

CHAPTER FIFTY-ONE

THE NEXT DAY Michael found himself on his horse at a gallop heading down the old Indian path towards Milledgeville to put his name in for the lottery. He hadn't participated in the first lottery, and he didn't know his chances, but if he could get a plot, he could easily trade it for a 40 acre plot next to Hank, and that would put them almost to 130 acres. And with the money he had saved up, and that large gold nugget he had found in the sleuth this morning, he could easily buy another 30 acres of so. With two hundred acres in cotton, they would be well on their way to a profitable business. The nugget would stand for a down payment on the cotton gin. They would need it with that much cotton. He started thinking about the road they would need to build to get the cotton down to the river. Hank had talked about it often, but he didn't know anything about laying out a road or what it would take. Michael, whose father had built such a road along the Lee River, not far from Cork, had watched the progress as a youth, and had carried a lot of stone from the hillside down the winding path toward the Lee for his pa.

When Michael's turn to return to Mrs. Johnston's boarding house finally arrived, he got a big shock as he entered the front door. There was Martha Johnston, waving her hands up in the air, screaming "she's gone, she's gone! Twelve hundred dollars and she's gone!" Her distress was readily apparent, and she didn't know whether to worry or be enraged. There had been a lot of talk lately at the women's circle about something they called "the railroad". Them niggers escaping up North. And Southerners, and some damn people from up North, helping them. It was outrageous. Anyone who understood anything could understand what a thousand dollars was in value. When a man might make $50.00 in a year working in the new mining industry beginning to take shape. Fifty dollars a year in some of the jobs around town. A thousand dollars. It was a fortune. Just one person. One healthy Negro slave. Or Creek slave, for that matter. A fortune in gold, out the window.

Michael was unstable. He ran to the proprietor, grabbing her by the arms. "What happened? Where did she go? When did you last see her". His thoughts immediately went to Amato, and the baby. "The baby", he shouted at her, "where's little Daniel."

"Gone too" was the reply.

Michael went to his room, dropped of some of his gear, changed clothes, and grabbed his rifle. He headed towards the river, looking for the ford that would take him across the Ocmulgee and to the Creek camp near the Flint. He was beyond being careful, driven by the loss of Gold Dust and his love for her. As he approached the small village, he spotted a paint which he had seen Amato tie to the pole outside the Gray Tavern. It was standing next to a square cabin made of white pine with no windows, only a door and a chimney, which took up most of one side of the structure. He put his full weight against the door, and burst in. There, in the middle of the room, was Amato's wife, and next to her was a child, about ten years old or so. A grandchild.

"Where is she?" Michael demanded.

"Who you want", replied the woman, pushing back her grey hair, and showing a curious look between a large gap in her front teeth. "What you do here?" she demanded.

"The woman, Gold Dust. Your husband has taken her. And her baby!" he hollered.

"What Gold Dust?" she replied. "I know of no Gold Dust. We have no gold dust here."

"Don't lie to me!" Michael screamed back at her. "Don't lie to me!"

At that moment, the door which he had slammed shut as he walked into the cabin, opened with a crash, and there stood Amato, with his hatchet out, and a large knife in the other hand.

"What you want?" he demanded.

"Gold Dust", he replied. "Eliza. She's disappeared, and her child too. Disappeared, and you better tell me where she is, or there'll be a lot of trouble for you."

Amato thought for a moment. He didn't recognize the man, but he knew who he was talking about, without question. It was the first time he had heard her called Gold Dust, but Eliza, yes there could be no mistake. Eliza had his property, and he knew exactly where she could be found. Or so he thought.

"You must be from Martha board house", he said.

"Yes, Mrs. Johnston. Gold Dust was her servant. And she's disappeared. And I figure you have taken her, and the baby, and if you don't tell me where they are, you are going to have more trouble here than even you can handle."

"The baby, that baby of hers, that boy is mine" said the Indian. "My property. She just take care him for short while. I come to get him, maybe very soon. But not got him yet. Where they go?"

"Where?" Michael shot back. "You know where. Where have you got them hid?"

"Me no have child, or Eliza. That her name. No Gold Dust. That not her name. I raise her. Raise her. And she have my child. She just slave girl. Child just slave child. Now go, go now or I will take your scalp and put it on a tree by the river for the birds to make nest in - they make good nest with that all that black hair."

There was something about the way Amato reacted, and his wife, and the perplexed look on the young girl who had hidden behind her grandmother that told Michael that Gold Dust was not there, and that Amato was telling the truth, at least about not knowing where Gold Dust or the child were. He was so sure that he would find her in the village that he was completely lost about finding another place to look. She was gone. Without a word.

CHAPTER FIFTY-TWO

THERE WAS NO trace of the girl or the baby. Eventually, Mrs. Johnston resigned herself to the fact that she had run away, taking the baby, and the only logical place they could have gone would have been up to Decatur, and then further on north to Nashville, on the Underground Railroad, as they called it, on their way even further north and to freedom. It was a long road, there were many risks, and only a few were willing to take the chances, because when you got caught, and most did, the return trip was not pleasant. Martha hired a man to look for her lost property, and paid him Fifty dollars, but he had been gone a long time, with no results. Eventually she travelled to Milledgeville and bought another servant at the Capital Square, next to the Presbyterian Church. This time she was determined not to pay more than Seven Hundred Dollars. Too much to lose if they run off, she declared to herself and to her friends at the women's circle. The replacement was older, with a bad left leg, and she had bad breath. But she could cook, and that little bit of skill sealed the deal. At least the auctioneer said she could cook. The damn railroad was driving down the price of a good slave, when it should have been on the uptake. Something just had to be done.

Michael was beside himself. He talked to everyone around the town, but no one had seen her or the baby since they disappeared. Her belongings seemed intact, and there was talk from the Sheriff that she may have been murdered. A distant cousin in the Winthrop family reportedly told the Sheriff she had been involved in the murder of his uncle, and she had friends who were known to be Yucchi. There were few Yucchi in South Georgia, and everyone knew it was a Yucchi arrow that took Winthrop's life. The Sheriff considered the cousin a suspect, but there was no body.

Without a lead, Michael travelled North along the Sandtown trail to where it met up with the Shallowford trail, both known Indian paths. There was a

Creek trading post at a place called the Standing Peachtree, but he could get nothing from the Creek or the Cherokee who frequented the place. From there he crossed the Utoy Creek and made his way to the Whitehall tavern, a meeting place for whites, and the only place in fifty miles painted white, hence its name. No one had heard or seen of the woman or her child, but there had been plenty of talk about slaves trying to get north. The problem was that no one who might know anything was going to trust this gold prospector with any information. If they were known to help the runaways, their neighbors, at the very least, would shun them. If they were known to aid and abet a runaway, the law would be coming, if not a mob. The complexities of slavery upon a society which had been so totally re-defined by it, and in such a short period of time, waxed heavily upon every family, and the laws were written to deal with the moment, the immediate needs of the rapidly growing economy. And people's greed, and above all, their fears.

The trail became cold, and the first sign of Fall was in the air. He had to get back to Hank, who'd had the stake by himself now for over three weeks. Torn, he turned his horse Northeast toward the gold fields.

CHAPTER FIFTY-THREE

"I TOLD YOU SHE was trouble, now didn't I".

Michael had to admit that Hank was right, at least about that. His heart was troubled, day and night. He couldn't sleep for the worry. He fell into the stream twice in one week. It seemed to help.

Martha was unhappy with her new employee, but you can't change a personality with a whip. And she wasn't one to do well as a disciplinarian. But the new girl would do. And the food was a little better, and, after all, it was the food that was the backbone of her business.

Amato, unhappy with the turn of events, sent his own feelers out trying to find out what had happened to Eliza and the baby, and he had heard the girl had been seen on the road to Macon in the back of a wagon. But the rumor proved to be false, and he too gave up looking, at least for now, and feared the worst for his property. He planned to travel north, and talk to the Yucchi. The Yucchi knew everything.

Michael got his land from the lottery, bought another 40 acres, swapped all of it for land next to Hank's, and the partnership now had over two hundred acres along the Ocmulgee. Michael began to lay out the road that would lead to a place they could load the cotton, and Hank surveyed the land and began to clear it. Another road was planned to connect their place with the main road leading north to the state capital, but that would have to wait.

CHAPTER FIFTY-FOUR

WORD HAD REACHED Gold Dust that Amato was coming for Daniel. Michael would fight him, of course, but the Winthrop lawyer who handled his Estate aftert being killed by the Yucchi had let it be known that their was an unaccounted for child at the auction, and so the Sheriff was going to have a difficult time siding for the white man over the Indian because the Indian had the white lawyer working for him. So she ran.

There was only one place for her to run with the child, and that was to the Gullahs, to Poot and MayMay. She felt safe among the Gullas, and May and Poot loved their new grandson, and built him a canoe. They taught him to swim, and watch out for the alligators. Amato would have to be careful here if he showed up looking for Eliza and her child. The Gullahs would have no problem with killing a slave hunter, and there was no local Sheriff to provide protection for the man and his property. As a slaver, Amato was a natural enemy of the Gullas and the Seminole.

Eliza was down by the creek, remembering about the magic powder and her days with Jonah, went she began to throw up, for no apparent reason. She was also missing Michael, who she had come to love and care for, but her first priority was keeping Daniel safe and out of the hands of the slavers.

MayMay, from whom few secrets were safe, knew the signs and talked to Poot.

"She with child again". Poot nodded.

Life sometimes makes us make difficult choices, and Eliza now had to choose whether to return to Michael or remain with the Gullah's. She had never revealed the location of the Gulllah camp to Michael, so he had no way of finding her, even if he guessed her destination.

When the baby began to kick, she knew she could not deny Michael his child. Nor could she return to Jonestown and risk losing Daniel to Amato.

So, it was decided. Daniel would remain with Poot and MayMay. She would return to Michael. As white as she was, and with a white father, the child would surely look mostly white.

MayMay and Eliza discussed the situation one night at one of MayMay's late night excursions into the swamps. They laughed when they thought of how her return to Michael would work out. "That child will be born to confusion" said MayMay. "He can pass fo' white much better than yu!" she declared. "But still slave child. Under law. He yo' chil', and that make him slave".

"Michael doesn't care", she replied. "And besides, it might be a girl".

"No, that son yu' carry. Boy baby. MayMay know." And, usually, she did.

"Care or not, he not be safe or free. Not till all white men dead, or heart of white man change. Always slave child. You, always slave child". When MayMay discussed the matter with Poot early the next day, he nodded in agreement.

Gold Dust's heart was breaking when she began her journey back north to the Ocmulgee. She knew she had to see Michael, and at least let him know that she was going to have his baby. "If he has no feelings for the baby, I'll be back" she told MayMay. Poot, who had been hollowing out the log for the little canoe, smiled. They had a grandchild to raise and spoil, and things, in one way, couldn't be better.

Gold Dust knew she had to plan a return that would convince Amato that Daniel was dead. She would by-pass Jonestown, travel to the gold fields, and find Michael. She would explain the situation to him. If he was going to treat her and the child like the slaves they were, then it would be a simple matter to return to the Gullas, and she would be perfectly happy raising the two children together. Fathers were overrated anyway, she thought. If, on the other hand, Michael wanted her on an equal basis, and was willing to treat the child as his own, she would stay with him and they could raise the child together. Maybe it would be a son. Time would tell.

"Life not simple, sometimes", said MayMay, feeling her sadness at leaving Daniel behind. "He be safe here. Safe from Mato. We make him good warrior. Very fierce. Afraid of no thing."

"You do and I'll turn you into a hog with your own magic", replied Gold Dust, smiling. But, in a way, she did want her son to grow up and be a warrior. A fighter, a fierce fighter, for his freedom, and for hers, and for all of the people owned by other people. It was the Creek in her.

CHAPTER FIFTY-FIVE

MICHAEL WAS PANNING down by the stream when someone came up behind him and put their hands over Michael's eyes. Spinning around, with a fist pulled back, ready to swing, he suddenly couldn't believe his eyes. There she was, smiling widely. She had been riding a small buckskin horse, and the horse stomped it's foot and whinnied. She had been riding with only a bridle, and her back was sore along with her legs. She stretched out by the bank of the stream, letting her feet dangle into the cold water. The weather had turned, and it was now cold when the sun dropped below the horizon. But the days were still warm, and she was hungry.

"You should see the place!" he exclaimed. "I've already started building a house. It's only one room now, but before I'm done, it will be a palace. Hank is making me into a real entrepreneur."

"I'm pregnant".

"You're what?" The words didn't seem to register.

"I'm pregnant".

It was only then that Michael realized that Daniel was missing. "Where's your son? Where's Daniel?"

"Dead, He died on the road to the Yucchi camp up North. I went there to escape Amato. I hid with the Yucchi. Daniel got the fever, and died. In my arms".

"Oh my God, Gold Dust. I can't imagine how you must feel".

"I feel tired, and hungry. The question is, how do you feel? About this baby I'm going to have. How do you feel about that? That is the question."

Michael, who had thought about nothing else but Gold Dust and what he feared might have had happened to her, was having a tough time processing this new information about a baby. He was so happy about Gold Dust being alive, and now, his mind went to what would Martha Johnston say about her lost property. Then, in a fit of anger, he turned on her. "Why, why didn't you tell me you were running off. Why? Why?"

Gold Dust smiled. "You would have come, come after me. And you would have to leave behind all you have worked for. Your chance to have a life better than poverty. I couldn't take that from you", she said.

Michael turned to her, looked down the creek, then up towards the small encampment where Hank was starting a fire.

"I feel like the luckiest man alive, Gold Dust. The luckiest damn man alive. That's how I feel."

With a sense of mixed emotions, because it meant she would not be returning to her Daniel, she pulled Michael close to her, put his hand on her belly, and looked up to him "Your son, Michael. I have it on good authority it will be a boy."

"And on whose authority is that", replied Michael.

"Oh, a little bird told me. A bird, sent by God. That bird told me, and we'll call him Moses. Robert Moses Downing. He will lead us to the promised land.

It was going to be necessary to keep Gold Dust hidden, away from the curious eyes of the townspeople of Jonestown, at least until Michael had enough money put aside to get Martha Johnston her $1,200.00 back. He would make up some story about how she had gone mad losing Daniel to the fever, and that a she would never make a good slave for her business, and that he felt sorry for her. And Martha would take the money, and be happy, and pretend she felt sorry for Gold Dust. It wasn't her fault that she had run off. And the new help, though older and crankier, at least didn't have that child to slow her down and take her away from her chores at what seemed like constant intervals during the day. Michael could be convincing, and he would convince poor Martha that this was for the best.

Michael took Gold Dust to the place where he had started to build his cabin. He put up a lean-to, a small corral for the horses, and continued to work on the main house. He laid it out so, in time, it could double, maybe triple in size. Hank, who had also begun work on a cabin, could see the smoke from Michael's newly built kitchen rising above the trees. Between them they would build the road down to the river. With help, of course. Slave labor. And money from the bank. The bank at Milledgeville was practically giving it away to those who had land. And land was selling for $1.25 an acre. Cotton prices were on the rise, and now was commanding ten cents a pound in Savannah.

"Why, with the gin, a negra knowing what he's doing' with a helper, can do 50 pound in a day" said the general store manager, Bob Franklin, whose store on the corner, next to the Mason lodge, was selling out faster than the stock could be put on the shelf. "Before, a pound maybe a day was all a man could make. It's not the pickin, it's separatin' what takes the time. Why they can't bring enough slaves up here from Savannah. Cotton now, it's like gold itself. Pure white gold."

The cotton gin, instead of reducing the labor market for slaves, made the commodity so plentiful that the market exploded. The South had, in a matter of a few short years, become the cotton capital of not just Georgia but the entire world, and the O'Malley Downing partnership was no exception in the lucky group of entrepreneurs that feasted on the burgeoning market. Their first wagon load to the river terminal was a grand event for the enterprise, and the barge captain, who had just been spotted a small gold nugget, courtesy of the partnerhsip, knew that this would become a regular stopping off point on his way down river to the sea.

With their successes there was talk, talk about the Irishman and his growing plantation, and the talk was also about the mulatto who went by the name of Eliza, who was living openly with him. And the white child they were raising, but who was suspected to be the child of the Mulatto – thanks in part to Hank getting drunk down at the tavern and spilling the proverbial beans. That they were living openly together was not as bad as him treating her as he would a white woman, and the women of the sewing circle in town did not approve. In fact, they mentioned it to the Priest at the Catholic church in Mobile, where it as rumored the man was a member. The woman, of course, was never seen with him there, or on his trips to town, but if you visited the place, she would bring you a cup of tea served on fine china, and she wore the best clothes sold in Macon or in Decatur. It was unhealthy, they said.

Their child was routinely ostracized from local society, except of course from those who could care less about such things. The bartender at the Gray Tavern, the lawyer from Savannah that had recently settled in town and was living at the Hotel, the Master Mason at the lodge – they couldn't give a damn about who someone chose to live with, or the color of their skin. They were, however, in the distinct minority when it came to racial feelings in the State of Georgia. A very small minority.

"Why, what difference does it make?" The bartender was in fine form, having had a couple of shots of liquor himself, and not minding if his words upset the regulars sitting and standing across from him. "It's his right. Who are we to say what he can and cannot do? It's a free country, goddamnit."

"Yes, and I've heard that his woman looks a lot like that lady that disappeared from the boarding house awhile back. Mighty similar. Though this one, she looks a bit whiter and her hair is short and cropped around her shoulders."

This type of talk was common enough to eventually grab the attention of one of the bar's regular customers, the Creek trader, Amato. Amato was still smarting from the loss of his young property, and the thought that his mother could be the same person living in the large cabin on the Downing property was too much for his curiosity. He went down to the river and followed the old Creek trading path upstream until he could see the smoke rising from the dwelling in the distance near the top of a hill. He slipped a canoe into the river, crossed over, and climbed the bank. There was a large cliff with a number of unusual rock formations, created years back when a mighty rumbling of the earth shook the area for hundreds of miles. He was young, but remembered it well. The mico of the tribe said it was a sign that the white man was coming to take their land from them, but that was a long time ago now, and he climbed the path up the side of the steep rock cliffs until he got to the top. There, two giant rocks were propped, one against the other, and they looked so fragile, one could imagine if they ever moved but just a little they would come tumbling down upon each other, sealing the large, cave-like hole below them. Amato almost slipped as he reached the top. He stared deep into the hole, and saw no bottom. "Probably snake in bottom of pit", he muttered to himself, and he thought about the rattlesnake pit he had come upon one day while exploring other limestone caves along the river and seeing the snakes practically standing on one end and dancing, weaving in and out with each other in some mythical rhythm that only the snakes themselves could understand. Sometimes hundreds would live and dance together in this way.

On reaching the top of the hill he crept toward the wisp of smoke he knew would be coming from the dwelling, and he waited. About an hour later a woman appeared with a small child. But this was a white child, or at least a child who could pass for white. It wasn't his child. His property. The woman, however, was Eliza. He would know her anywhere. "Ah, she has returned", he said to himself. Another person, a negro child about 12 years old, came out of the door, and then two dogs. Amato was downwind, but knew if the wind changed, they would start barking and he would be caught. So he waited, still as he could be, and in about an hour the dogs, the child and woman all went back indoors. "No Daniel" he said to himself.

The next day Amato was up before the sun and struck out North, along the Flint, and headed for Cherokee territory. He traded with the Cherokee and had been to the Standing Peachtree village many times. He wanted to visit the Yuchi camp, and he needed a Cherokee to show him the way through what was now Cherokee country.

Amato carried a new hatchet with him, and offered it to any man who could take him to the Yucchi encampment. There were several who stepped forward and offered to show him the way, but Amato was hesitant and distrustful. Then, a young boy about 10 or so said he knew the way, and Amato handed him the hatchet, and they were on their way. The boy's mother was Yucchi, and his father Cherokee. They lived with the Yucchi, but his father had to leave a year or so ago due to bad blood between his father and his mother's brother. The journey, with both riding the tan gelding of the Creek trader, took three days, but they finally arrived. Amato had brought ten beaver skins for trade, along with a flintlock pistol. He would not trade the pistol for anything, but the fact that he had it, and could at least promise to find another and bring it on his next trip, was enough to get him a meeting with the tribe's mico, and it was then he learned that Eliza had not been there with Daniel. In fact, she had not been there at all. Not in recent memory. One older Indian remembered her, and remembered she had fought with the Red Sticks. Her story, the one he had heard at Gray's Tavern, and which had come out of Hank O'Malley's own mouth, that she had hidden out amongst the Yucchi, and that Daniel was with her there, and had died in her arms, was not true. And if the story of her being there was not true, then maybe the story of Daniel dying in her arms was also not true. Maybe she lied about that as well. Maybe the child was still alive. His child. His property. He had become obsessed with the child, and would find him. Take him. Own him. Why, even Amato did not fully understand. But it consumed him, down to the bottom of his very unhappy soul.

CHAPTER FIFTY-SIX

MAYMAY HAD A bad feeling. There was something wrong in the air. Something she could not put her finger on, but something was wrong. There was a stillness. The birds were not singing. Something told her to get the child and Poot and go to the swamp. They got in the small canoe Poot had made for the child, and paddled into the abyss. A maze of inlets, waterways, trees beginning it seems underwater. A complex maze of no return if you didn't know where you were and where you were going. They had no sooner made it to the safety of a small island within the maze when they heard the first gun shot. Then more shots, and then a cannon burst, hitting the Gullah village dead center. A fire started, and the Gullah warriors began to fire back. Soon there was a full stage engagement between the soldiers and the Gullah. Forty men or more were on horseback. The cannon burst again, and the entire village population began to make their way toward the safety of the swamp. Many were slaughtered by the grapeshot from the cannons and the incessant roar from the rifles.

Poot and MayMay watched with horror as the scene unfolded. The Gullah camp had somehow been partially surrounded by several hundred armed men, and the only thing that could be done was to retreat into the alligator infested waters to the East and West of the camp. The soldiers followed as best they could, but the soldiers knew the dangers of the swamp and entered it with reluctance. MayMay scooped up the child as Poot pulled the canoe up alongside them, and the canoe gently slid along the edge of the island, and then further East.

By the end of the attack, half of the village had been killed or wounded. The remainder of the tribe had managed to escape into the swamp, but the village was burned by the invaders. MayMay and Poot decided to continue to move East, leaving the canoe behind as the swamp receded, and they headed on foot toward the great sea, seeking another Gullah settlement they had heard about along the banks of the ocean. It was a long way, but their legs were still strong and they had the child to protect, to motivate them, to give them strength. Along the way a dozen or more survivors of the attack joined them, and at last they reached the sea and the relative safety of a Gullah community near the border between South Carolina and Florida. An island, and safety, at least for now. Pollawana, the leader of the group, welcomed the newcomers with open arms, and listened sadly to their story of misfortune. He knew of their settlement and its history. "White soldiers", he concluded. "Want rid of Gullah. Never any peace". MayMay gathered in a few herbs, and began to make a concoction to help celebrate and give thanks for their deliverance. Daniel and Poot began work on a new canoe.

PART FIVE

CHARLESTON, SOUTH CAROLINA - 1835

CHAPTER FIFTY-SEVEN

THERE WAS A round wooden knob at the foot of the elaborate staircase leading to the second floor of the Springer home. John Springer loved the feel of the wood, and grasping the knob as he descended the stairs from his second floor bedroom gave him a sense of calmness and assurance. It was one of those little things, as silly as it may sound, that a person does that seems to give the day an ordered meaning that it wouldn't otherwise have. From the home's vestibule, he would enter a world of privilege, wealth and power. It wasn't always like that. The early days, growing the business, had been difficult. Money was hard to come by. The banks weren't lending. Born in 1758, he had developed a chronic foot disorder as child, and had great difficulty getting around. Now, he had outlived most of his contemporaries. His oldest son, Mathew, had long ago assumed command of the family shipping business, and was currently in England, negotiating a contract to supply three new ships to the English fleet. Their ships were circumventing the world as each new day arrived. One of their companies sailed regularly to the Caribbean, trading for sugar and now, in ever expanding numbers, the new white gold of the Southern colonies, cotton. Cotton in every increasing quantities, more than his father could ever have imagined. It was the substance, the heartbeat, the rhythm of the South, the basis of her currency, and the envy of the world.

The Springer family had found wealth, wealth beyond its wildest dreams. John Springer's wife, Margaret, had given the family seven children, and all but two had entered the family business. One child had moved to Boston, and another, somewhat to the family's dismay, had become a priest in the Catholic church. The family was, in almost anyone's terms, the picture of success.

The growing Catholic community now had a new church, Pope Pius VII had canonically erected the Diocese of Charleston, and a new Bishop, an Irishman from Cork, was sent to found the new diocese. The Springer family donated a sideboard to serve as the first alter, and made a substantial contribution toward the building fund. It was the right thing to do.

But, for the aging magnate, something was missing. Something deep within him, something he could not explain. As the friends of his generation began to pass on, an emptiness seemed to envelop him. Something was not right. Something was out of tune. Something made the walnut knob at the foot of the stairs of the magnificent home feel hollow, and its charm, capable of exuding order, was losing its power. He tried to get his arms around it, to understand what was happening. But to no avail. His wife, to her credit, tried to console him, explore his uneasiness with him, and bring him out of it. But she found herself time and again walking away, exasperated, unable to comprehend this man who, by all appearances, had all that life could bestow upon a person, and then some. Tomorrow they were going to name their newest ship, a tall, three masted schooner, built to the finest specifications, the Seven Seas, after their seven children, and Susannah, Mathew's second wife, was to break a hundred dollar bottle of champagne upon her bow at the ceremony.

Susannah called him for tea, but the aging magnate declined. Instead, he asked for his carriage, put on his top-hat, grabbed his cane, and went to visit his son, the one who had become a Priest.

The priest, Abraham Springer, had found a home in the growing Catholic community of Charleston, and had become celibate, choosing a life of service over the life of wealth and privilege. The Church had assigned him to a small parish in one of the poorer sections of the city, and from there he had begun a life of devotion to the church, administering to the disenfranchised and unfortunate of the city's poorer citizens. He had drawn the attention of the area Bishop for his devotion to his faith. Unlike the Bishop, he owned no slaves, and deemed the practice deplorable.

The aging grandfather looked at his son, Abraham. "How ironic", he mused, "that I have come to my child to make my confession".

"Long ago", began the financial magnate, "before your brother married his wife Susannah, when you were still a boy yourself, your older brother married a woman by the name of Juliet White. She was the only child of another shipping family, the Whites, a family that was part of one of the first families of Charleston. She had a child, a negro girl, and after the child was born, your mother insisted that the child be sold, or given away. White's daughter, Juliet - her name was Juliet - was heartbroken when the child was sent to Georgia in the care of a Creek trader. I instructed the trader, a man by the name of Amato, to raise her as a free black woman. Whether he did or not, I don't know. He said he would. For several years the Creek trader would come, and I would provide him with money for the child's care. However, a number of things happened, and I lost track of Amato and the girl. There was an embargo imposed against trade due to the problems the colonies were having with the British, and in 1812, another war with Britain broke out. Shipbuilding was affected, and so was the cotton trade. The British put a blockade around Charleston, and nothing could get out. About this time, the Creek nation had a civil war, and no Creek traders were making it down the Altamaha. Amato sent word that the girl had run off to fight with the Red Sticks, and that was the last I heard of her. Quite naturally I quit sending any money, and when it stopped, so did any news of the child.'

The old man cleared his throat and spat into a nearby spittoon, and then continued.

"The girl was named Eliza, and her mother, Juliet, just disappeared from society after the child was taken. Your brother could never find it in himself to forgive her, and the White child, Juliet, was ostracized in the Charleston society. There was a divorce. The Whites and the Springers had been partners in one of the first shipping enterprises in this city, and after the birth of the child, the Whites, who had remained loyal to their disgraced daughter, and the Springers, fell out, and the two families went their separate ways. The Whites were eventually ruined financially due to the embargo, and moved south, on down to Savannah, to try to rebuild their shipbuilding business. Our family joined up with the Hamptons, and got into cotton. Mathew's marriage to Susannah, why it was more a merger than a marriage, but they have been happy together and raised a fine family."

Abraham remembered that there had been talk about his older brother and another woman, and there was something he recalled about a disgrace to the family and, in an action so foreign to his Catholic teachings, a divorce. The priest reeled back, stunned at the brutal honesty coming from his father about matters which had never been discussed publically or privately to his memory. Savannah and Matthew were a merger more than a marriage? But Abraham was not so naïve as to ignore the fact that marriages in the early days of the colonization of America were often structured by families, and marriage for love was more for the poor and outcast than for those who considered themselves part of the best society. The elder Springer paid no attention, oblivious to the effect his words were having on the clergyman, and continued on with the tale.

"With their heightened position in society, the Hamptons gained access to the royalty of Europe, and with that, the window to the cotton trade was swung wide open. Along with it came the slave trade, and the tobacco and sugar markets. Charleston's place as a point of entry into the colonies was established, never to be surrendered. The Caribbean, and Nevis in particular, became the center of commerce with the European markets, which then expanded out to India and around the world.

The old man stumbled, and as he stepped back, Abraham hurried to get him a chair. His father drank a long glass of water, and seemed to shudder as his mind wandered into hidden places. "There is something, something that I can't put my finger on, but something that is keeping me alive", he went on. "Something about that girl. That negro girl. You must help me to find out what is so important about that girl. My soul is not a rest. Please, you are a priest. You can….you must help me!"

"Of course, pa-pa", replied Abraham. "But what could that possibly be? And where could the girl possibility be? That was, what, well over thirty years ago."

"No one knows. Maybe the Whites can tell you. The girl's father is long dead. But there is an Indian shipbuilder who is rumored to be part Creek. You might try him. He lives in Savannah now, near the mouth of the Ocmulgee River. I remember Juliet White's father talk of him. As family. As family, as I remember it. Imagine that, a Creek Indian, as family."

"I will see what I can do", replied Abraham, "but no guarantees, you understand". The old man reached over to the table next to the door, took his hat and cane, and turned to address the priest again. "Please", he said. The two men then parted, and the aging ship magnate returned to his mansion overlooking the bay. The walnut knob had no effect on his state of mind, and he kicked at the dog as it ran between his legs, almost knocking him over. "What a waste of time", he murmured to himself. "Those damn Catholics!" He could not comprehend what had driven him to seek out his son the Priest, much less open up about one the deepest of the families many secrets.

CHAPTER FIFTY-EIGHT

AMATO WAS ON a mission. And he had the perfect opportunity. The missing child consumed his thoughts every day, and one day, sitting on the porch of a cotton trader outside of Mobile, the trader mentioned to him that he was looking for a man to travel to Charleston to find someone who could eventually rise to the position of oversee'er for his massive cotton holdings. He needed somone he could train, someone who could master the workings of the cotton gin, and for that matter, the labor side of the cotton business. And to find that person he was in need of someone to travel to Savannah, or perhaps, Charleston, and try to find a slave capable of meeting that need, a highly skilled and intelligent slave, able to oversee the manufacturing process. Whoever went would have to be trustworthy, as he would be carrying a good bit of money as he travelled downriver to do this business.

"Why, I'm just your man!" Amato almost shouted. "That's what I do best. And I have people who can speak for me, people who can vouch for me to take care of your money."

And yes, Amato thought, while in Chalreston, I will seek out an old friend. An old friend. It was time to pay the family a little visit. It had been a long time since he had spoken to John Springer. And speak to him he would. Perhaps there would be word about the missing child. Daniel. Perhaps John Springer would like to know where the mixed offspring of Juliet White was living. Perhaps.

The old white horse was long dead, and had been replaced by a buckskin and then a paint. But the paint was in fold, and he was getting much to old to consider a journey all the way to Charleston by horse. Travel by boat was his preferred method of travel, and he picked two strong men from the village, and began his journey down to the Altamaha. The weather was getting cold, and the river was running fast, and they made good time. He had purchased a new rifle, and he would fire it each morning, learning how it operated, its ticks and its tricks. He worked on his reloading time.

The Ocmulgee, they say, has more twists and turns than a lifetime, maybe two lifetimes, and the canoe was old, but it was well made and it held up until they reached the Altamaha. There, they had to do some major repairs, and it held them up for almost a week. The first sign of winter was in the air and the squirrels could be seen running from the base of the walnut trees and scurrying toward their winter homes. When they reached the Charleston trail, they were already miserable, and even with the rented ponies it was a good three day journey from the river to the good road leading to the port city. Amato wondered if he could talk the elder Mr. Springer into paying for the upkeep of the child who had so long ago been entrusted to his care. "I'll tell him she came back from the Red Sticks, and I've fed her and cared for her all this time. Fifty dollars a year should be a reasonable price, and then I'll say she ran off again, and now no one knows where she is. That should be good for a least Five Hundred Dollars. He should be good for that." Amato, well pleased with himself, drifted off to sleep, confident he would be in for some extra money when he found John Springer. If, of course, he was still alive.

The sun was getting toward the horizon and they were still twenty miles from town. They stopped at a tavern. The two native helpers slept outside in the barn, and Amato, carrying his hatchet with authority, quickly convinced the inn-keeper to give him a room. The money was good, and while he smelled bad, most travelers did, he had paid extra for the horses to stay in the barn. Outside of town, and beyond watching eyes, money spoke stronger than prejudice.

The next morning the Creek trading party reached the outskirts of Charleston and made their way to the Sheriff's office. They showed their papers authorizing them to purchase a negro slave at the auction, although they intended to make their purchase in private and be on their way. "Ever hear of John Springer?" Amato asked the deputy inside the policeman's office.

"Here of him, why he's one of the richest, if not the richest, men in this whole town. Why, everyone knows of John Springer."

Amato's eyes lit up and he was doubling the Five Hundred Dollars for the care of Eliza in his head. "Well then, can you tell me where his Lordship might be living? I've got business with the man."

"Business, you say. What kind of business would a man like you have with the likes of John Springer? Besides, the man is old, and his son does his business now." The constable was growing irritated at the Indian, who acted uppity and spoke like he was an equal. Nothing made him madder than an uppity Indian, lest it was an uppity Negro, which was worse in his mind than the Indian could ever be. Of course, he had lived in the area only after it was mostly settled, and the Indians hadn't been something he grew up fighting, like his forebears. Amato dropped a sixpence coin on the table. The Sheriff stepped in.

"Go to the river. You will see a small island not too far from the shore. They are building a fort there, and moving granite over there onto a sand bar. By the ton. If you travel to the far Eastern part of the town, you will see a large white house closest to the water. You can see the fort being built from the road in front of the house. That's the Springer place. Can't miss it. Lest you are blind." The Sheriff laughed at his little joke and picked up the coin. "Don't make trouble", he warned. "I would hate to have to take that money pouch you are carrying away from you." He smiled broadly, and Amato got the hint, moving quickly out of the office and waving his two men on down the road. "What a son of a bitch", he said under his breath.

When Amato arrived at the location described by the constable, there was a long line of carriages leading from the road all the way to the front door of the large white house adjoining the harbor. When he got to the front door, he could see two large wreaths, made of carnations and various greenery, one on each of the two massive wooden doors leading into the home. That generally meant only one thing. Someone had just died. "Too late", he murmured to himself.

Fully expecting the deceased to be the elderly Mr. Springer, Amato turned and started back to where one of his helpers were holding his horse. There, leaning into one of the carriages, was an old man with a topcoat and cane. Amato couldn't believe his eyes. It was – could it be – the late John Springer. There could be no mistake. The old shipbuilder himself. He was still alive and kicking. A short white beard, and little hair, but still strong in the jaw and still moving with a great deal of grace for someone his age. "Why, he must be amost 80!" Amato said to the Indian standing next to him. The Indian grunted, not understanding a word of English.

CHAPTER FIFTY-NINE

A BRAHAM SPRINGER HAD barely made it to Savannah, courtesy of the Bishop's own coach, when word of the death of his brother, Mathew, reached him. He was stunned, but he and his brother had never been very close, and his mind went to Mathew's wife and his other siblings. There had been a major storm thundering across the Atlantic, and the ship carrying Matthew home from his trip abroad had gone down with all aboard. Fortunately, none of his children had accompanied him on the trip. The company's financial manager and its chief operations officer, however, had not been so lucky. And they had taken their wives. A holiday for them. It was a serious blow, not only to the Springer family, but to Springer and Hampton Ltd. as well. The City itself was feeling the loss.

Abraham debated whether to return immediately or to seek out the mulatto shipbuilder before returning. The funeral was being postponed temporarily in the hopes a search might uncover the bodies of the deceased victims and in order for the relatives to be able to make the trip to Charleston, so it would be a week before his appearance would be required back home. The Bishop had left it up to him to decide whether to return immediately. Abraham thought about the long trip back, and decided it would be best to stay on for a few days and look for what remained of the White family and their shipbuilding business. There was a new Baptist church which had just been completed, but the Catholic population was still recovering from the prohibition against Catholics which existed when Savannah was founded. That prohibition was lifted following the American Revolution, but the diocese was still too small for its own governing body, and was under the auspices of his own boss, the Charleston Bishop. From their small office in Savannah, the presiding priest directed Abraham to a large, stone waterfront building. The smell of yellow pine was everywhere, as was the unmistakable odor of turpentine and black pitch. The sign in front read "White and Sons, Shipbuilders and Supplies".

A short, be-speckled Indian with long black hair, braided down his back, appeared from behind the counter. He was heavily tattooed across his face and arms. "I'm looking for someone from the White family", Abraham inquired. The Indian, seeing the carriage and driver in front of the building, simply nodded and disappeared behind a door made from an old blanket. Before long, another Indian, this time a woman, appeared and motioned Abraham to follow her, and she led him to a staircase which led to a second story. There, behind a desk, was a mulatto, mostly white but with some clear Creek features, and behind him was a painting of a large, three masted schooner, painted while at anchor in Charleston Bay.

"I'm looking for someone who knows about the Harriet and John White family, formerly of Charles Town", inquired Abraham.

"And what be your business with that family?" was the reply.

"I'm looking for a child of John White. A young woman by the name of Juliet. She would be in her 50's, maybe, by this time. She had a young child when she was married to the son of a shipbuilder in Charleston. Perhaps you have heard of the family. John Springer?"

With that the man behind the desk leaned forward, grabbing the priest by the collar. "Best you get out of here before you find yourself on the wrong end of a sharp knife, Mr. Priest!" The Indian let go, and Abraham stood up, and began to leave.

He turned back in the direction of the mulatto. "Mathew, Mathew Springer. Mathew Springer has just died. A shipwreck."

The Indian behind the desk suddenly changed his countenance. "Mathew Springer you say? He's dead?"

"Yes, Matthew Springer. He is, was, my brother. I am here on a mission for his father, John Springer. He is trying to find a child. A negro child. The negro child of Juliet Springer. A woman by the name of Eliza."

"Why, why?" replied the Indian, "Why in the world would he care about that child. Of what interest is that to him, now? They sold that child to a Creek Indian. The Springers did that. The child is dead".

"Dead? replied Abraham. "How do you know that? When did she die?"

"Who knows? Who cares? The child hasn't been heard from in over twenty years. She was caught up in the Red Stick war. I am a grandson of a member of the old Yamacraw clan. We are just a few left, most of our clan joined the main Creek confederation. We believe, as you do priest, in the afterlife and the existence of only one god. But we do not believe is senseless miracles. The daughter of Juliet Springer is, barring a miracle, dead and gone. She is at one with the Nunnehi. She rests with the spirits in the afterlife. You are wasting your time looking for her."

"I would like to talk to Juliet Springer. I would like to talk to her, face to face. I would like for her to tell me that her child is dead. My father, his soul is not at rest, and he will be dead before long. He wants to know what became of the child. And I am going to find out for him. He is a powerful man, and he can ruin your little enterprise here if he has a mind to. Please, please help me help his soul find some peace."

The Indian shook his head and got up from his chair. "Juliet Springer is mad. She has gone mad, and lives with the women of the church. Your church, father. She lives in a home cared for by the sisters of the parish here. You'll get no answers from her. She hasn't spoken a word in twenty years. She's completely mad. Best you go home and tell your father that he accomplished what he set out to do when he sold that child to the Creek. He killed Juliet, and he killed her child. Tell him that, and let his soul rot in hell. Where it belongs. Now get out!"

Chapter Sixty

"WE WANT TO establish a convent, we just don't have the resources. So we make do with what we have." The priest over the Savannah district looked into Abraham's blue eyes, and knew he was going to have to tell him where the woman was. The man was sent from the Bishop, and was in his carriage. "The woman is in a small village about fifteen miles from here. It is a small Indian village, and she lives there with two Spanish women. Catholic women. They care for her. She makes moccasins for the children of the parish. I will have a guide lead you there. But you can't go by carriage. The road is nothing more than a trail, and you will have to go by horseback. You can take one of the horses from our stable. The gray horse, he knows the trail. Take him. He's a gelding and very gentle. You must be careful. The road is very dangerous to travel, especially at night. Even a priest can be robbed or killed, or both, along these roads."

The guide spoke little English, and there was no conversation as the two men covered the 15 miles from Savannah to the little Yamacraw village. It didn't take long, but the trail wound around between swamp land and marshes. Within a half day's travel they were entering the small village. There were wooden enclosures, some tents, and a long, log house which was the tribal center. There was no apparent fortifications or defenses, and the inhabitants did not appear alarmed or concerned as the two men rode in and tied their horses to the tall pole in front of the main structure. The guide went in, came out, and motioned for Abraham to follow him.

He was taken to a small cabin at the edge of the village. There was a community well about ten feet from the entrance to the cabin, and an old woman wearing a brightly colored headdress was carrying a large cistern on her head. She pushed the door to the cabin open and went in, moving the cistern to her side as she entered.

"Come, come, follow." instructed the Indian guide.

Abraham went inside, and there, next to a fireplace, sat a woman who appeared wrinkled and forlorn. She was dressed in a faded blue calico dress that came well below her knees. She was sewing, and didn't look up when the two men entered.

The woman who had carried the water into the room looked over at Abraham. "She knows why you are here".

Abraham sat down next to the woman, who put down her sewing and looked at him. Tears were flowing down her cheeks, and her hands were trembling. Sitting next to her was a Springer, and she knew it. She began to cry uncontrollably. A second woman came into the room, went over to Abraham, and tried to pull him away by the arm. But Abraham resisted, and held to the edges of the chair with both hands. The woman retreated, and he just sat there, watching the woman until the wailing stopped, and became nothing more than a sniffle, and then quiet.

"I am Abraham Springer, Mrs. Springer. Mathew is dead. I wanted to tell you that, to let you know that he's dead. He died at sea, in a storm. His body has not been found. It is lost at sea, at the bottom the ocean. There will be a funeral service for him in a few days. The law has declared him dead. His father came to me, before the news of Mathew had reached us, and begged me to find you. To tell you that his soul could not rest. That he wanted to know what had become of the child. The negro child. Eliza."

The woman turned and looked at him. This woman, who had not spoken a word in twenty years or more. This woman who most people considered mad. This societal outcast. Harlot. Worse! This sad, sad human being. She turned to Abraham, and smiled. "That negro child you speak so flippantly about a moment ago is your niece, Mr. Springer. Your niece. Your flesh and blood. Your blood! Do you hear me? She is not some piece of property who is lost and whose retrieval can wipe away the sins of your bother or your father. She is your kin. Your blood kin. And by the heavens above, she is living today. Somewhere, someplace. She is alive, I know it in my heart. And she is your blood."

Abraham looked at her in disbelief. She was, obviously out of her mind. That would be impossible for this negro child to be his niece. This slave child. This, what exactly was she? A descendant of John White, his grandchild, but a mulatto. A black man was her father. A black slave. They had different mothers and different fathers. She was obviously out of her mind. Abraham had heard all he wanted, and got up to leave.

"I have proof, Mr. Priest. Mr. Better than me. Mr. White man. I have proof."

"That's impossible. How could you have proof. You cannot prove something to exist that is impossible to exist.. You are as crazy as they say. I came to get something I could tell my father before he dies. Something to give him some peace. And all I get is a pack of lies from a demented old woman. Thank you for your time. I will be going."

Abraham hurried to the door, mounted his horse, and the two men left the village at a canter, headed down the trail toward Savannah. He did not look back, not even once.

CHAPTER SIXTY-ONE

THE FUNERAL FOR Matthew Springer was an elaborate social event for the City of Charleston. Many in the city were in mourning, for there were twenty local families affected directly by the sinking of the ship. Its destination was, after all, Charleston, and, coming from London, it was by no means an inexpensive voyage, even for the lesser classes. There was talk that the owners, from Boston, were being called to Charleston for an inquiry. Was the ship safe? Were there enough lifeboats? Had she been properly inspected? The newspaper, the wharf barrooms, the church circles, all had opinions, accusations, and condemnations. It was always that way when there was a great loss. Someone other than fate, other than God, had to be at fault. Someone needed to be sued.

John Springer, upon learning of Mathew's death at sea, called in his lawyers to advise him what to do. The entire Springer fortune centered around the business enterprise, their one-half interest in the Springer-Hampton partnership. The elder Springer had given his interest, consisting of 51% of the entire family interest, to his oldest child, Mathew. This was a European concept, the oldest child takes everything, or at least control of everything, and it was so entrenched in the Springer mindset that no one questioned it when the transfer had been made. So control of the enterprise, from the Springer side, would depend on the way Mathew had provided for it to pass upon his death. His will was examined, and it was concluded that he had left everything in trust to his father, John Springer, if indeed Mathew died before his father, and which now was obviously the case.

The elder Springer was delighted with this wise and mature decision of his son, and now he would have to re-design the future knowing that Matthew would not be in the picture to run things. Then, word came from one of the company's employees, it's Controller, who had missed the fateful voyage home from England and had arrived a week later on a subsequent sailing, that Mathew Springer, while in England, had written a new will. The father was exasperated, but confident his son had made the same provisions, probably changing a few things here and there, but nothing of any major importance. The will itself was to be arriving on the Thursday next on the company's flagship, the Hopewell. Those British lawyers. They were so peculiar.

Abraham had not spoken to his father following his return, other than to inform him that he had, indeed, located the woman, Juliet, at considerable trouble, and who had proved to be quite irrational, insisting that the negro child was Mathew's child and his niece. "She's not in full control of her faculties and has been living among a small out-band of Creeks known as the Yamacraws. She had become a mute for twenty years, but had suddenly broken her silence when I told her about Mathew's death."

"Ridiculous!" was the elder Springer's only reply.

Alive, yes - Juliet Springer was alive. But competent, no. He didn't go into further detail. His father seemed distracted, and perhaps the loss of Matthew was more than his father could easily bear. He had, somehow changed, and had seemed to have lost interest in Juliet and the whereabouts of her daughter Elizabeth. His mind had turned to business matters, and he was obviously distraught over the loss of the head of the Springer financial empire. So Abraham retreated, and resumed his duties for the Bishop. He had been careful to clean, immaculately, the Bishop's carriage before returning it. A door handle had been broken, and he asked his mother for the money to have it repaired.

When Mathew's will finally arrived, the family arranged for a reading of the will, a custom handled by lawyers for the family, and which in this case was to be accomplished at the family home, in the parlor, on a Saturday afternoon. All of the potential heirs were in attendance, and especially the children, brothers, sisters and of course the father, of the deceased. The family, excited to see what, and if anything, they were to receive from the Estate, mulled about the room waiting fo the lawyers to arrive, which they did, finally, and carrying the document rolled up and tied with a ribbon. John Springer, who had taken ill with a cold and had not managed to discuss the will with his lawyers during the week, was feeling better and went for an afternoon carriage ride with his wife and had discussed where they would take a vacation when all this business of Mathews' estate and the continuation of the partnership had been concluded. It had been so stressful. And they, of course, had already met with the lawyers and knew what the will contained, and were satisfied that all would go smoothly.

The lawyers filed in, taking a position along one side of a large table which had been brought into the room for the occasion. Major Horace Wilson, the son of one of the local Revolutionary War heroes, headed the legal team. The will was read. No one seemed to be alarmed or upset, and tea was brought in. The men soon retired to the salon for cigars and liquor. Everyone but Abraham. And of course, that could be expected. He would not be expected to take much from the estate, and what little he might have, he would surely give to the parish for the benefit of the poor.

Chapter Sixty-Two

"FATHER, MY BISHOP, I need to borrow the carriage once again. I must return to Savannah. It is urgent. Family business."

"Of course, my son. But take a bit better care of the carriage, will you? And don't race the horses. I will send William with you as your driver."

Abraham then went immediately to Major Wilson's office. "I have a question about the will, Major. Nothing serious, but a question. Do you have someone, a colleague perhaps, who might be able to advise me about a certain portion of the will?"

"Of course, my dear Abraham. Of course. In the building next, the lawyer Franklin Jefferson. One of the finest lawyers in the Charleston, and with whom I have an excellent relationship. He and I have been on opposite sides many times, and he won't admit it, but I have rarely bested him on a major case. In fact, I'm a bit surprised at myself that I've admitted that little fact. Oh, well, at any rate, he is very good, and I'll be happy to recommend you to him."

The priest left the Major's office, and the lawyer turned to his secretary. "Odd", he said, "that Abraham Springer would want to see a lawyer. About the estate. What in the world could that be all about? Matthew left him nothing, but he did make a donation to the Catholic church in his honor. Could he be wanting more? Just a bit odd, don't you think?" The secretary nodded her head in agreement.

Mathew disobeyed his Bishop, and raced the horses. Something that Jefferson had told him had him worried, concerned, even desperate. He had shared it with no one, especially the Bishop, and was thankful as the carriage careened through the night on its way to Savannah. Arriving, he met the local priest. The horses were lathered, and the driver was a mess.

"I want to see the Juliet girl again. Please, it is very urgent. You must arrange it."

"I am sorry, but the word came back that she was so upset at your visit that she had gone into seclusion. The sisters will not let anyone near her. The fact that she broke her silence, after all these years, was a shock to everyone. She had been such an example to one of the sisters who had taken a vow of silence. It was felt that perhaps, she too, was wanting to become a nun. Impossible, of course, but she had set such an example. Twenty years without a word. And then you. I'm terribly sorry. It's just impossible."

Abraham turned to William. "Let's go". Abraham went to a small room in the back of the parish church and collapsed from the long trip. William took care of the horses and carriage and returned, slumping down beside the door to the room where Abraham lay sleeping, and he too, fell asleep. When Abraham awoke, he saw William fast asleep on the floor. It was still dark outside, and he had lost track of time. He tried to figure if it had just become night, or if it was early morning. He stepped over the driver, and went to the stables behind the church. There he found the horse he had ridden earlier on his visit to see Juiliet. He grabbed a bridle, then a saddle, and led the horse out of the barn and along the alleyway leading to the road in front of the church. He mounted the horse, and headed for the Indian village.

The trail, while narrow, was well worn and easy to follow, but it led through a deep forest, and in the night, with little more than a quarter moon to brighten the sky, it was difficult going. He had made it about half way to the village, and it was still dark, but he could see signs of the sun beginning to break the horizon. He heard the sound of hoof prints coming from behind him. Several horses, he figured. Coming at a gallop.

Abraham let up on the reins. "Let's go!" he commanded to the horse, but the horse was not responsive, and it took several kicks to the horses' side to get him moving. Even then, the horse did not seem to want to go into a gallop on the narrow trail. The sounds of the horses behind him grew louder and louder, and in a few minutes the riders had pulled up, aside and in front of him. One grabbed his bridle and the four horses all pulled up and stopped, almost at once.

"I have no money. I am a priest!" Abraham cried out. I have nothing but a few silver coins. You are welcome to them, but I have no other money or valuables."

A tall Indian dismounted, and then motioned for the priest to dismount, and he obeyed.

"My name is Amato", he said. "A friend of your father. I am not here to rob you. I paid your dear father a visit, after your brother Mathew died. He was not very cordial, and he refused to pay me for all the hard work I had done taking care of Juliet Springer's child. Downright inhospitable, you might say. But he did tell me that you had been looking for her, and that you knew the whereabouts of her mother, Juliet Springer. So I have followed you, and I suspect you are going to her now. So I think we have something in common, Mr. Priest. Something very much in common. You want the daughter, and I want the daughter's son."

"The daughter's son? The daughter of Juliet Springer has a son? How old is he. Where is he?"

"If I knew where he was, my friend, I would not be here after a very long ride following you up this ragged trail in the middle of the night. He is but a child. But I do know where the mother is. The child of Juliet Springer. The woman they call Eliza. I do know where she is."

"She's alive?" responded the priest.

"Oh, yes. Oh, yes, very, very much alive. And doing quite well, I might add, for a negro slave girl. She owes me, she owes me big, and she has my property, and I intend to get it from her. One way or another."

"Your property?" replied the priest. "Oh, you mean her child. How is that your property, may I ask?"

"She is a slave. I took possession of her in Savannah. She became the property of a well to do businessman in Georgia, who, as part of the bargain, gave me the child she was carrying as part of the trade. Now that child has disappeared. She says the child is dead. But I am not so sure. I think the child's grandmother may know something. Something about the whereabouts of the child. Whether the child died of the fever, as her mother claims, or whether the child has another fate, so to speak. So, let's all of us continue on this little ride, and have a talk with the mother, the mother of the woman they call Gold Dust. The infamous Juliet Springer. Let's go."

CHAPTER SIXTY-THREE

THE SUN HAD well broken the horizon and the last few miles of the trip were made in daylight. The three Creek riders were recognized as such by the aberrant Creek band that comprised most of the village. There were some Spanish occupants, but the Springer woman was the only white. The Yamacraw spoke a different dialect than most Georgia Creeks, but the language barrier was hardly a problem. The mico, who was, for such a small band, hardly more than a figurehead, acknowledged a tribal loyalty to the Creek visitors, and quickly pointed out the woman's cabin to Amato, who was told the white woman had been taken to another location by the Spanish nuns. The mico offered to show them the way, and the five men then headed South. Traveling for about four hours, they came to a small stream leading Eastward, toward the sea. Over a rocky hill, past a small cemetery, and hidden by large cypress trees – there, sitting on the small porch of a wooden cabin, was Juliet Springer.

"This is my place, and you're not welcome here". She showed a rifle that had been hidden behind her calico dress, and it was clear that the woman was not quite the weak, displaced and helpless figure she had earlier appeared to Abraham. "Now get out of here!"

"Now, now, Ms. Springer", replied Abraham. "I must talk to you. It's important, and it's something you need to know. It's something about Matthew Springer. Something very important. You said you had proof that Eliza was Mathew Springer's daughter. I need to know what that is. What evidence you have. Whatever it is, it must be irrefutable. It must be authentic. It must be something that can be proven in Court. If you have it, you must tell me what you have."

"Why now, Mr. Abraham almighty Springer? Why now? Only a short time ago you could have cared less about what evidence I have or may have.

You weren't even interested in what I had to say. You rode off without even showing an idle curiosity. Why now?"

The woman raised the rifle, pointing it in the direction of Amato, who she clearly saw as the biggest threat. Amato pulled up his horse, and dismounted. "I'm not armed", he said. "My name is Amato, and I know where Eliza is. She is alive. And I know where she is. I know exactly where she is."

The woman on the porch almost fell back, then, gathering herself, she looked over at the Indian who was now only about fifteen feet away. An easy shot. She could blow him away and not think twice about it. "You're lying" she shouted. "You're a damn liar!" she exclaimed again. "How would you have that kind of information?"

"I am Amato, if that name means anything to you. I saw you on the porch of your former home. My wife took Eliza from your arms. She nursed her, raised her as a Creek in my home. I am her father. Amato. The father of your child, Eliza".

"Father, hell you say." she replied. "Mathew Springer is the father of that child. Mathew Springer". She looked at the Indian, and tried to remember that day. "What was she wearing? Your wife? What was she wearing?"

"A buckskin dress, and she had a woolen blanket. She wrapped the child in that woolen blanket. It had many colors, and it was a Creek blanket. Given to us by the white man. In our camp, along the Flint. Your daughter, she look white, but she black too."

"What. What's become of her.? Where is she? What has become of my child?" The woman suddenly burst out crying, and dropped the gun. She fell to her knees, and collapsed.

A Spanish woman wearing a nun's headdress emerged from the cabin and bent down over the woman lying on the floor of the porch. She held a cup of cold water to her lips, and the white woman began to come around. Abraham came up to her, and put his arms around her. "Juliet, you must know what I have to say. You must listen. But first, you must show me your proof. What proof do you have that my brother Mathew is the father of your child. How can that be? We all know she is a mulatto. We all know that."

"A mulatto, Mr. Springer? A mulatto you say. Why, we are all mulattos. Weren't we all born from the same two people? Weren't we all descended from Adam and Eve? Isn't that in your precious Bible, your book given of God, your book without error? Aren't we all God's children, Father Springer? Mulatto, you say. Yes, Eliza is a mulatto. We are all mulattos. We are all descended from the same family. We are all children of the same God. But your brother is Eliza's father, and I will show you my proof, and you can judge for yourself. You can see for yourself that you are kin to this mulatto child, if indeed that is the right word for it."

With that the woman rose from the porch, and motioned for the Spanish woman to follow her into the house. In a minute or so, they emerged, carrying an old wooden trunk. Its straps were leather, and the brass buckles still held the lid tightly against the body of the wooden box. "This chest belonged to my mother. She is buried on the hill over there, next to my father. They got this place as a retreat when they moved to Savannah. Inside the house was this chest. When my mother was dying, she told me about the chest, and what it contained."

"Open it!" she instructed the priest. "Open the chest, and you will see my proof."

Inside the trunk was an old leather pouch. Inside the pouch was an old leather strap, which, when he unfurled it, also contained several pieces of paper. On the paper was the story of Adam, and Big Toe, and the love story of Adam's mother and father, and the truth. The truth about the baby. Written by the first Adams White's own child, Billy. The baby was not the baby of some field hand. The baby was Mathew Springers. It had just brought out the gene. It had just finally brought out the gene. And now the truth was known. And now Juliet Springer could be forgiven. Could be forgiven for a crime she never committed. A sin. A sin she never committed. She had been loyal. She had been faithful. She had been true to Mathew Springer. The child was his.

CHAPTER SIXTY-FOUR

"**I** WENT TO MATHEW and told him about it. I told him, but he still wouldn't believe me. He laughed at me", sighed Juliet.

"No one will believe this silly story", he had said to Juliet when confronted by the strap and the writing. "No one will believe that story over me. And I will deny Eliza until my dying day."

Juliet continued. "I was so hurt that I simply removed myself from society, and I never spoke about it, to anyone. Then I learned that Eliza had disappeared and was feared dead. After that, I never spoke another word to a living person. Not until you told me that Mathew was dead." She looked about the room, and her eyes found Abraham's. He looked at her incredulously.

"And now, Mr. Priest, it is your turn. Your turn to tell me why now, why now this is important to you. Son of a wealthy businessman. Part of one of the most powerful families on earth. Why is it now so damn important that you know the truth about Eliza Springer. Why?"

The priest drew back, contemplating whether, in the present company, he should share what he had learned from the lawyer in Charleston. Confronted as he was, he opened up.

"Juliet, when Mathew went to England, he wrote a new will. The will has only recently been read, and I was present for the reading. In the will, the Estate of Mathew Springer, well, it consisted of many things, but the most important thing was a controlling interest in the Springer half of the Springer Hampton partnership. The ability to vote 50% of the business. In essence, the ability to control half of the most powerful business interest in Charleston and perhaps all of the Southern states. Political power comes with such wealth. Political power, Mrs. Springer, as I'm sure you are aware. There is a bitter line being drawn between the American colonies. A very bitter line. A line in the sand, if you will."

"Anyway, when the new will was written, the scrivener wrote the following words. And I copied them, and took them to a lawyer. And they mean exactly what they say. The will said, and I quote: Upon my death, I give to my oldest child all of my interest in the Springer Hampton Ltd. partnership, to be that child's property, absolutely, per stripes."

"What that means, Mrs. Springer, is that, if what you say is true, and Matthew is the father of your daughter, Eliza, the lawyer drafting the will made a terrible mistake. He obviously believed, as did everyone else, that the first born child of Matthew Springer was Susannah's son, Michael. So he didn't make it clear that he meant Michael Springer was to inherit the business. In fact, the lawyer I went to says that, if it could be proven that Eliza was indeed Mathew's child, then Eliza would be the heir to his fortune. She was the first born child of Mathew Springer. Hers is the Springer fortune. It's just too much for anyone to comprehend. How can a black slave be heir to one of the largest fortunes in the South. How could that have happened? But it has. It has. If what you say is true. If these documents can be authenticated. If what you say is true, Eliza your daughter is a very rich woman."

No one had noticed Amato, who had quietly picked up the rifle from the floor of the porch, and who now pointed it in the direction of the priest. "I'll have that strap, and pouch, and letter, if you please, Mr. Springer. I'll have that. Give it to me!" he demanded.

"No!"

It was the Yamacraw. "No", the Indian repeated. "Not go against church. Not hurt priest."

"He's right, you know", Abraham responded. "If you go against me, you go against the Springer family. And you know what that can mean. No more trading. Your name would be banished from trade from Georgia to Ohio. And if you kill me, which you will have to do to get this pouch, you will be hunted down like a wild beast. Now, you don't want that, do you?"

Amato knew he was beaten. All he had left was the whereabouts of Eliza. Someone, surely someone, would pay dearly for that information. Someone, and the price would be high. Only Eliza could lay claim to the Springer fortune, if indeed the law would allow such an act, given the apparent mulatto history of the child and, perhaps, a legal challenge to the new will.

"Ok", he said, lowering the weapon. "We go to see John Springer. Your father, he will know what to do".

"Now you're being reasonable," piped in Abraham.

"The pouch stays here", demanded Juliet. "Here, in my possession. I don't trust either of you, especially you, Abraham Springer. You will do whatever your father says. You say you have religion and you answer only to God. But the truth be known, you still answer only to your family. The almighty John Springer. The devil incarnate."

CHAPTER SIXTY-FIVE

JOHN SPRINGER CALLED in his lawyers. "Just how is this possible?" he insisted. He wanted an explanation. He would sue. He would own all of Britain before he was done. They would pay dearly for their screw-up. They would not get an ounce of Charleston cotton until the damage was undone. "Major, I'm holding you and the partners in your firm personally responsible", he bellowed. It was a hollow threat. Together, the three lawyers were not worth the revenues of a dozen voyages to Nevis. And besides, they hadn't written the will. They didn't even know of its existence until recently. No, the answer had to be found elsewhere. Disputing the evidence was not the correct approach. Destruction of the evidence seemed the more rational approach. But then, could she be telling the truth? Could the evidence be valid? Could the girl be his own granddaughter? It was too much to contemplate. It was too much to handle, period. His own grandchild. A Negro!

Margaret Springer, his wife, was equally confused, but she gave no credit to the evidence that had been presented, the pouch, the leather strip, the letter. "Impossible. To say that child is Mathews' is a disgrace to his memory. I will hear nothing of it." However, in private, when she was alone, the thought of the child, Mathew's child, haunted her. What had she done? The child was her flesh and blood. The child of two white people. "Impossible", she repeated to herself, and anyone else who would listen.

John Springer was at complete odds with himself. "I want to see the evidence for myself!" he insisted. But the journey was long, long on his arthritic limbs, and, after all, Abraham had seen it. Seen the pouch. Powhatan. Looked genuine. The strap, the story on the strap, the story as told by Adam White's son, all there in his own handwriting. It seemed legitimate. Could Juliet have been telling the truth all along? And what did it matter. The will would have to be disproved. Someone would have to travel to England, disprove the will, and let the estate revert back according to the prior will of his son, Mathew.

"It won't work!" Abraham declared. You just can't pretend that this woman, Juliet Springer, is going to go away. I talked to an attorney. The will's existence is known. It's simply a matter of the daughter making a claim. Supported by the mother, a court could declare Eliza Springer the heir. No Matthew Springer there to challenge her. To deny it. The attorney was of the opinion that the new will would stand up. Even if you disprove the will in England, it would have no effect on the Courts of South Carolina. We're not England any more, remember! We're America. And our courts don't have to recognize the English law. We make our own! And as any good lawyer will tell you, a jury's decision can never be predicted with absolute certainty. Unless of course, you are able to control the jury."

"Damn the law". The old man slammed his fist down on his desk. "I'll be damned if I'll let that Juliet White, or Springer, or whatever the hell her name is, or that black bastard child of hers, have what me and my family have built up for a hundred years. Damn her and her child. Damn them all. I'll kill them first". Never had John Springer been more serious, and it frightened him, and what he saw he had to do. "Call for the Creek trader. Bring him to me."

Amato was delighted when he got the news. It was just as he thought. Eliza's whereabouts was the key, and no one knew where she was but him. He sent his two braves to the auction to find the slave overseer for the gin man. He packed the horses, and readied for the trip back to the Flint. He would be a rich man this time. The price would be high. The price for Eliza Springer would be very high. He held the high cards this time. Ace high. Royal flush. Victory, at last.

John Springer looked at the Indian. He barely remembered him from the young brave who arrived at his doorstep some thirty years or so before to take the negro child away from Charleston. Away from the embarrassment, the humiliation of his son, the indignity of it all. At the time, he was certain he was doing the right thing. And now, with death watching him closely and not far behind, he was still resisting the call to embrace the child. In fact, every fiber in his body told him she must be destroyed. She represented something evil in his world. Something that had to be eradicated. She represented the destruction of slavery as an institution, for he could not love Eliza Springer as his own grandchild and embrace slavery at the same time. Not his own grandchild.

"Five thousand dollars. That is my price. For five thousand dollars I will take you to Eliza Springer." Amato did not know where he arrived at that price, but as soon as he said it he was sure he had gone too low.

"I don't want you to take me to Eliza Springer. I want you to kill her. To destroy her. To eliminate her from this earth. I want that, and if you can do that for me, I will give you your five thousand dollars, in gold, and a thousand acres of land along the Ocmulgee to boot. A thousand acres of land, and five thousand dollars in gold. Just bring me proof she is dead, and it is yours".

Abraham heard the conversation, and so did his lawyers. No one said a word, and the Indian found his men, approved and signed for the purchase of the slave they had selected, and headed toward the river. "This would be easy" Amato thought to himself. "So very easy. I should have gotten some money up front", he said out loud as he placed his paddle into the waters of the Altamaha. "I should have insisted." The great-grandson of the wealthy businessman, the boy Daniel, would have to wait his turn. Firsts things first. Something brushed up against his arm as his paddle stroked the river, and then slid away. "Goddamn gator!", he shouted.

Abraham didn't know what to do next. He could not stand by and watch this murder take place without trying to stop it. His family would be of no help. The girl meant the end of their fortunes. The church would be of no help. It was not equipped to deal with such things. The Sheriff could do nothing, as he had no jurisdiction in whatever faraway place Eliza was living. He would have to tell Juliet of the danger that Eliza, and Juliet herself, were now facing. Maybe she could think of something. But where was she? The cabin, he mused. "I must go to the cabin".

The Bishop's carriage was not available, but the Springer stables had plenty of horses, and he took one he knew was trained for endurance, an Appaloosa, and headed to Savannah. From there he headed past the Yamacraw village, and followed the trail towards the sea. When he arrived at the cabin under the cypress trees, to his dismay he found it empty. She was gone. The wooden trunk was standing open. There was nothing inside. She had gone. Gone with the pouch. Gone with the paper. Gone with the leather strip. Gone, and with no trace as to where she might be.

CHAPTER SIXTY-SIX

EVER SINCE SHE heard that her child had disappeared and had joined the Red Stick groups of clans in the Northern part of Georgia and Alabama, and that Amato didn't know where she was, Juliet quit talking. Some said she had lost her mind. The divorce from Matthew Springer, while unheard of in Charles Town at the time, was an easy step for her. Understandable, under the circumstances, said the Judge granting the divorce. She hated herself for not speaking up when Mathew's father took the child and gave it away. She didn't understand what had happened to have caused the child to have a different skin tone, but it was nothing she had done. Her only sin, if you want to call it that, was not to speak up and fight the Springer family's decision to send the child with the Indian. She didn't say anything, and when she realized that her child, as young as she was, had disappeared and was no longer being taken care of in the Hawkins compound, she quit talking. There was no reasoning with Matthew, even after she learned about the contents of her mother's trunk. And now Matthew was dead. Dead. And then, Amato's words. Those incredible, beautiful words. "I KNOW WHERE SHE IS." She was alive. He knew where she was. She had survived the Red Stick War. She had survived, and was alive, somewhere.

So, when Amato and Abraham left, she packed up what little she could put on the back of a horse and headed to Savanna. There she found the local priest, and he told her that Abraham had come from Charlestown several times in the Bishop's carriage, and that he had returned to Charlestown as soon as he had found and spoken to Juliet. The priest was completely taken aback by a Juliet he never knew. A talking Juliet. He had learned a little from Abraham before he left. He had learned about the fact that Juliet had a child. That the child was a negro, and had been taken by a Creek Indian by the name of Amato to live with the Englishman, Benjamin Hawkins, on the Flint River near a town called Jonestown. Jonestown, Georgia. That was many years ago, and the child, if still alive, was fully grown by now. Abraham had said that the child had disappeared and only Amato knew her whereabouts. There was a road, a decent wagon trail, from Savannah to a town nearby Jonestown, a place called Macon. "It's in the center of Georgia, the heart, if you will, of Georgia. A woman can't make that trip alone. You will need a man with you. Someone to protect you."

"I have God and justice to protect me", she said to the Priest. "Draw me a map". Reluctantly, the priest showed her a map of the trail, and he drew it on a piece of leather, marking the major road and waterways. 'It's a long journey. You will need this.' He handed her a Bible and a small pistol, a flintlock which he pulled from the drawer of his desk. "Left here by a sinner who had killed his wife with it. I have no use of it, but it may come in handy as you head North. There are many dangers upon the highways – thieves, savages, wild animals. God be with you, Mrs. Springer. It's not my place to say this, and the Bishop would be very angry if he knew, but I would advise you, when you get to Macon, to find the Masons. They're your best bet in finding your daughter. I am forbidden by Papal edict to encourage you in that direction, but they do seem to know quite a bit more than most. And they may be more sympathetic to your plight. Good luck."

Luck. What did the priest know about luck? She had all the luck in the world. Her daughter was alive. Alive. She could find her. She would find her. And beg her forgiveness for giving her up. If Amato knew where she was, it was most likely near where he lived.

The trip along the Macon road would take less than a week, assuming the horse held up and there were no accidents. That's moving at a pretty good pace, and making thirty or forty miles a day. By the time Juliet had made Macon, Amato was starting up the river by canoe. She would have a little time, but not much. And she had no idea of the urgency of the situation.

Jonestown, she learned, was a half a day's ride north out of Macon. The local Mason building was empty, but she was told by the town's blacksmith that a Mason lodge existed in Jonestown, and the horse, with his new shoes, felt and responded much better as they set out again. By nightfall and a week out of Savannah she was on the outskirts of Jonestown. A wagon, headed South to Macon, was stopped in the road with a broken wheel, and Juliet pulled up and offered some water and a piece of deer meat. She got some free advice for her trouble. "There's a boarding house in town, but it only caters to men. Your best bet is the hotel in town. Gibson Hotel. Don't venture into that saloon next door." And, yes, there was a Mason lodge in town, on the town square. The lodge was run by a lawyer, John Wilson, whose law office was also on the square, although on the opposite end. He drank quite a bit, but was said to be honest. From Virginia. His father had fought in the war, in Tennessee, against the British.

Juliet was not completely broke, and she had a little money with her. She had kept it in the pouch, for an emergency, and the situation definitely fit the bill. She received a small yearly sum from a trust her father had set up before he died, and, while she gave most of the money to the poor, she had kept back a portion, just in case. And now, she was glad she did. Tired and hungry, she found the hotel, and collapsed on the straw mattress, completely exhausted.

CHAPTER SIXTY-SEVEN

WHEN SHE AWOKE, the sun was high in the sky. She had to remind herself where she was, as she had been dreaming. Dreaming of something, she didn't know quite what. It wasn't disturbing, the dream, but it wasn't revealing either. Sort of a fun dream, and, as she went about the room, she realized she was happy. Happy for the first time in a long time. She was going to find Eliza. She just knew it.

The mason's office was closed, and the note on the door was signed J. Wilson. She hurried down the stairs of the two story building, and went out into the road. Like many town squares of the time, the courthouse was at the center of the square, and various offices, stores, taverns, and other buildings, like the Gibson Hotel, were located around the square. She headed for the lawyer's office. Opposite end of town, she remembered.

A stage was arriving, and the store keepers and other occupants of the town square were coming out, looking to see who was arriving, whether any mail was being delivered. The kind of things that people do on a regular basis when they are isolated. The lawyer's office was no exception, and Juliet gazed at the three gentlemen, all standing at the doorway to the office, each looking with some excitement as the stage made its way down the town's main street, kicking up dust and with every dog in town barking to beat the band. She tried to pick out the lawyer, and settled on the man in the middle. He was short, balding, and seemed well dressed, although he had no jacket on. The other two men looked like they were laborers, one in buckskins and the other was wearing heavy cotton pants and a woolen shirt. He had a beard, and his hair was long and braided in the back. He looked to be in his forties, which was no youngster on the frontier. Life expectancy was around 50, and even that required a bit of luck. There were some, however, who lived to be over 100, so the end of life was, for some, a long ways from the average end point. Most, however, never made it that far.

The three men watched as the stage rounded the corner and then wandered back into the office. By the time Juliet got there, the two men she had figured for the clients proved her calculations to be correct – the short balding man was the lawyer all right. The other two men headed straight for the tavern next to the hotel. She scraped the mud off her boots and went in. There was no secretary or other lawyer working out of the office. The office itself consisted of just one room, with a large, roll-back desk near the window overlooking the square. There were several comfortable chairs on the client side of the desk, and a big stuffed chair next to the back of the room. A coat and hat stand was next to the entrance, along with a rather dirty brass spittoon.

"Howdy, ma'am." The lawyer looked Juliet over. The woman was very plainly dressed, and showed signs of having recently spent a good deal of time on the road. Her hair was brushed, but had not been washed in some time, and there was dirt around her ankles. Nevertheless, she seemed intelligent enough, and, beneath her ruddy exterior, she still showed signs of having been rather pretty in an earlier day. "And what brings you to Jonestown, Mrs......., ah, what did you say your name was?"

"Springer, Juliet Springer", was the reply.

"Ah, Springer, there's a Springer we know in these parts from Charles Town. Very successful. You're not kin to him, are you?"

"I was. At one time I was the wife of Matthew Springer, son John Springer. He's a shipbuilder. Of Charles Town, or Charleston as they now refer to it. We had a child together. A little girl."

"A little girl, you say."

"Yes, a little girl. Then we divorced."

"Whoa, whoa there. Nobody gets a divorce in Charleston. It's unheard of. Especially high society folks, like the Springers. Now just how did that happen? And just how legal was that divorce?" inquired the lawyer, politely.

"You should know that, Mr. Mason Wilson. Isn't that your job to know things like that?"

"Mr. Mason?" She knew he was a Mason. Smarter than he had given her credit for. Her demeanor drew him in, and now he was now interested. "And so, the former Mrs. Springer, just what brings you to these here parts. Not looking for a husband, I venture. No, I'd say you are looking for something, but it's not a husband. What then, what has emboldened you to travel all this way from Savannah to the middle of Georgia by your lonesome self? To find what? There's gold, but it's North of here, and you don't look like a prospector. What of value do we have out here that is so important to you? What in the world….."

"My child!" she blurted out. "I'm looking for my child. My child with Mathew Springer. That….that's why I'm here. You must help me. My priest said you would. The priest said you would understand. You must help me. I can pay. I have $10.00 to give you now, and more later."

The prospect of a paying client, albeit not a lot of money, was enough to make the lawyer offer the woman a cup of coffee and ask her to sit down. The coffee was a real luxury, and usually reserved for special occasions, but there was something about this lady that intrigued the be-speckled attorney. The woman took the coffee, took a sip and sat it on the desk, and sitting across from him, looked out, past the lawyer, into the street. Then, her eyes focused back into the room and returned to the lawyer, who sat, patiently, waiting for the story to come.

"So you've lost track of your daughter, have you? I suppose your former husband took well care of her, gave her a proper education and so forth." The lawyer was trying to piece together, in his mind, how the child could disappear, and this woman, even if divorced, could appear to be so poor and without any significant means. The means a person who was of quality, of quality enough to marry into the Springer family, would certainly have at this juncture in her life.

"No, you don't understand. You don't understand at all. The child, my child, was given up by the family at birth. You see, they, everyone it seemed, thought my husband was not the father. Everyone but me, of course. The child had a slight brown skin tone. No one could understand where it came from, and everyone assumed I had been unfaithful. So the child was sent out to these parts with a slave trader. A Creek slave trader, to be raised. To the family, she no longer existed. When my mother passed, I discovered an old chest that contained a long, handwritten story that explained the child's light brown skin tone. And now, now I have found out she is still alive, I've come to find her. To beg her to forgive me for letting them take her, so many years ago."

The lawyer sat back, amazed at the incredible tale brought to his office by this incredible woman. "Come to find the child? Now, after so many years?"

The woman sighed, and the lawyer, sensing her despair, continued. "There are several women here, in and around the County here that might meet that description. Thirtyish, somewhat mulatto, light skin color. The pretty ones, many end up, at least in their youth, as concubines. An easy life, in some ways, for some."

Juliet had no idea what her daughter looked like, and whether she was pretty. But she did know the name Amato, and when the lawyer heard that, he perked up. "Amato, you say?"

"Yes, Amato was the name of the Creek slave trader that said he raised her. He said he knew where she was. That she was alive".

"Well, Amato is known in these parts. He trades in slaves and guns down the river. And he did, at one time, have a young girl, I thought she was a white girl, a white girl that he raised in the Hawkins encampment. But she disappeared from what I was told. Fought for the Red Sticks. No one could understand why. Dead now most likely. They lost, you know. The war. They lost the war. And now, it looks like they will be run out of these parts all together. All the Creeks. Whites and Reds. It's just a matter of time. What with the gold and all. People moving in. Taking the land. The state – just giving it away. And cotton, cotton. King cotton. Ruling everything."

"You said there were several women who met that description. Who might they be?

"Well, there's the wife of the overseer at the gin making place. Out of town. She could fit. Very pretty. Then there is, or should I say was, the negro bought to help take care of the widow woman Johnston's bed and board establishment. She was light skinned, and pretty too. But she disappeared. Might have gone North on the Railroad. You've heard of the railroad, haven't you? No rails. No cars. And it travels underground. Takes the darkies right out of the country North to freedom. Then there's several women light skinned over at the Brown plantation. Bill Huggins has one. Two north of here, I believe, up near Graysville. You got your work cut out for you, Mrs. Springer. Here's your ten dollars back. I just don't think I can be of much help."

"The priest, he said the Masons, the Masons would understand. Understand why I need to find my daughter. You're a Mason. You do understand, don't you, Mr. Wilson. I am desperate here, and I have no one. No one to help me. Please."

The lawyer leaned back again in the oak chair. It had swivels, and he swirled around in a circle, coming back to the Springer woman, face to face. He saw her desperation. Her anguish.

"Come to the house and I'll have the Missus make you some tea. And I'll bet you're hungry as well. Come with me to the house, and we'll see what Mrs. Wilson has to offer. She knows everyone around these parts, and she's in the sewing circle, so she's good with the gossip. Come on now, and stop that crying. I just can't stand to see a good woman crying."

Chapter Sixty-Eight

MRS. WILSON WAS just finishing the morning dishes and was calling for the cat when her husband came down the short walk to the front door of their home. She opened the door, saw the haggard woman, and offered her some tea. There was to be a party, a real hum-dinger, over at the Brown plantation on the Friday next, in celebration of Thanksgiving, and she was beginning to put up some marmalade and peaches just for the occasion. Her peach marmalade was said to be the best in the County, for which she was justly proud. She listened to the sad tale of the lost Eliza. "Why, that's the name of the lady that run off from Mrs. Johnston. Her name was Eliza. They said she went on the railroad, but I know different. Mrs. Johnston told me herself that some boarder had gone sweet on her, and that she went North to live with the Yucchi's. The man came and paid for her, paid almost a thousand dollars to hear her tell it. All that he had at the time. She said the woman was pregnant at the time she run off. Pregnant with a second child, and she was glad to be rid of her with those two children to care for. Said she's much happier with the replacement, though she chews tobacco."

The lawyer, who knew Mrs. Johnston well, piped in. "Give me a minute to hitch the carriage, and I'll take you over there. Mrs. Johnston's. Maybe she can help you. No refunds, now, on the ten dollars, what with this door to door service."

"Best ten dollars I've ever spent", replied Juliet, "assuming of course that's my Eliza."

"We'll see. Her place is right close."

Mrs. Johnston too was busy preparing for the upcoming event at the Browns, and had just returned that morning from taking a side of pork and the better part of her squash and pole bean supply to the plantation kitchen. "Yes, that Eliza was a feisty one. And the man, why he had a deep affection for her. She run off, and from what I know, her boy, a young child, died of the fever. Then she got pregnant with this boarder, and off she run. He's still around, and the word around here is that she's living with him, just like she was a white woman. In the same house. And they got a little one, a little boy. That's what I hear. He's still working the gold fields too, to pay for it all. Till he can get a good crop in. It's all going to cotton. Before long, the color of gold will be white."

The ages seemed to match up. The name. The town.

"Where's his place, where is this man living? What's his name?" Juliet said excitedly.

"Why, his name if Michael Downing, Mrs. Springer. He's Irish, you know. One of those Catholics. I understand he has a place on a hill near the river. Puttin' in cotton, like everyone else. Yep, and living openly with that negro woman. Just like she was a white woman. Just like she was same as him. And that child, he's so white, you know he will pass for white one of these days."

CHAPTER SIXTY-NINE

THE FALL PARTY at the Brown's plantation was looking to be a major event. All sorts of decorations were being made to the main house, a sprawling three story monstrosity which was the largest house in the County. Invitations had been sent out as far as Decatur and down below Mobile. There was kin in Milledgeville and a family from Savannah was said to be coming for the party. There was excitement everywhere, and the Wilsons had been invited, even though they weren't planters, but Mrs. Wilson, by virtue of her position as mistress of the sewing society, knew who to ask to make sure her family was on the guest list. The Springer woman had been staying with them for over a week now, and it was their intention to take her with them as well. After a good bath she had begun to show signs of recovering her strength, and the refinement that had been her birthright, something she had grown up with, had been once accustomed to, and which she remembered, if only vaguely, was showing through.

"There's a chance the O'Malley's will be there, and maybe even Mr. Dowling himself. I've heard he's back from the gold fields, and he's buying more cotton seed." The lawyer was, at times, a better source of gossip than his wife. But his news came from different sources, and was generally more accurate.

Juliet tried to prepare herself for the event. If this was the right Eliza, then the father of her grandchildren might be at the party. The location of their home, her history, there was so much to be learned. She could hardly contain herself with the anticipation. "He won't bring the woman", commented Mrs. Wilson. "He can live with her. Nothing can be done about that. But he can't bring her into society. That would be going too far. No, she won't come. But her boy may come with the father. He holds the boy out as his own kin and takes him everywhere. A good looking boy. Can't tell he's a slave child. Not by looking at him. Looks just like his father. Spittin' image."

More information came in from Mrs. Johnston about the girl. She had heard the name Amato, and knew about the child, the one who disappeared and was assumed dead. A black child. "Yes, she was carrying the child when I bought her," said Mrs. Johnston. "She sure loved that little thing. It's so sad, what happened. The Indian, Amato, was saying it was his child. Laid claim to it. Said he had bought the child from a planter. He came to the house here, looking for the child. Dirty old man. I told him to get off my property, that I wasn't afraid of him. There are plenty in this town who wouldn't think twice about killing a Creek."

A week at the Wilson place drew Juliet and the lawyer closer together. She finally confided in him about what Abraham had said about Eliza being the beneficiary of Matthew Springer's will. She showed him the evidence, she had carried it with her. The pouch looked genuine. The writings on the paper. The leather strap. It all made sense. "But you know, Mrs. Springer, they will never let this stand. Legal or not, no court is going to give a black girl any white man's inheritance. It's not an issue of right or wrong. It's an issue of what society will tolerate. How much it can stand. And no Judge in his right mind is going to find for your Miss Eliza. You just need to understand that. It may be legal. The will may be upheld. But at the end of the day, your daughter is going to lose the case. Somehow. Someway. Believe me, this is a hopeless endeavor, trying to prove your daughter is the rightful heir to the Springer money. It's just not something that South Carolina can handle. Not in a hundred years. But look, she may be alive. Maybe we can find her. Maybe that will be enough. Maybe that will be justice enough."

Somehow, deep inside, Juliet knew that the lawyer was right. It was one thing to take on the power, to take on the courts, the judges, the rule of law. It was one thing to go up against all that. But it was another to ask the State of South Carolina to rule against a prominent white family in favor of a child of color. Any drop of blood that was not white. Just one drop, even if it went back two hundred years. You can dilute blood, but you can never eliminate it. And it wasn't her decision, anyway, now was it? It was Eliza's decision as to what to do with the knowledge of Mathew Springer's will, once she was made aware of it. For now, all Juliet could do was hope. Hope this Eliza, this woman living with this Irish planter, was her Eliza. Her sanity, what was left of it, depended on her finding her daughter.

CHAPTER SEVENTY

THE MAMMY AT the Brown's plantation was having all she could stand. That morning she had tied a new cord around Mrs. Brown's five year old with a little bag of asafoetida to keep diseases away, but the child had already lost it. The kitchen had never seen such a feast. Turkey, duck, opossum, ham, pork, large samples of nearly all the meat and game to be found in the county had been loaded onto a long, wooden table. Piled high were mince pies, puddings, fruit cakes, nuts and raisins. The food was cooked in a large, broad fireplace, heated with hickory and oak wood coals, some of which were piled on top of the oven lids for added flavor. The racket was continuous, and everyone seemed to be in good humor. There was a big pot of whiskey stew which was making the rounds when the first wagons and carriages began to arrive down the long winding dirt road leading from the main road to the house.

Outside the front of the house was covered in pots filled with snow-on-the-mountain, coxcomb, phlox, rosemary and sage. As evening approached, and in the distance, the stage from Savannah could be heard blowing its horn, letting the town know it was coming in. For three days preceding the event there had been an early winter fox hunt, and the fields in fence were filled with over two dozen horses, all excited, running from here to there, anxious to see where the new smells and noises were coming from. A tall black stallion was fighting to get near the mares.

The lawyer's carriage was more of a wagon, with two benches and a top fringed with silk. The wheels had been painted a yellow color, and two horses, one white and the other a sort of milky white, pranced proudly as she came down the roadway toward the house. Juliet had to share the back seat with a keg of fine Irish whiskey, Mr. Wilson's contribution to the affair, and a small dog with brown and white spots had followed the carriage all the way from town. This was no match for the likes of Charlestown, but it was bold, exciting and lively. In fact, much livelier, in Juliet's mind, than the stodginess of her former hometown.

Greeting the guests as they arrived were the Browns and eight of their ten children. The five year old was being punished, and was in the kitchen shelling beans. The youngest, still crawling, was in the kitchen as well, being watched by Nancy, the White's chief helper. Singing could be heard from the slave cabins behind the main house.

"This is Juliet Springer, Mrs. Brown. She's from Charleston and she's come to Jonestown for a visit. She's related to John Springer, the shipbuilder."

Mrs. Brown looked over the woman and smiled graciously. The woman appeared to be preoccupied, something had her attention, and she turned to address the next guest. "Springer", she said, turning to her husband, "Springer. I know that name from somewhere", but she just couldn't place it.

The sun began to set and most of the guests had arrived. There was a near full moon and plenty of stars, and the sky was cloudless. A fiddle and mandolin had begun to pick up next to a large bonfire, and people started dancing on a wooden platform that had been built just for the occasion. Some fireworks could be heard and it startled one of the horses, who broke through a fence and had to be corralled.

The O'Malley's arrived on horseback. Behind them, in a two person buggy, was Michael Downing. He was alone. Mrs. Wilson pointed them out to Juliet, and she was suddenly overcome with emotion. The man, the man who was father to her grandchild. He was standing fifteen feet away. She was too fearful to approach him, and she begged Mrs. Wilson to go over to the man and bring him over and introduce him. Mrs. Wilson was more than glad to accommodate her, and before long the former mute and recluse was learning enough about the Eliza who belonged to Michael Downing to be certain it was her Eliza. Downing, comfortable with the assurances of Mr. Wilson that this woman was who she said she was, and was, indeed, the likely mother of the mother of his son, was agreeable to take her with him, in his carriage, when he left the party, to his place on the Ocmulgee. O'Malley was helping the lawyer open the keg of whiskey, and a crowd was gathering around. Wilson had an important client who peddled whiskey, and that client always made sure that Wilson got the finest bourbon available in Georgia.

The younger set had taken over the dancing and most of the food was gone when a one-horse carriage came racing down the dirt road toward the house.

Alone, and driving the carriage, was a whiskered man wearing a black shirt with a Roman collar. Pulling up to the front door, he entered the main room of the house, where he was approached by the senior Mr. Brown. Brown, a Baptist, was not particularly fond of Catholic priests, but the man had a sense of urgency about him, and the planter approached him politely and asked him his business.

"What brings you to our home, Father ____, ah, what did you say your name was?"

The senior Brown left to find his wife, who was socializing with Mrs. Wilson and two other members of the sewing circle in the parlor of the home. "There's a man here, says his name is Father Springer, from Charleston, and he's looking for a relative. He says it's a matter of great importance that he talk to her."

"That's strange, said Mrs. Brown. We do have, I remember, a Springer here, she arrived with the Wilsons. Mrs. Wilson, you know, Lady Springer is in your company, I believe?"

"Yes, she's had quite a day. She's around here somewhere, I'm sure, probably with that Mr. Downing. They seemed to have some history together and have spent most of the past hour talking to one another."

The priest burst into the room and addressed Mrs. Wilson. "My name is Abraham Springer, and I've come by stage from Charleston, arriving this evening. I am looking for a woman by the name of Juliet Springer. She is a relative of mine. By marriage. I'm afraid she may be in grave danger, and I've come to warn her. Please, please tell me where I can find her."

"She's outside, near the dancing platform, and talking to a tall Irishman in a blue jacket. She's wearing a green dress, and her hair is greying, in a bun. There, there through the window. There she is, right over there."

The priest ran out of the room, out the front door, and in the direction of the woman in the green dress. They spoke for a few minutes, and then the tall Irishman headed for his carriage. The horse was still harnessed, and he pulled the carriage up to the door of the house. The woman he was talking to, in the green dress, jumped into the seat next to the Irishman, and the carriage took off down the dirt road at a gallop.

"What, what did you say to her that made those too take off like that?" asked Mrs. Wilson of the priest.

"There's a man, Amato, a Creek trader. He's got instructions from my father to find and kill Eliza Springer. He's going to kill her. He's been paid to kill her."

"Eliza Springer? Well, I declare!" piped in Mrs. Wilson. "Why she's nothing but a slave girl living with a white planter. Why would anyone want to harm her?"

"It's a long story", replied the priest. "She's the daughter of Matthew Springer. The Matthew Springer, who until recently was chairman of the largest, most prosperous shipping business in South Carolina, if not the whole United States. Your cotton, everyone's cotton around here, travels, more likely than not, on a Springer ship. Built by a Springer shipyard. And financed by a Springer bank!"

"The man, your father, wants to kill his own granddaughter, Father Springer? His own flesh and blood? This is all rather confusing."

"And disturbing", added Mrs. Brown. "Most disturbing".

CHAPTER SEVENTY-ONE

A MATO HAD PLANNED it all out. He had heard about the big to do at the Brown plantation, and had learned that O'Malley and his wife were planning to attend. He had also learned that Michael Downing was back from the gold country, and it only made sense that he would attend the party as well. That would leave Eliza alone, or at least without a male companion, for the better part of the evening and at least part of the night. Plenty of time for him to cross the river, climb the ridge, and find Eliza Springer alone and defenseless. He worried about the fact that, if she were dead, he would have a problem finding out if her child was alive, her first child, the one he claimed and believed to be his, and if alive, the child's whereabouts. So his first plan was to approach her, try to get her to confess as to the child's whereabouts, and then earn his $5,000.00 from John Springer. He could not rationalize his desire to find that little boy, because, in light of what he had learned about Eliza Springer, that black child seemed to be of little import. But he was a man obsessed, and as everyone knows, rational thought and obsession don't travel together. Where had she hidden him? He would use the second child, the Dowling child, as a hostage. Surely she would tell him the location to save the white boy, and she had no way to know his true intentions with regard to her. He had bided his time, and now was the time to strike.

He waited until the sun had reached the Western horizon before dipping his canoe into the water to cross the river. By the time he was on the Eastern shore, the sun was completely down. There was plenty of light, however, as the moon was bright, and the way up the steep bank was no challenge to the Creek warrior. He arrived at the spot where the two large boulders met, and shivered at the thought of the rattlesnakes dancing in the black pit below. He had brought a tomahawk and a large bowie knife for the occasion, not feeling a need for his trusty pistol.

The house was well lit, and the lower windows were covered with thick wooden shutters. He would need to find an entrance, perhaps from the roof. There were two open windows on the second floor, along the Western wall, letting the cool breeze from the rushing river below air out the house. She could see Eliza looking out one of the windows, then closing it. She shut the second window, but didn't close it all the way, leaving a small gap. That would be his way in.

Amato waited until the lights in the upper part of the house went out. There was, he counted, two candles and a lantern, and the lantern had made its way down to the first floor. He worked his way up a tree near the house and gained the roof from a strong limb. From there he tied a piece of rawhide to the stone chimney and lowered himself to the cracked window. Easing the window up, he slid inside. It was dark, and he didn't know what room he was in. He heard the child breathing, and crept down the hallway to the stairs leading to the main room below. It was there he figured he would find Eliza, waiting for her man to return from the party.

Eliza was standing by the stove, heating some water, when she felt the strong arm of the Indian around her neck. "Scream if you want to, my little Eliza. There is no one to help you. Scream all you want. I'm not here to harm you, I just want to find my little child. You know. You call him Daniel, I understand. It is time for you to give him to me. It is time. You have known all along I would come, and now I have. I know he's alive, and you have him hidden. And now you must tell me where he is. I will kill the white child if you refuse. Kill him, you understand. So tell me, and I will go, and I will leave you and this white child alone. For good."

"Ha!" replied Eliza. "You will never leave me alone, and if you take my Daniel, I will never leave you alone. Nor will my husband. He will find you, and you will be sorry you ever came after my child."

"Hush, my little Eliza", said the Indian, squeezing tightly against her throat until she couldn't breathe. "Just the child's whereabouts, that's all I want. Just where you've got him hidden. No need to worry. I have no intention of harming him. But he's mine, he's mine. And I will have him!"

Eliza reached for the pot of hot water boiling on the stove and tried to sling it around her body into the Indian's face, but she missed, and the water fell mostly to the ground. Some had landed on the Indians left hand, and he let go of the woman momentarily, reeling backwards. She raced for the door, removing the heavy wooden bar, and attempted to open the door to run outside, but the Indian had recovered and was too fast, and he grabbed her by the wrist, pulling out his knife with the other hand.

"Don't make this too difficult for me, Mrs. Springer". The Indian was wild, angry, and ready to pounce. A dog began to bark, and the sound of a horse drawing a carriage could be heard coming up the road leading to the house. Coming at a gallop. Amato hit the woman with his fist, knocking her to the ground, and senseless. He dragged her body into the corner of the room, and hid behind the front door. Downing came rushing in, pistol drawn, and the Indian struck him on the side of the head with the hatchet. It was a side blow, but enough to drop the large man to the floor, unconscious.

Amato leaned over, pulling Eliza up by her hair. "This is your last chance. Tell me where Daniel is or I will cut your throat from ear to ear". Eliza looked at him in terror, not knowing what to do.

A voice came from the doorway. "Go ahead, Amato. You plan to kill her all along anyway. So go ahead, earn your money."

Amato turned. "Juliet. Juliet Springer? What, what you do here, Mrs. Springer. This not your business. This just slave girl. You go before I kill you too, Mrs. Springer."

Juliet reached into a pocket on the front of her blue dress and pulled out a small pistol. The gift from the priest in Savannah. She was only a few feet away. She aimed at the Indians forehead and pulled the trigger. Amato fell, into her arms. She fell backwards, the two bodies crashing against the floor. Eliza rushed to the woman's side, dragging the Indian off of her. Amato started to get back up, rose to his feet, staggered a bit, and fell again to the floor.

"You've killed him. You've killed Amato. Who are you? You've saved my life. And my child. My children. Who are you?"

"I'm your mother, Eliza. I'm your mother."

CHAPTER SEVENTY-TWO

"HERE, MRS. SPRINGER, a cup of my best coffee."

They were in the lawyer's office, discussing what had happened. "Now what you tell me, that's in confidence." The lawyer was trying to be assuring, and supportive at the same time. The killing of Amato was in self-defense. There was no disputing that. But the Springer family was powerful, powerful almost beyond belief, and Eliza could be blamed, and she was not even permitted, under the law, to testify in court in her own behalf. Juliet, of course, could relate the story, but she would be seen as biased, as she stood much to gain if her daughter was determined to be the rightful heir of Matthew Springer. Michael was credible, but also biased in favor of Eliza. They were the only witnesses. The best thing, concluded the lawyer, was to just remain silent about what had occurred on that dreadful night of the Brown's party, and go on as if Amato had never crossed the Ocmulgee that night and attempted to murder Gold Dust. The body of the Indian would never be found. Michael had taken care of that.

"I think we had best turn to where you should go from here." Abraham had remained in town, and it was felt he could be trusted with the news about Amato's attack. It was his turn to speak.

"I don't really think that Amato's death changes anything from the standpoint of John Springer. He won't rest as long as the threat to his family's fortune remains. He will eventually conclude that Amato was unable, for whatever reason, to carry out the murder, and he will simply get someone else to do it. He will never give up on that. I know my father well enough to know that. As long as he lives, Eliza, you will never be safe. And from what has happened, I don't think you, Juliet, are safe either. They will track you here. They will find you. And they will kill both of you."

The lawyer had carefully gone over his evaluation of the effect of the late Mathew Springer's will. Amato had kept the Springer family connection from Eliza as a child, and she was unaware of her family heritage until her mother laid it all out for her. Rightfully, and legally, she was heir to a fortune. But practically, and in reality, she was a negro slave. She had been bought and sold. At any time she could be taken, sold, and transported practically anywhere in the American hemisphere. The laws were changing. Fears were growing. There was a cry in the North for emancipation. To win she would have to eliminate the blackness of her skin, that slight color discrepancy that separated her from the white class. And of course, that was impossible. They had no option but to run. To disappear. To vanish.

Abraham would return to Charleston, and report that he had been informed that Eliza Springer had met with a terrible accident as was killed. That would last for a while, but when Amato didn't come to claim his $5,000.00, the senior Springer would become suspicious and send out feelers. He would eventually conclude that Amato had failed in his enterprise, and would resort to other means.

Juliet, well no one really cared about her whereabouts, and Juliet was adamant that she would never be separated from her child again, so she was staying, and would go wherever Eliza went. As long as there was breath left in her body.

Michael was also on board, and met with his partner, Hank, to discuss the transfer of his lands and property over to him. Hank, in exchange, agreed to buy his partner's share of their gold stake and to give him a fair price for his property in Georgia. It would not be a lot of money, as Michael insisted that any slaves working his place be given their freedom. They met with the lawyer, and the papers were signed. The lawyer would let it be known that Downing had returned to Ireland due to the ill health of his mother. Not everyone would believe it, but it was better than no story at all.

There was just one thing missing. Daniel. Eliza would head South, to get Daniel, and then they could try to make it into the mountains, where they could disappear.

"He's with MayMay and Poot", she finally revealed. The threat of her child being taken by Amato now being gone, there was nothing preventing the child from being reunited with his mother, and no reason to continue the charade of his unfortunate demise.

"You had us all fooled, Gold Dust," replied Michael. "I really thought he had died of the fever."

"Juliet can remain here with us until you return", added Mr. Wilson.

"Not on your life", responded Juliet. I'm going. There's no ifs, ands and buts. I 'm going too. I've been separated from my baby long enough, and I won't be separated from her again. For no reason, and by nobody."

"Alright", sighed the lawyer. "Best we keep what has happened and these going ons away from the Missus. You know that sewing circle, they do talk." Gold Dust didn't hear the end of the conversation. Her mind was hundreds of miles away, in a Florida swamp, dreaming of her little Daniel.

"Damn shame", the lawyer reflected when everyone had left and he was alone in his office, trying to put all the pieces together in his mind. "Damn shame. There just isn't any justice in the world. No justice whatsoever. But even the best lawyer in the world couldn't win that case for Eliza Springer. Not even me", he laughed. "Not even me." He threw what remained of the coffee out into the street, and returned to his office, pulled out his finest bourbon, and poured himself a drink.

PART SIX

NEWMAN'S RIDGE, TENNESSEE - 1865

Chapter Seventy-Three

GOLD DUST SWEPT off the front porch and looked into the Eastern sky. It was a Sunday, and she was going to church. Michael had the wagon ready, and the team of mules knew the routine and were waiting impatiently to get started. They had fallen in with a tribe of castaways, known as the Melungeons. The Melungeons were a fascinating group of people of various skin colors and temperaments, a people who were able, barely, to hold onto their bottomland in the area of Northeastern Tennessee and along the Eastern Kentucky border. That was due, primarily, because of their tenacity and ability to adapt in order to survive. Their skin color was a mixture, in various degrees, of Indian, English, Portuguese, and African - just a pot load of colors, ethnicities, and opinions. Most of the darker colored Melungeons lived on the ridges, where it was so deep in timber, and the lacking of roads, that there was travel only by foot, with an occasional deer trail that a mule or shore-footed horse could follow. The Melungeons were not a proud people, at least back then, and they were known only as FPC's, or free persons of color. They couldn't vote. Some couldn't own land. The good land in the adjoining counties was reserved for the "pure" whites, and so they stayed mostly together, drifting from county to county as the good land was taken from them. Some planned to travel out west to Arkansas, Oklahoma, Texas and even California where there existed a hope for a future. Michael's family, with its bottomland, large fields, and access to plenty of water, did well compared to many around them. And the fact that Michael was white made it possible for him to own land, land which he could keep and protect in a legal society that remained segregated and which offered no protection to non-whites, whether they be Indian, Portuguese, African or otherwise.

Gold Dust, in her own way, was content with her lot in the valley. She was not too big on climbing the high ridges, but would do so to visit family. Her son,

Daniel, whom she had found, after a six month hunt, along the outer islands of South Carolina, was living on the Ridge with his wife and four children. Her other two sons, Robert Moses, who preferred to be called just Robert, and Patrick, both of whom could pass for white, shared the valley with her and her husband. Three daughters made up for the total of six children who had survived childbirth and the rugged first few years of life.

As "free persons of color", most of the Melungeons really had no identity. They would have been better off labeled as Indian, or African, than what they were, people of no identifiable ethnicity. Some had blond hair, some blue, brown or green eyes, skin colors ranged from near white to brown to red to an ash looking color. The Dare clan claimed they were from South Carolina near Charleston, and some claimed to be from Turkey and others from Portugal. There was a lot of Indian blood. Gold Dust felt right at home, because, she too, was an outcast. A person with no identity. She had roots, but her roots had denied her. She had an identity, to herself, but it was called a lie. When she and Michael had left MayMay and Poot at the Gullah camp, and headed inland, they became as much a lost people as those they found in the isolated mountains.

By the time Michael and Gold Dust had arrived at Newman's Ridge, the Melungeons as a group had been stripped of their rights of citizenship. They were not slaves, but they were, in every sense of the word, outcasts. The Downing children grew up in the bottomlands and along the ridges and knolls of the sparsely settled Southern Appalachians, and while they did not, as a whole, prosper, they did learn to survive and, for the most part, live happy and somewhat enjoyable lives. As the years passed, the thoughts of Charleston, the Springers, and the family wealth became a distant memory. This was one place that the Springers would never find them, look as they might. They had managed to disappear.

By the early 1840's the mountains were becoming more populous, and a few Cherokee began trickling in, having been run out of Northern Georgia, southeastern Tennessee, and North Carolina by the white settlers. Many had died during a harsh winter as they travelled West under government direction and insistence. Tennessee, with its own man in the White House, led the cleansing of the Southern Indians from their lands. The Melungeons, themselves, suffered from its own ethnic cleansing by the federal government.

In the 1860's, a few of the Melungeons had gone to fight in the war. Some sided with the North. Others the South. Some had joined a group of marauders that took advantage of the chaos created by the war and were feared in the white neighborhoods and were referred to as the Hannibal's. In these parts, what side a person fought for was really based more on their families and relationships than anything else. Billy and Henry Mullins had signed up to fight for the Confederates, but were rejected, as they were seen to have too much negro blood in them. So they went to fight for the North. Billy had been killed in Pennsylvania, and Henry hadn't been heard from by his family for over a year. He was schooled and knew how to write, but there was no regular mail anywhere now, and especially in the deep mountains of Northeastern Tennessee. Patrick, Eliza and Michael's youngest child, had run off and joined a Confederate cavalry unit, and was rumored to be somewhere in Virginia. The war waged on, and affected, in one way or another, every family in the hills.

CHAPTER SEVENTY-FOUR

I T WAS AT church on a cold Sunday when Gold Dust learned a terrible and awful truth. Patrick, the youngest, who had left and joined up with the Confederate unit in Virginia, had been killed defending Petersburg. Their cavalry unit had been ambushed in a gully outside of the city. The tragedy of this loss was soon magnified when Robert, learning of his brother's death, had crossed the mountain and gone to Roanoke, where he had joined a unit being sent up to Richmond to defend the city. He wanted revenge. And to make matters even worse, Daniel, who had grown up alongside Robert and who had grown very close to him, had followed Robert and joined up along with him. He said he was Melungeon, but they enlisted him as a free negro and assigned him to Robert's company. Initially he was to be a cook's helper, but with things turning desperate for the Southern cause, he was given a rifle.

"What could Robert and Daniel be thinking?" Gold Dust was pacing, throwing things, angry and worried at the same time. "I'm going after them", she told her husband. And she began to pack a knapsack. "Get my pony out from the South pasture."

"Are you crazy?" replied Michael. "You can't go chasing after grown men who are serving in the Army by their own decision."

"I'm not going chasing after them to Richmond!", replied Eliza. "I'm going to Charleston. I'm going to get the Springer's to find them and get them back to me."

"That's madness. We have spent the last thirty years evaporating from the Springer family. And you want to go back there? That's crazy."

"It's been a long time, Michael. John Springer has got to be long dead. There is no danger that some court is going to try to re-write the Mathew Springer estate at this point. When we left Jonestown, the Springer family was one of the most powerful families in the South. There is no reason to suspect that is still not the case. If anyone can get my two children out of Virginia, it is the Springers. And that's where I'm going. They owe me, that family. They owe me big. But I'll be satisfied if I can just get my children back. Alive, and in one piece."

"It's madness, Eliza."

"It's my blood, Michael. Get my pony."

"You're not going without me," was Michael's reply.

Eliza mounted the painted horse with its brown and white spots, and rode up the knoll to the East a short distance from the house. She dismounted, placed some freshly picked flowers on the grave of Juliet, her mother, said a prayer, and got back up on the horse and headed South. Michael rode the buckskin mare, and had Smokey, the mule, along on a lead.

The trip South was a lesson about the war. Every town had its cemeteries with fresh graves. They travelled down into Georgia, through Milledgeville, the Georgia capital, which had been burned. The only structures in the town spared from devastation were the churches and the insane asylum. They called it a medical hospital, but the first patient that was brought in was chained to a wagon. They went through Jonesboro, which had been spared by the Yankees, but the gin factory had been raised. They crossed the river at Macon, which had also seen the destructive hand of Sherman's troops. When they got to within thirty miles of Savannah they learned that it had fallen into Northern hands. It was just after Christmas, and they celebrated the holiday together in a small tavern along the road to the famous port city.

They couldn't believe their eyes when they saw Charleston, which had been under bombardment for 4 months. Sherman hadn't burned the city – he hadn't even come here, choosing instead to go to Columbia and burn it to the ground as he moved North through the state. The city was in shambles. Most everyone had abandoned the town fearing the threat of Sherman's army, including the Springers, and their whereabouts were unknown. With the Southern cause is total disarray, it was unlikely they could do any good at this point anyway. The economy was in ruins, the fields were overgrown, and the people were starving. There would be no help coming from this quarter. Eliza was devastated.

"Nothing to do but head back", said Michael.

The spotted horse was worn out and Eliza traded for an Appaloosa where the Savannah trail picked up on the road to Macon.

CHAPTER SEVENTY-FIVE

THE TWO MEN marched for what seemed like a year through the foothills of the Appalachians as they sloshed in the Spring rains along the muddy road toward Richmond. In fact it had been less than two weeks. Their newly formed unit had been ordered to go into the city and place a guard around the capital building and state house. They were going to protect the President, along with what remained of the Confederate leadership. The fall of the city was imminent. Sheridan had overrun Confederate forces at Five Forks, and Lee had abandoned Petersburg. He was now withdrawing his protection of the city, and panic was spreading by the minute throughout the Southern capital. On a Saturday night General Lee sent a telegram to the President. "Leave the city tonight". President Davis read the telegram as he was leaving church the next day. The military could protect the capital no longer. By two o'clock, troops were burning large stacks of Confederate documents out in the streets. It was a race against time as a large Union Calvary battalion was approaching the outskirts of the city.

Robert and Daniel had seen no action since their enlistment, but had witnessed a lot of death as the wounded and dying seemed to be everywhere. The hospitals were non-existent, the doctors were non-existent, and medicine, bandages, and chloroform were non-existent. The South was falling apart in every way. Their company of raw recruits was sent to the railroad station. There, two trains were waiting. The first train was to carry the fleeing Confederate leadership, including the President. A guard of young, unseasoned naval soldiers was assigned to protect them. Most had never fired a gun. Into the second train was loaded what remained of the Confederate treasury. Robert and Daniel's platoon was ordered onto the train with instructions to protect the gold, at all cost. The trains pulled out of the station, headed for Danville. It was midnight.

On reaching Danville the two trains were evacuated. Northern troops had cut off further retreat South by rail. A series of wagons, heavily reinforced, were brought up. The gold was loaded into the wagons. Half headed South, with instructions to get the gold on board a ship for Europe. The remainder headed West, toward Georgia. The President and his family accompanied the second wagon train. When it reached the Georgia line, a portion of the gold was distributed to what remained of the Confederate cabinet, with instructions to pay the troops and try to maintain their loyalty. The remaining gold, almost a third of the entire Confederate treasury, along with a few of the remaining dignitaries, headed further West into central Georgia. News of the Northern President's murder and the surrender of Lee's army reached them as they neared Milledgeville. The Southern President, fearing capture and possible hanging, continued South and was near Jonesville on his way to Mobile, where he hoped to escape by sea. Four wagons of gold remained. "Enough to start the rebellion again", the beleaguered President said to his wife. "The South is not done yet."

Daniel and Robert had heard the stories of Jonesville from their parents. They had heard about the old Indian trails, and their excitement grew as they approached a split in the road which led further South to Macon, or directly West toward Jonesville. The Captain in charge of the convoy pulled up and ordered the troops to settle in for the night. The wagons were pulled off the road, and Daniel and Robert were ordered to man a post at the crossroads. The rest of the troops, including the President and his wife, were about a half mile further down the road.

The first few shots sounded to Robert like fireworks. The two men looked at each other. They had been ordered to man the crossroads, and were torn whether to leave and go towards the gunfire. The intensity of the hostilities picked up, but the two men continued to man their post. Then everything went silent.

"Surely they'll send someone for us". Daniel checked his weapon. The two men looked at each other, and began down the road toward the encampment. When they arrived, there were four wagons standing in line. The gold wagons. Two wagons which had carried the President and his family were gone. The platoon, the guards of the four wagons of what remained of the Confederate treasury, were all dead, along with what appeared to be a large group of thieves, cutthroats and stragglers. Robbers. The two groups had killed each other off. The area was deathly silent.

"There's enough gold here to start another war", remarked Robert to his brother.

"What'll we do now?" replied Daniel.

"Look at all that gold. Just sittin' there. What do you think will happen to it?"

"The Confederates, when they realize what has happened, will come looking for it. The Yankees, they will too, if they ever figure out it's out here. A whole slew of people will come looking for it. Another band of robbers and cutthroats. We might as well get out of here."

"Where'll we go? The South's dead. Lee's given up. There's no sense in us carrryin' on with this foolishness. Let's clear out. Go back to Newman's Ridge. As far as the war's concerned, we was just killed here at this intersection along with everyone else."

"And leave all this gold? For the Springers and their kind to find? And start the war all over again? Rebuild and fight again? We can't do that. There's a ton of gold here. We gotta hide it. Bury it. We gotta make sure that it don't find its way to start another war."

"That's not our problem, Daniel."

"Maybe not your problem. You can pass for white. You don't have to live up on the Ridges. You don't have to scrap for every meal, every piece of bread. You don't have to live like something that don't have no rights over their government, over their courts. You live within the rights. I live without them.'

"Damn, Daniel. I never knew you felt that way."

"And my kids. What about them? What kind of world do they have to look forward to?"

"Well, they're going to make slavery against the law. That's what they're talking about. It'll be illegal. Your kids won't have to grow up worried about that."

"There's a lot more to slavery than being owned by a person. If you got no rights, no land, no money. You live in poverty. That's a form of slavery too."

Robert thought the situation over. He looked at his brother, and thought of his struggles up on the mountain ridges. He thought of what he had, what more he had, and he thought of the only reason his lot was better than his brothers. It was just the color of his skin. A lighter shade of brown. That was all. A slight alteration of the way the human being was constructed. A few drops of blood. "Ok, Daniel. Let's hide it. But where?"

The two men worked through the rest of the night loading the gold onto two of the remaining wagons. They hitched six mules to each wagon, and headed toward Jonestown.

"You remember dad telling us about when they left Jonestown? And how he told us of the Indian, Amato, and where he hid his body?"

"Yes, I remember", replied Robert. "Up at their old place, on the ridge overlooking the Ocmulgee. Up where the earthquake moved the hillside, up where the two boulders met. Yeah, I remember him tell of it."

"Let's take the gold up there."

"How will we ever find it? The place where he threw the body."

"All we got to do is find the old homeplace. People will remember. Maybe Hank O'Malley. He was dad's partner. Maybe we can find him."

"No, we can't tell nobody. Nobody can know we was here. Nor see these wagons. We go to get that gold up on that hill and then set the mules free. If anyone knows we done this, they'll track us down all our lives. This has got to be our secret."

Daniel hid the mule teams and wagons outside of town, near the cemetery leading East.

Robert walked into the town. Past the Baptist Church. Past the hotel. Past the jail and the Parish house, and the silversmith's, and Sullivan's Bar. He stopped at a three story brick building, the Mason's Hall. There was a skating rink on the ground floor. He walked up the steps. A note on the door. Down at Judge Gray's office next to Johnson's store. He walked around the corner of the square to the storefront with the Judge's name on the door.

"I'm looking for the old Downing place. On the river. Ever heard of it?"

Oh, yes," replied the Judge. "Remember it well. I had to sell the place when O'Malley was killed last year in the Battle of Atlanta. I told him he was too old to go to war. He just laughed and joined anyway. He must have been in his sixties. Nice gentleman. But he should have left the fighting to the younger men. But what do you need with that old place? The Downing house was never fixed up by O'Malley after Downing left, and it's pretty rundown. The old road has still held up, however. That Downing really knew how to build a road. Must have been the Irish in him. Him and O'Malley. You just go North, on the Peterson Road. When you get to the Grayson turnoff, you go West about two miles. There you'll see the old road cutting in at a spring. You take it up the ridge, and you'll have to search for the place from there, but it's findable. Good luck. By the way, what's your interest in the place?"

Robert was out the office and headed to the rendezvous with Daniel and didn't hear the question.

"I got the directions. I'll take the lead."

"We'll need some dynamite, or gunpowder. Something to blow up those boulders."

"The gin factory. Remember, dad said they had converted it to a cannon factory during the war. That's why Sherman wanted it burned to the ground. They had to test those cannons. And to test them, they would need gunpowder."

They found the old gin factory. A couple of slave cabins still stood on the property, along with two walls of the old factory. "Now if I was an overseer, where would I store the gunpowder?"

A small storage building remained intact behind one of the remaining slave cabins. Several people were still living in the cabins, and Daniel approached them. He pulled out three American dollars he had found in Richmond. "This here is the only money that's any good now. I'll trade it for a keg of gunpowder."

Within a few minutes, a small keg, containing about forty pounds of black gunpowder, was tied to Daniel's mule, and he headed back to find Robert.

The two wagons pulled to the top of the ridge. A log was across the road and the two men had to walk the last half mile to the old abandoned house. Daniel searched the barn and found an axe. He returned to where he had left the wagons and cut the tree, and the two wagons proceeded to the ridgeline. They walked along the ridge until they could see the river below.

"There, there it is. That must be it."

Before them were two large rocks, leaning against each other, both perched over a large hole in the earth. Limestone. Not the sturdiest of rock. A pit. Deep and dark. Robert threw a rock into the abyss, and heard it rattling down until it no longer made a sound.

"It must be fifty yards or more down into that hole. Maybe even below the river. It's some sort of aberration created by the earthquake. I didn't hear the rock land. It's like it's got no bottom."

One of the wagons lost a wheel moving toward the hole. They cut the team loose and began to carry the gold by foot. The hole was big enough to engulf the wagon, and they pushed the wagon that still rolled, loaded with the gold, into the hole. The remaining gold they carried, and it was late in the day when they had tossed all the gold into the pit. They pushed the broken wagon into a thicket. The mules were all gone by now. With everyone hungry for miles on end, they would likely be stew before the week was out. They loaded their charge, lit the fuse, and watched as the two giant rocks collapsed on top of each other, sealing the opening with tons of rock and earth. It was almost like the earth had opened up and swallowed the wagon, gold and all, and then closed back upon itself, leaving no evidence of what had just taken place. The two men looked at each other, picked up their few belongings, and began their journey back to Newman's Ridge.

When their mother, Gold Dust, heard the story, she smiled quietly. There was justice, she thought, it's just not for us to control it. "It's bigger than we are. It sets its own course, and has its own end. It carries us along, as the wind carries the seeds in Spring. It is stronger than its enemies, and it always lands on its feet."

The chickens were squabbling in the yard, and it was time to feed the hogs. The buckskin was in foal, and Michael was mending a fence on the back pasture. "We won't tell Michael about the gold, Daniel. Let's keep it to ourselves. Just the three of us. Let the rest of world wonder what has become of the South's gold. For us, we have all the gold dust we will ever need."

Late that night, as Gold Dust was sitting alone in a rocker on the back porch of Daniels mountain cabin, she heard the wind whistling past her and she looked into the night sky. The stars were everywhere, millions of them it seemed, and then, suddenly, a bright streak of exploding dust streamed across the heavens. A shooting star – igniting the sky. Gold Dust watched with amazement, then walked out into the field. "Ye nevr part, even tho ye di. Ye liv lik star in ski for all tim as one". It was Jonah, coming to say hello.

Printed in the United States
By Bookmasters